Landing Party

I0550405

by:

Cole Machia

LANDING PARTY

1

(ORDER)

---PROLOGUE

AS BUSTER MACREADY trudged hesitantly toward the supply marker, taking tentative steps over the rocky terrain on his second trip outside of the ESC Carolyn Summers in the last half hour, he thought to himself, it's almost as if they don't want us to leave.

Good God.

The supply marker's beacon light flashed strobe-like as he approached. The beacon light had been the subject of several rather serious debates among the crew of the ESC Carolyn Summers over the past three months. Buster held it as fact that the light was blue, and exhibited as proof to this fact the Supply Marker's provided directional manufacturer's handbook which clearly stated the light was indeed blue. Mission Specialist Thompson Scurry, American, argued, sometimes passionately, sometimes unconcernedly, but always steadfast in his opinion that the beacon light was white. The third and final member of the crew, Agronomist John Felps, mediated by offering an explanation to satisfy both men, which was that the light was indeed blue, but giving the absence of the light within the ten second intervals of its flash, the initial information relayed to the brain by the optic nerve amounted to misinformation on the part of the brain to give the seasoned response that the light was white based on the rational belief that no light equals darkness; black, and the opposite of darkness is light; white.

Either way, blue or white, the beacon was on the fritz, flashing continuously every .05 seconds. At that rate, the light would burn itself out in a matter of days, essentially leaving them stranded.

It'll work, he said to himself.

Ridiculous, replied another part of himself. That's an eighteen mille-meter bolt on the marker, you only have a seventeen mille-meter socket.

He had had to return to the ESC Carolyn Summers the first time having inspected the supply markers casing and realizing he had the wrong tools. It was only a short distance, but incredibly strenuous.

I'll make it work, he thought. I'll use my body weight and force it to fit.

…

He had to fight against the wind as he approached the marker, a large, roughly square shaped contraption that mildly resembled a refrigerator.

Leaning against the wind, he held his hand out in front of him as if fearing the wind would suddenly stop, leaving him to fall over his own body weight as he came upon the marker. Then, against his own inclination, he pulled the tabs at his collar and removed his helmet. It was required of every crew member to go without their helmets for at least forty percent of their time on touchdown, using only a breathing apparatus (if needed), in order to acclimatize.

Tears came to his eyes and immediately dried up as the wind rushed in followed by an almost searing cold. Able to hear now, the sound of the atmosphere came to his ears. Static emissions in the upper atmosphere sounded eerily like that of a thousand babies screaming.

Jesus, he thought. And it's like this every day.

He squinted his eyes against the wind. Already he was being blinded by specks of dry orange dirt that hadn't felt moisture in billions of years and were finding it now for the first time, maybe, ever, in his eyes.

"Damn it!" He shouted loudly in order to hear himself over the screaming sky.

There was no way the socket was going to fit. He had been silly to try. Stubborn. But they didn't have an eighteen mille-meter socket.

How do they expect me to fix anything without the proper tools? He asked himself.

Maybe they don't want you to fix anything, said the other part of himself. Maybe they lied, knowing you wouldn't have come if you knew there was no way back. None of us would have.

He was still for a moment.

I would have come, he thought.

Of course you would have.

Caesar or nothing, he thought.

Your motivations, yes, said the other part of himself. They are heartening.

"Caesar or nothing!" he shouted, holding his arms up high.

The wind seemed to die down a bit as if…understanding? Or, at the very least, maybe, hearing his proclamation. He motioned his body to correct against the slight give in oppositional force. Felt for a moment…important.

Suddenly, to his right, about ten yards away from the supply marker and its blue/white .05 second flashing light, a large circular section of the ground gave way, disappearing in a violent swirl. Buster Macready stared in fear, and a little bit of awe.

I've never seen one that size before, he thought.

Return to the E.S.C. Carolyn Summers immediately, said the other part of himself.

He did so.

~1~

FORDY MACLENNON CURSED under his breath as he took a sip of his morning coffee. Too hot, he thought bitterly as he pinched his bottom lip between two fingers. It was a tedious disappointment. And so early in the morning. He poured the too hot coffee into the sink, watched it swirl down the drain and immediately regretted it. What an ignoble waste of water, he thought. Crickets, she can't even use the automatic brewing machine properly, he lamented, referring to his wife of six years, Abigail who at that moment walked into the kitchen, a towel wrapped around her waist and another draped over her head. Droplets of smoky grey water still clung to her soft skin.

"The filter on the shower head is clogging up again," she said, rubbing the towel over her head furiously to dry her blonde (originally brunette) hair.

"You made the coffee too hot again," said Fordy, bracing himself against the kitchen counter, unable even to look at his wife.

"Really?" she asked, cocking her head to the side quizzically like an interested canine. "I set it on two, just how you like it. I even double checked."

Fordy indicated a grooved knob on the side of the automatic brewing machine. "Does that look like it is set on two?" he asked, a tone of overt rationality in his voice.

Abigail leaned over for a closer look. The knob was set at six.

"I practically destroyed my taste buds," stated Fordy MacLennon. "And my bottom teeth hurt."

Abigail responded quietly, somewhat bemused, shaking her head, "I could have sworn I had it set on two."

Fordy said, "That was yesterday. Crickets. You just can't be consistent, can you?"

Abigail gave no answer.

He turned to face her, his face incredulous. "Just because it's set on two one day, doesn't mean it's going to be set on two the next, Abigail. You know how these things act up." He paused, sighed. "I want a divorce," he said.

A wave of sadness seemed to overtake her, rippling through her like a rough tide, but she quickly recovered, stared at the ground. "I guess it couldn't have lasted," she said as if speaking through a cloud. Then, opening the refrigerator, she pulled out a cylindrical plastic pouch containing a mixture of egg and milk, drank it slowly and said, "Should we report it?"

Fordy hesitated.

It was a big step, divorce. Reporting it would make it official. No turning back after that. He'd be throwing away the last six years of his life.

Everything he had worked for...right? They would lose the apartment. That went without saying. He would have to move into a cramped studio apartment. One bedrooms were only made available to married couples. And even then, only if they could afford the hefty down payment. Abigail, too, would have to move into a studio. It wasn't quite fair to her. It seems like such a waste, he thought.

Quietly, he turned the knob on the automatic brewing machine back to two, waited a few seconds for it to heat properly, and then poured himself another cup of coffee. He took a sip, appreciating the subtle warmth as Abigail once more stared down at the floor.

"Let me think about it," he said.

Abigail nodded, adjusted the towel around her waist. "It might be best to give it a few more years," she said evenly. "At least two."

Fordy repeated, "Let me think about it."

"Honestly, though, I should have guessed where you were at," she continued, "mentally. You wouldn't even fill out the paperwork to get us a dog."

A buzzer went off. It sounded for a full thirty seconds, coming from a solar clock mounted above their television monitor.

Fordy stood motionless and said, flatly, "Now I'm late for work."

"I'm sorry," said Abigail, moving in and, out of habit, kissing him on the cheek. "It was my fault. I hope you won't be in any trouble." She spoke automatically, without conviction.

Fordy picked up a thin, brown, imitation leather

13

briefcase from a chair at the kitchen table and made for the door. "It'll be okay," he said, opening the door a crack and sliding through.

Stepping to the curb, Fordy groaned, remembering his wife's complaint about the faulty shower head filter. He turned, walked back up the steps to the building's front entrance and pressed a button next to the frosted glass paneled door.

After a pause, a mechanically garbled voice came through the speaker. "Superintendent Uhaul Malone," said the voice, elderly yet vital. And proud. All building superintendents were proud.

"This is Fordy MacLennon. Room 1, 873," he said loudly, pressing his face close to the speaker. "My shower head filter is out. When can I expect--"

The voice of Uhaul Malone interrupted. "No maintenance requests from outside the building," It said. "Too many scammers. You'll have to call direct from your apartment."

Fordy sighed, checked his watch. He didn't have the time to go all the way back up there. He was late enough as it was. "I'll call later," he said.

Walking with a measured pace through the parking lot, past the rows of analogous ovular vehicles, Fordy reached his own vehicle at space 1,873, corresponding with his apartment number. He typed in a numerical code above the door handle and stooped to get in. The vehicle started automatically as soon as the safety belt was clicked into place, and Fordy pressed the letter 'A' on a plate containing the letters A-E next to the steering console. A small, square view screen lit up under the plate containing a simplified road map and the route from his apartment to his workplace was highlighted. The vehicle rolled into motion, following that route.

Fordy eyed the monitor as the vehicle traced along the highlighted streets. Sensors clicked and whirred from deep inside the vehicles brain; its informational guidance system, stopping for red lights, speeding through yellow, yielding to pedestrians; insuring a safe, comfortable ride.

Within minutes, Fordy was transported the entire length of the Corporate City of Springfield, Massachusetts; his vehicle coming to a slow stop at the Office of Development, a fifty-six story high rise straddling the Connecticut River.

As he approached the building's front entrance, he gazed at the large color coded key that listed all suite numbers, directing visitors to their desired office, and leered as his eyes glanced over a name stenciled in red; 'Lincoln and Son LLC'. Every day he turned his nose up to that name. And every day he hoped it would be removed. What business did a private firm have in a federal building, he asked.

Stepping up to the door, he slid his name badge over a magnetic strip, then placed his right index finger onto a scanner. Removing his finger, he grabbed the door handle and pulled. The door remained locked and a rotating red light above the door began to blink.

"Oh, give me a break," he mumbled, placing his finger once more on the scanner.

"It's been happening a lot lately," said a jovial voice. Fordy turned to see a man he did not

15

recognize. He hadn't even noticed the man was behind him. He was well into old age and wore a brown chequered suit that seemed a bit too short at the sleeves. He had a friendly smile and stood an appropriate distance back, in keeping with building policy. When a worker or visitor entered the building, it was required for any others waiting to enter to stand back several feet. It was supposed to keep anyone without clearance from entering the building by slipping through before the door closed, without having been scanned.

Fordy kept his finger on the scanner five full seconds, giving it time to properly read his print and tried to keep his composure. When you're late, you just get later, he thought. The old man giggled quietly. As if he found it all to be great fun. As if it were a toy. Or an adventure. Fordy looked back and studied the man's face. Makes sense, he thought. The guy was probably around long before any of this.

The rotating red light stopped blinking, clicked, and turned green. Fordy took a breath and pulled the door open.

"I don't believe we've met," said the old man, moving closer suddenly. Too close.

"Hey," said Fordy, blocking the entrance, a startled, paranoid expression on his face.

The old man held out his hand. "Name's Edward Lincoln," he said.

Fordy reached out, shook Lincoln's hand, nodding, and then quickly shut the door behind him. Once inside, Fordy allowed his eyes to adjust to the dull lighting and spotless grey interior and watched the old man's heat signature on the infrared screen next to the door. The yellow and red globulous shapes surrounded by a deep blue seemed to show the old man scanning his print. Fordy turned slowly and made his way down the hall, his heels clacking on the floor. He hadn't walked twenty feet before noticing a security guard approach. Holding up his name badge, he stopped in front of the guard. "Fordy MacLennon, suite fifty-three," he said automatically. "Office of--"

"We know," said the guard, taking the name badge and pulling a short plastic tube from his pocket.

Of course they know, thought Fordy. And if I were an impersonator, I'd know too.

The security guard unscrewed the lid of the plastic tube and pulled out a cotton swab. "Routine, sir. You understand," said the guard, holding up the swab.

Fordy nodded. "The door, yes," he said, opening his mouth and allowing the guard to swab the inside of his mouth, around his teeth and under his tongue.

Meanwhile, Edward Lincoln walked passed the two men, almost hobbling, smiled and tipped his hat.

"Good morning, Mr. Lincoln," said the guard, taking the swab and placing it into a blue mixture. Fordy turned red with embarrassment as the old man continued on. He stared at the security guard, feeling contemptuous over the man's total calm; his seeming disinterest. Just doing his job, he reminded himself.

After the swab had soaked up the blue mixture, the security guard inserted it into a flat aluminum object, pressed a button and waited as a series of letters and codes flashed across it, followed by the appearance of

Fordy's picture; the same as that on his name badge.

The guard gave a satisfied look, handed Fordy back his name badge. "Thank you, Mr. MacLennon," he said. "Have a nice day."

Fordy smiled ineffectively and continued down the silent hall. Stepping into an elevator, he pushed the button for the fifty-third floor and felt his stomach drop as the elevator hurled smoothly upward, Holst's Mercury playing softly in the background.

He entered his office, averting his eyes instinctively from those of his co-workers. He always felt a measure of guilt whenever he was late. He was in much too high of a position with the company to be giving such a poor example. If someone were to come in late the next day he would blame himself and, knowing this, he began to castigate himself in advance.

He glided into his office without much of a stir and slumped into the chair at his desk, dropping his briefcase at his feet. If he had had a door he would close it. He laid his head down on the desk feeling incredibly drained. Those security checks really suck the life out of me, he thought as he blew into a stack of papers and watched them lift slightly into the air. Then, picking himself back up, he smoothed his hair and walked over to a water cooler in the corner of his office. Lifting the top of the filter unit, he checked to see if the salt neutralizers had been refilled. They had. He poured himself a cup and leaned against the wall, looking back at his desk and all the work he had yet to start on. As he drank the water down he lamented the rationing of fresh water. Ocean water did the trick, but it just wasn't the same.

He sat back down at his desk and began sorting through the large stacks of paperwork when his partner, Cole Strinager stepped in and tapped on the wall with his fist.

"You're late," said Strinager.

Fordy looked up, noticed the rolled up set of blueprints Strinager held in his hand and beckoned him into the office. "I know," he said. "Have a seat."

"No time," said Strinager dropping the blueprints onto the desk, unrolling them. "Have a look at these," he said. "I'd like to know what you think."

Fordy looked over the blueprints, cocking his head and turning them occasionally to get a better view. He narrowed his eyes. "It's Flavian's Amphitheatre," he said. "The Coliseum."

"Wrong," said Strinager. "It's the new Cheyenne Megaplex. Or so they hope. They want you to sign off on it."

Fordy pushed the blueprints away. "Absolutely not," he said. It's unethical."

Strinager rolled the blueprints up again and placed them under his arm. "I thought you'd feel that way," he said backing out of the office.

"The Coliseum was the scene of horrific crimes, sexual carnage, degradation and excess," said Fordy, leaning forward on his elbows. Strinager stopped to listen. "These are not things we celebrate today. As a matter of fact," he said, reaching into his desk, taking out a pad and pencil. "What is the superintendent's name? He should know better." He was obviously agitated.

It unnerved Strinager who was more or less used to Fordy's usual monosyllabic answers. He flipped back the first page of the blueprints, scanned the corner for the superintendent's name; the man proposing to run the Cheyenne Megaplex. "Hollis Kincaid," he said. "Draughtsman's name is Kitty Kampai," he added for good measure. "Are you going to file a motion?"

"I might."

Fordy wrote down the names, hesitated with the draughtsman. What kind of name was Kitty Kampai, he wondered. Possibly a pseudonym. Or it should be. Drafting a recreation of the Coliseum bordered on the illegal. What kind of idiot would sign their real name to something like that?

"By the way," said Strinager, stretching back into the office. Fordy looked up. "Did you hear about the explosion this morning?"

Fordy shook his head, a blank expression on his face. "No. Where?"

"Town called Rotenberg. Somewhere in Old Germany," Strinager said evenly.

"Industrial accident?" asked Fordy.

Strinager shrugged. "Probably. But people are dead. I think twenty, last I heard."

Fordy nodded as Strinager went back to his own desk. What could he say? Explosions happened; not often, but not unheard of. He went back to his work, sifting through papers, signing off on appropriate planned building construction, recommending contractors.

Twenty people.

It was horrible.

When a teardrop landed on his desk, smudging the ink of an order form, he realized he was crying. Wiping his face with the back of his hand, he stared at his wet knuckles, utterly confused.

~2~

OTTO SHULTZ FIDGETED in his seat, allowing the cool air coming through the vents to wash over him as his squad vehicle turned right off Kanonenweg onto Bruckenstrasse. His gaze alternated from the file folder sitting on his lap to the neighborhood passing by outside his window. This was the Neubauten District of Rotenberg. Very cheap, affordable housing built specifically for singles. Mostly minor clerks. They were cramped, but in good shape. No high-rise over two years old here. Stifling a sneeze, he double checked the address on the file.

This has to be an error, thought Otto Shultz. No pertinent suspect would be caught dead in such living conditions.

His vehicle pulled to a stop next to a row of towering ewe trees. Shultz inhaled deeply, taking in the scent as he stepped out and advanced toward the building in front of him. The building supervisor, informed earlier of his arrival eagerly opened the door for him and followed as Shultz headed for the elevator.

The superintendent, a spindly man in his early forties rubbed his hands together, quickly reached out and pushed the 'up' button, saving Shultz the trouble. Shultz looked down at the man and smiled, hiding his annoyance.

"You will tell them I cooperated?" asked the superintendent in a raspy voice.

Shultz responded, "You've been very helpful."

The elevator reached the lobby followed by a metallic DING. The doors opened.

"Good day to you, then," said the superintendent with a bow before scurrying back to his office. Shultz waved politely, then stepped into the elevator.

He rang the bell to apartment 915 and waited patiently for a response. There was none. He checked his watch, waited two minutes, then rang again. The door opened revealing a young woman. Very pretty. Healthy frame, blonde hair, blue eyes with (Shultz noted) black circles. She said nothing.

Shultz double checked the number on the door. "Mister Ersterblumen?" he inquired.

The young woman lowered her head in resignation and opened the door wider for Shultz to enter. An immediate claustrophobic sensation overtook him as he stepped inside.

Turtles, he groaned to himself. Smaller than I thought. And this woman, who is she? Girlfriend? Possibly a live-in. I can't conceive of how two people can live in such a small space, he thought. But it happens.

A large man, at least, large to the five-foot eight, one hundred-fifty pound Shultz, lay sprawled out on a couch in the corner. He seemed to waken as Shultz walked in. Rising partly, he stared drowsily as Shultz flashed his badge.

"Mister Ersterblumen," he said. "I'm Friendly Neighbor Otto Shultz. I'm investigating the explosion that occurred in the Warehouse District earlier this morning and your name has come up in possible connection. Might I have a look around?"

Ersterblumen smiled sardonically and waved his hand as if brushing Shultz off. "Sure," he said groggily. "Why not?"

Shultz put away his badge. "Thank you," he said, looking around, feeling lost in the scattered mess. Where to start, he wondered.

Looking to the girl, he asked, "Dirty laundry?"

"Sure," she pointed. "That pile there."

Shultz reached into his shirt pocket and pulled out a pair of dark glasses with protruding conical lenses meant to detect unwarranted amounts of chemicals. Putting them on, he began searching through the dirty laundry; he could already tell there was nothing out of the ordinary. Just to be sure, he looked carefully at both Ersterblumen and the girl before taking the glasses off.

This is a complete waste of my time, he thought. There is no way this man had anything to do with the explosion.

Once more, to the girl, he asked, "Any closet in this apartment?"

Again, the girl pointed. Ersterblumen shouted out, rising off the couch, "Yeah, go ahead. Give him all the help he needs."

"Drunk?" Shultz asked the girl.

"How?" she responded.

Shultz shrugged. It was a stupid question on his part.

Ersterblumen paced around the tiny room. As much as he could pace; the room was only three strides wide. He seemed fully awake now, but he was still wobbly. "Friendly Neighbor," he stated patronizingly. "What a name. Why don't you just call yourselves Police? Like the cops that you are, you pigs?"

Shultz remained calm as he lifted the closet door on its rollers. "Because we're not police," he said. "The Friendly Neighbors' are a crime solving outfit, not a crime divergence unit. There's nothing here," he said as several items fell from the overflowing closet.

"I'm sorry," said the girl, sensing Shultz's disappointment.

"What are you sorry for?" screamed Ersterblumen. The man was so incensed his voice cracked. "Stupid! It's good that he didn't find anything."

Grabbing the girl by the arm with incredible force, he gave her a hard back handed slap to the face. Shultz watched in silence. That explains the dark circles, he thought as Ersterblumen knocked the girl down and pressed his foot down on her attractive buttocks.

"Swine," said Shultz dispassionately, grabbing Ersterblumen's arm and extending it. Ersterblumen froze as Shultz slapped the cuffs on him.

The girl looked up, bleeding from the nose, and pleaded, "No, please. He's not himself. He has a vitamin deficiency. He takes a supplemental. Sometimes it changes his mood."

Shultz looked at the girl, then punched Ersterblumen square in the nose. "You'll never marry," he said, hoisting Ersterblumen's heavy frame onto his shoulders with ease.

As his vehicle raced down highway A-73, carrying him and the still unconscious form of Mister Ersterblumen toward the Corporate City of Munich and the main headquarters of Friendly Neighbor International in Tower 2-D, the largest high-rise on the continent at one-hundred and eighty stories, Shultz pondered his life as a Friendly Neighbor.

What was it exactly that set him on the path? Most people had their lives decided for them by the time they entered early puberty. The school system was remarkable for finding a child's niche. Taking into account any subjects the child excelled at, which activities held their focus, any particular fancy or passion; it was all considered and fostered, insuring that child would grow up to be exactly what it was his very nature demanded he be. It was an extremely effective system. And very productive. Every child can be considered a prodigy of some sort. Even those who grow up to be clerks. They're the very good clerks.

But, he asked himself, what could I have done as a child to predispose myself to a life of crime solving? What opportunity could I have had, at any given moment, to show such a nature? Perhaps, he conjectured, my father was prone to losing his car keys. Or my teachers their lesson plans, and I found them.

There was one occurrence that came to mind. In fourth grade, primary school, he had a teacher, a certain crotchety old man who had fought in the war, who seemed to sadistically enjoy torturing his students with pointlessly difficult tests. One particular day, several students approached Otto with an offer. They had somehow come across an answer key to the tests and were offering to hand it over to any other student willing to part with a week's worth of lunch tickets. Otto declined the offer. And, at the end of the week, he unreservedly informed his teacher on why it was the other students seemed to be performing so much better of late. Needless to say, the teacher had responded harshly. Several students were publicly paddled and all were given essay assignments. Otto Shultz was never a popular student after that. But he was apprenticed to a forensic pathologist the next year.

He curled up his lip, shook his head. Funny if that were it, he thought. That one single act as a child. One tiny moment. And they had used moments like that to decide every child's fate.

There had to be more. He found it hard to believe that his whole life could be prejudged by one ninety second conversation he had held with his teacher. But maybe it had. Maybe there was nothing else.

Ninety seconds.

That's all it took for them to answer every man's eternal question. "What am I?"

In Otto Shultz's case, it was simple. He was a Friendly Neighbor.

After passing through the rather elaborate security check of Friendly Neighbor International (now including a bomb screen) Shultz lugged Ersterblumen, dazed but conscious, to the main offices on the one hundred and forty-second floor. Leading him by his cuffed hands, Shultz brought Ersterblumen to a stop in front of the desk sergeant, intending to hand him over to be processed. All vital information, including finger prints and DNA samples were already on file for just about every person on the planet, so the only thing left for Shultz was to file the charge.

The sergeant came from around his desk, ready to lead Ersterblumen to the holding cells on sub-level 3 when Deputy Director Friedman Rose stepped off the elevator and, observing Shultz, walked passed the sterile landscape pattern paintings lining the walls of the corridor to stand next to him.

"Dietrich Ersterblumen?" he asked. It was more of a statement than a question.

Shultz nodded. "Yes."

Friedman Rose looked Ersterblumen up and down, observed his red, swollen nose, and grimaced. "You brought him in, then," he said. "What's the charge, suspicion?"

"Sixteen thirty-six dash A," said Shultz. "Assault on a female."

Friedman squinted, tilted his head from one side to the next. "Assault on a female? What happened to his involvement in the explosion? I thought I sent you over there to question him in regards to that." There was a disappointment in his voice that stung.

The desk sergeant sat back down. Ersterblumen leaned against the desk, not really sure where he was at.

"I'm telling you he doesn't know anything," said Shultz, defensively. "It was a long shot at best. I don't even know how his name came up. There's nothing in his file to suggest he would be involved in any such activity. Now, instead of running around grasping at straws, we should be looking in one place and one place only, and that's Nuremburg."

Friedman sighed, rubbed his forehead. "Nuremburg again," he moaned. "You're assuming the explosion was an act of terrorism," he said, warily. "Now who's grasping at straws? As far as we know, with what we know, the Rotenberg explosion was home grown. Nothing political about it."

"In any case," said Shultz. "I'd like permission to investigate Nuremberg direct."

"You can have all the permission you want," said Friedman, throwing up his hands. "But that doesn't mean they'll let you in. They don't let just anybody in. And certainly not us." He looked once more at Ersterblumen. "Did you hit him before or after you put the cuffs on him?"

"After, I think," Shultz replied, tiredly.

Friedman sighed. "Well, I'll have to make a phone call," he said. "Go ahead and take him down sergeant, thank you."

The desk sergeant once more stood up and came around the desk, tapped Ersterblumen on the head, bringing him to focus, then led him into the elevator and down to the holding cells. Friedman put his arm around Shultz's shoulder, walked with him down the pristine corridor toward their neighboring offices.

"Look, I know how you feel," said Friedman, his voice quiet and friendly. "Nuremberg is not a nice place. And the people are even worse. But we can't run around pointing fingers at them whenever something bad happens. Now, the government says they have a right to exist as a separate entity. Frei Stadt Nuremburg. They don't want to risk that. Would you?"

"I wouldn't want to stand apart, separate from the whole," said Shultz, stopping at his door. "But they do. I can't conceive of even that part of their mentality. So how can I know what they might be willing to risk?" He took a deep breath, lowered his voice. "All I know is I have a hunch. And I'm going to   follow   it."

~3~

MARVIN DENNIS STEPPED into the waiting room at the office of Doctor Louis Judd, hunched over and out of breath. Too impatient to wait for the elevators which were always full in such establishments, he had taken the stairs in order to keep his appointment. Judd's petite young secretary stood up from her cluttered desk as he entered. Her brown wavy hair sticking out from under her white beret in tufts and her breasts barely noticeable in her oversized sweater, she knelt down beside Marvin Dennis as he bent at the waist, trying to catch his breath.

Patting him on the back, she asked, "Mister Dennis, are you feeling okay?"

"Can I take off my shoes?" he asked, beginning to untie them without waiting for an answer.

"You should have a seat," said the secretary, helping him to a row of multi-colored plastic chairs. Slumping into a chair, he pulled his shoes off and kicked them away. The secretary patiently gathered them up and set them onto a chair beside him. "Did you take the stairs again?" she asked, putting her hands on her hips.

Marvin winced, nodded as he massaged his feet.

"All fifty-three flights?" Her eyes bulged out of her head. Sometimes she just couldn't understand men.

"The elevators are always full here," he snapped, as if it were her fault. "Full of women. It's like men never have to come here."

The secretary went back to her desk, pushed a button on the telephone, waited, then turned her attention back to him. "Men come here voluntarily," she said, matter of factly, resting her chin on her hands. "Anyway, Mister Dennis, an elevator full of women doesn't really bother you, does it?"

"It does here," he answered, a slight quiver in his voice. "They're always...," he circled his hands, "crying. Always upset. It's depressing." Poor Flora, he thought, If I hadn't married her, she wouldn't have to come here. She could have continued going to one of the smaller firms. Not this place, so full of sterile professionalism.

Before the secretary could respond, a voice came over the loudspeaker on the phone. "Yes, Jenny, sorry about the wait. What is it?"

Pushing the button on the telephone, she responded. "Mister Dennis is here for his three o'clock, Doctor Judd."

A pause, then, "Send him in."

Overhearing, Marvin stood up, straightening his back slowly, then limped down the hall to Louis Judd's office. Before he could stretch out his hand and turn the knob, the door opened inward and Louis Judd stepped out. A tall man with slicked back hair, pencil thin moustache and an aristocratic demeanor, Judd held out his hand and shook with Marvin, smiling affably. "Mister Dennis," he said with a deep voice. "I'm afraid you'll have to pardon me for a moment. Just have a seat in my office and I'll be right with you."

Marvin watched Judd disappear down the hall before limping into the office. It smelled of cleaning fluid and potpourri and was decorated with exotic items from all corners of the globe. Marvin envied Louis Judd; his power, money, and--his job, in a sense, even though it held a certain aura of sordidness, regardless of the Government's complete support. When Judd returned after several minutes, Marvin stood at the far end of the office, scrutinizing a large 3'X5' framed picture on the oak paneled wall.

Pulling a wheeled chair out from the desk, Judd sat down and swiveled. "Are you an admirer or an enthusiast?" he asked, locking his thumbs and pressing his upper lip with his index fingers.

Marvin turned slowly and sat down opposite the desk, chewed his thumbnail. "I was just looking at it," he said, sounding penitent, as if he had been caught doing wrong.

"It's called 'Bestowal of Privileges'," he said, beaming with pride. "Have you ever heard of it?"

Marvin shook his head unsurely, tried to recall. "No?" he said.

Judd smiled. "Not a lot of people have, Mister Dennis," he said, attempting to lift the man's spirits. In the eyes of Louis Judd, Marvin wasn't unique. Most men felt an overwhelming need to give him all the correct answers, even when asked the most trivial questions. If he asked them what color their eyes were, most men hesitated. "It's from a medieval work called the Laienspiegel," he said, scrutinizing the picture. "It is, of course, only a copy," he said, lowering his voice considerably as if owning only the print hurt him deeply.

Marvin lowered his eyes, stared at Judd. "Medieval?" he asked.

Looking away from the picture, Judd pursed his lips. "Fifteen hundred and eight," he explained. Marvin pretended to understand. Judd shifted several small items on his desk. "I also have 'Custer's Last Stand'," he said. "Unfortunately, also a print."

Marvin, perking up, said, "I've heard of that."

"What is it, again, you do for a living, Mister Dennis," asked Judd.

Taken by surprise, Marvin fumbled over his words. "I work in the...I'm in waste management," he responded.

"And you are recently married?"

"Two years," stated Marvin firmly. He was offended. He and Flora had been patients of Doctor Judd since their marriage. They visited regularly. At least Flora did.

Judd closed his eyes, nodded. "That's right," he said. "I've turned myself around. You have only moved into a new apartment recently, correct?"

"Yes," said Marvin. "Our old apartment had rats. We've moved to a different floor. A higher level."

"To get away from the rats," Judd mused, then, cutting to the chase, he asked, "Why is it you wanted to see me?"

Marvin squirmed. This was it. "Well," he gulped. "I wanted to clarify whether or not you were aware that I've refinanced. I'm sure your files have been updated. But, I wanted to be sure that you knew and...wanted to check and see if maybe something has changed."

Judd sat up straight, his face a blank canvass onto which Marvin painted every conceivable emotion, then, as if it were a facial tic, he smiled. "I'll check and see," he said, pulling Marvin's file up on the computer. He studied the screen in silence for several excruciating minutes, then sat back in his chair. "Mister Dennis, it is true, you have refinanced. But your file continues to show significant debt. In fact, the apartment you have so recently moved into is considerably more expensive than your last." He folded his arms. "I'm afraid nothing has changed."

Marvin felt his body sag. Every ounce of energy-- of will, sucked out by those words. Tears welled up in his eyes. "Nothing?" he asked, piteously, trying not to show too much concern.

Judd raised his eyebrows in response.

Marvin slapped his knees and rubbed his face alternately. He wanted to leave. But simply rising out of the chair and walking out of the office seemed much too unassuming a gesture. He wanted to pick up the chair and toss it across the office, run through the halls screaming.

"Mister Dennis--Marvin," said Judd, his voice consolatory. "It is not the end of the world."

Marvin fought back his tears, asked in a strained

voice, "Can I at least fill out the paperwork for a dog?"

Judd shook his head. "What would be the point?" he asked.

Marvin nearly broke down. But doing such a thing would almost certainly condemn him. Emotional precariousness was frowned upon. A negative trait. He wrung his hands together behind his back.

"If it is an issue of instinct," said Judd, not fooled by Marvin's restraint. "I'm sure we can drum up some sort of a deal. As it is simply a matter of finance and as there are no genetic restrictions barring your wife and yourself, I am sure we can make an appointment with our labs to extract an egg. We can even use your sperm. There are, after all, those couples in stable financial conditions who, nevertheless, have negative genetic traits blocking them from receiving a license."

Marvin blinked rapidly to block the tears, looked up. "Are you kidding me?" he asked. "My wife and I want to raise our own child."

Judd shrugged him off. "Your situation as it is, that will not happen. But, I understand a woman has maternal issues. A…biological clock, as they say. Donation may be her only choice. At least," his voice became troubling, "as long as she chooses to stay married to you."

Marvin squinted and the blood raced to his head. He gripped the sides of his chair, trying to control his anger. Judd smiled once more, not frightened in the least. He had seen this sort of thing a hundred times. And the men never once followed through with their anger. "Then again," he said. "This is a Gynecology Firm and Licensing Bureau, not a psychiatric clinic. If I were you, though, I would have a serious talk with my wife tonight."

Marvin imagined Judd's head collapsing under an enormous weight, then let go of the chair. Suddenly, he felt all the anger flush from his system. He found it difficult to feel anything. After all, it wasn't Judd's fault he was broke. It had been his own choice to move away from the rats. It was almost as if he had woken from a somnambulistic sleep. Acceptance came quickly to Marvin Dennis, followed by complete denial. Standing up rigidly, he made for the door.

"Goodbye, then" said Judd, retaining his close lipped smile as Marvin walked out of his office without another word. As the door closed, Judd keyed up Marvin's file once more and added one short statement: 'Suffers bouts of anger, depression and stress; possibly hereditary.'

Hereditary was the parallax word in the Bureau. The line was clear regarding positive and negative hereditary traits. It meant Marvin Dennis would never be issued a Procrete license. He would never have a child of his own.

Marvin did not take the stairs down. Instead, he managed to squeeze into an elevator along with a handful of morose women. As he searched their faces, he was reminded of Flora. She had come back from her monthly check-ups with the same look of hopelessness; frustrated about the unfairness of it all. It was one thing to know you weren't legally able to bear a child; it was another thing all-together when they made sure of it.

A lanky girl pushed into the corner of the elevator caught his attention. She was crying softly, almost as if she were embarrassed to let the other women know. She was young. At least thirteen years old. This was probably her first visit, thought Marvin. I hear that's the rough one. The one that makes you feel the most shameful. The most cursed for being a woman, when they haven't even begun to think of themselves as women yet. The girl caught his staring, turned her face to the wall, hiding it.

She's probably right, not wanting these other women to notice her so much, he thought. After a few years, most women lost the ability to empathize with girls like her. They were lost in their own pain. A less obvious pain; more trained, seasoned from years' worth of check-ups. This little girl's pain had only just begun. But as far as the women were concerned, as bad as the first check-up is, the little girl could still hold a measure of hope, whereas they felt they had none. They imagined that to be worse, or insisted on it, almost proudly. The only way for women like them to adapt to the pain was to give up hope. If they managed to get used to the idea that they would never give birth to a child, it wasn't such a bad thing, after a while, when they were told they weren't allowed to. Strangely, it was the men that felt the most for the young girls. Like Marvin did now.

Once outside, he hailed a taxi, climbed into the back seat and gave the driver the address to his apartment building. After security checks, he took the elevator to the eighteenth floor. He hesitated at the door of the apartment, room 1,889, his key card hovering over the slot, knowing that once he went through the door and saw Flora he would lose all composure. So far, he had kept his emotions pretty well under control. He knew he would break down as soon as he laid eyes on her. And then once again she would see him weak.

The elevator dinged behind him and he turned to see his neighbor, Fordy MacLennon, step out. Marvin endeavored to smile, feeling awkward, and waved flaccidly as Fordy made his way down the hall to his own apartment. Marvin watched him as he turned the corner and felt like cursing him for acting as the impetus in making him go inside. He couldn't very well stand out in the hall all night. Not now that someone had seen him.

Flora was in the middle of dusting when he stepped inside. It was a superstition with her that good news came only when things were clean. She had been cleaning all day.

When she saw her husband's face, she knew there was no good news.

"I want to die," he said, standing in the doorway.

Flora dropped her dust rag and wrapped her arms around him as he wept.

~4~

AN UNASSUMING MAN sat alone under the patio of a café in the old city of Paris. He sipped his drink slowly, watching the steam rise from his cup as the rain fell evenly from the dark clouds above. The rain flowed down the avenue, mixing with the dirt and silt of the city streets until overflowing the gutters. Refuse, washed away by the rain, floated atop the dirty grey water, until being caught in the litter nets deposited next to the drainage grates. When the rain ceased, workmen would come and empty the nets, saving recyclables and burning the rest. But by the looks of it, the rain wasn't going to stop anytime soon. The City of Lights seemed to hold a more somber atmosphere in the daytime. Gloomy in its black and grey masonry, as if it had been built, or had grown to share a certain dreary affinity with the rain.

The man finished his drink and set the cup down on the table. His pale eyes noticed a young couple turn the corner and come racing toward the café. Once under the patio's umbrella, they laughed giddily as if they had just done something exciting. The young man shook out his jacket as a waiter came over to take their order. The unassuming man turned up his collar as the couple sat down behind him, chattering incessantly. A cold wind blew as he stood up to leave, dropping a few coins on the table next to the empty cup. The young couple watched him depart, smiled at each other, glad to be alone.

A moment later, the waiter came out with the couple's order. As he turned to go back inside where it was warm, he was surprised to find several coins had been left on one of the tables. Already he had forgotten the unassuming man. The young couple, too, had already forgotten. There was nothing worth remembering.

Several yards away, the man made his way down a deserted Rue D'Ulm, walking against the wind. He buried his chin in his chest as the rain pelted his face. An elderly woman living in one of the houses lining the street leaned out her window and held out a large plastic bucket with which to collect the rain water. Spotting the man below, she shouted down to him in a harsh argot something he did not understand. Ignoring the woman, he continued down the street where, in the distance could be seen a large structure. The Pantheon.

As the street widened, the man clung to a nearby wall on which had been posted dozens of recruiting posters for the Extra Solar Pioneers, and watched as a large group of people emerged from the front entrance of the old building. Tourists. A black mold rubbed off onto his grey rain coat from the wall as he slid closer to the edge of the building, nearing where the street interconnected with a parking lot. The rain slowed to a light drizzle as he waited patiently for the group of tourists to disperse, marching almost single file down the Rue Soufflot on their way to another attraction. Sticking his hands in the pockets of his rain coat, he walked swiftly toward the Pantheon, coming to a stop next to a large weather beaten Corinthian column. The day grew increasingly darker as he studied the front entrance. He seemed to be measuring something in his mind. Finally, he approached the building, stopped to order a ticket at the ticket counter, and then opened the door. As he opened it, he turned to see a bus pull into the parking lot. Another group of tourists streamed out, laughing and smiling; some tired and grumpy. The man politely held the door open, allowed the group to file passed him, before entering the building himself.

"Will you be joining the tour this evening?" asked an elderly man wearing a pompous uniform.

The man answered, not looking at the guide, "I want to see Emile Zola's tomb." His voice had an eerie, almost inhuman quality to it. As if the words were nothing more than directions written on a slip of paper.

The elderly man motioned with his hand. "The catacombs are straight ahead, monsieur. Just go down the steps." He started to walk away, but stopped. "Are you a devotee of Zola's?" he asked, hesitantly.

The man did not respond immediately. He appeared to be confused by the question. He nodded. The elderly man fidgeted. "It's just that so few people are these days," he said, almost apologetically. "Most people pass him by."

The man said nothing. He stared at the guide for a brief moment before heading down to the catacombs. The guide frowned suspiciously, watching the man disappear down the steps.

The unassuming man walked alone under the quiet luminescence of the hanging lights, passed the bones of Voltaire and Madame Curie, and then halted at the stone sarcophagus of Emile Zola. He lowered his head and closed his eyes. His lips began to move but no words came out. Then, with a subtle grace, the man pulled a thin, hexagonal shaped object from his coat pocket. Holding the object close to his chest he connected several loosely hanging wires, then stretched his thin fingers through the grating and placed the object at the foot of the sarcophagus.

An echo of voices was heard and the man looked up to see the group of tourists being led down to the catacombs. He rose quickly and made his way through them, nodding as he passed.

"Good day to you, monsieur," the elderly guide called out to him as he made his way to the exit.

Standing under the portico, the man lifted his arm to check the time on his watch, then looked to the right and the left as if trying to decide where to go next when he spotted a young boy squatting on the ground, leaning against a column. Two adults, obviously the boy's parents stood at the ticket counter.

The man knelt down next to the boy, stretched out his hand, waved the other hand in front of it, and slipped a coin from his sleeve. The boy smiled brightly when the coin appeared seemingly out of nowhere. The man smiled too and dropped the coin in the boy's hand. At the ticket counter, the boy's parents began to argue. The boy didn't appear all that surprised by it. He merely brought up his knees and lowered his head. The man looked back at the parents, then down at the boy and made a funny face, sticking out his tongue and puffing his cheeks. The boy lifted his head and mimicked the faces, giggling quietly. Having bought the tickets, the parents came over to retrieve their son.. Paying the man no attention, the father lifted the boy up and led him by the hand toward the entrance. The little boy looked back and waved as they passed through the doors.

Circling the Pantheon, the man continued down the Rue D'Ulm, whistling quietly to himself. When he crossed the Rue Des Ecoles, he reached into his pocket, pulling out a flat, square object and pushed a button on its front plate. Behind him, the Pantheon exploded, incinerating everyone and everything inside.

~5~

BUSTER MACREADY HAMMERED the protective covering of the outer circuit breaker with all his might but it refused to budge. He kicked at the dirt and swore, watched the dirt swirl back at him with the wind. At the moment, the E.S.C. Carolyn Summers was without power in two compartments. No electricity, no ventilation, no environmental control. If he couldn't get power to those compartments, the crew might as well consider their mission a failure.

Grabbing a wrench from his tool bag, he swung it at the metal covering. No use. Frustrated, he tossed the wrench with all his might into the vast desolation. Hoping, like a lunatic, that it might meet with some artificial structure, perhaps a gigantic projection screen, and shatter it, revealing the jagged horizon to be false; as if the earth lye there the entire time, hidden, but within reach. Instead, the wrench travelled farther than he could ever have thrown it on earth. It was the perfect reminder of his situation. Here he could throw farther.

From around the corner of the Carolyn Summers

came John Felps, the missions Agronomist. He walked slowly toward Buster allowing a handful of the orange dirt to pass through his gloved fingers. He spoke into the microphone in his helmet. "My guess is the outer core is cavernous," he said.

There was a one second time delay on the microphones, so Buster saw Felps' lips move before hearing his words. He responded, "I can't get the cover plate open. I think maybe the frame shifted on the landing. It's pinched closed." He squeezed one hand with the other, demonstrating his meaning, paused. "What about the outer core?"

Felps waved his boot on the ground, spreading the dirt. "I think it's cavernous," he repeated. "That may explain the sink holes."

The sink holes, Buster thought. What a benign description. A chill ran up his spine. He shook his head. "I don't think that's it," he said. He wanted to tell him what he thought they were. What he thought caused them. There was something under the ground. Something alive.

Felps said, "I'm the agronomist. I think I know a thing or two about geology." He moved toward the entrance of the Landing Craft, stumbled on a loose boulder and caught himself. "Try a cutting torch," he said as an aside. "You need to get that covering off somehow. And don't forget the Supply Marker."

I'll have to get a hydraulic lift and release the burden on this side of the landing craft, he thought as Felps disappeared inside.

The ground isn't hard enough, said the other part of himself. It won't be able to offer an opposing force to the weight of the Carolyn Summers. The hydraulic lift would be pushed into the ground before it moved an inch.

He shook his head. The Carolyn Summers weighs only two/thirds what it weighed on earth, he thought. If we removed the support beams, the crew could lift it by hand.

They'll never agree to it.

You're probably right. I'll use a cutting torch.

In the distance, the supply marker continued to blink. Supposedly, the government on earth sent out supply satellites every year in the general direction of space taken by the Extra Solar Pioneers. They began sending the satellites forty years before any Pioneers lifted off. The satellites were meant to pick up on the signals sent by the supply markers. Theoretically, there were thousands of satellites roaming the space ways in reach of any given Pioneer landing site, just waiting to receive a signal. Or, there might be none. Who knew anymore? Buster Macready certainly didn't. He picked up his tool bag and entered the landing craft to search for a cutting torch.

John Felps and Thomson Scurry, American, sat at the chrome table in the main communal compartment of the Carolyn Summers having a lunch. Scurry looked up as Buster stepped inside, pulled off his helmet and wiped the sweat from his face. "We drew straws," said Scurry. "You'll have to find another Pioneer Outpost and borrow an eighteen millimeter socket."

Buster squinted, confused. "What are you talking about?"

47

"Well, we didn't draw straws really. We picked numbers and rolled dice."

Opening a drawer to one of the many cabinets containing a variety of freeze-dried foodstuffs, Buster took out a sleeve of roast beef and had a seat next to the others. "I oppose this," he said, taking a shaky breath. "You can't decide another crew member's fate when he isn't even in the room."

Scurry shrugged. "We could do it again if you like. But you should know Felps and I picked the rolled number exactly. Even if you had been here, the odds are against all three of us choosing the correct number."

Buster broke the dried roast beef into pieces and stuffed them into a glass of water. After the water was soaked up, he took the pieces out and ate them greedily. He swallowed, coughed as a piece caught in his throat and drank what remained of the water. "It's not the odds that concern me," he said. "I just don't believe you."

Felps said, "I'm offended."

"Don't be," said Scurry. "It's perfectly understandable. We'll do it over."

All three men pushed away from the table and lined up against the wall. Scurry pulled the dice from his pocket and tossed them against the opposite wall on the far side of the compartment. They bounced and rolled under a cabinet.

Felps turned to Scurry. "Seven," he called.

"I'll take seven as well," said Scurry.

Buster looked at the both of them. "This is ridiculous," he said. "All three of us know the statistics involved. The odds are with six, seven and eight. None of us is going to pick two or twelve. Since the best guess is on seven, I'm going to pick seven as well and that forfeit's the entire point of this exercise."

Without a word, Scurry walked over and stooped down to read the dice. "Nine," he said, picking them up. "You could have chosen eight, nine or ten and you would have guessed closer than either me or Felps. Let's do it again until we can all be satisfied."

"I don't want to do it again," said Buster, pointing to Scurry. "You're the mission commander, it's your duty to take responsibility. You should be out there searching for another pioneer site, not me."

"And you're the engineer," countered Scurry. "It's your duty to fix things when they break down."

"Agronomy being my specialty," added Felps. "It would be unreasonable to send me. I'm still working on the green-house."

"Fine," said Scurry. "We'll do it this way. I'm the commander, so I'm ordering you to go."

Buster threw up his hands. "There are only thirty-six pioneer landing sites on a planet with a diameter of over forty thousand kilometers. I'll never find them." He was beginning to be afraid.

Jesus, he thought. They're serious.

"Anyway, I'm still needed here. We still don't have power in the rear compartments. We don't have an incubation chamber without power. How can we engineer progeny without power? That should be fixed first."

Scurry said evenly, "The supply marker is our

number one priority."

Buster shoved his hands in his pockets. "I'm not going," he said, definitively. "I can't do it. A person can't survive out there alone. There's the thing with the ground, and the winds and the cold. The lower atmosphere sounds like it's screaming! I can't take it for too long. Haven't you heard it?"

Felps grabbed Buster by the collar and gave him a smack. "Get a hold of yourself."

Scurry, meanwhile, opened one of the nearby cabinets and pulled out a pistol. Buster kicked up his leg, knocked Scurry down and pinned his arm to the floor as he pulled the trigger. The bullet narrowly missed Buster's head and lodged itself in the wall. Sighing, he lifted his foot and sat down at the table. Felps helped Scurry to his feet.

"A poor decision," Scurry ruminated, dusting himself off. "I apologize."

Buster waved him off. "No. You were within your rights. I broke the prime directive by not maintaining a constant pragmatic optimism." He picked his helmet up from the table. "I'll go," he said. "I'll find another pioneer site and get the tools we need. I suppose it's the only option."

"We'll pray for you," said Felps.

Scurry sat down next to him. "You can take the scooter," he said. "And as much food and water as you can carry. Take a bag of flairs with you too. You're bound to run into another camp in a couple days. Just launch a flair and they'll respond."

Felps shook Buster's hand. "We'll have vegetables when you return. That's a promise."

Minutes later, Buster had his supplies packed and cabled to the rear of the scooter, a electrically powered vehicle resembling a moped, only with much larger wheels with which to maneuver over rough terrain. Taking one final look at the ESC Carolyn Summers, he was ready to depart on this terrifying new mission. His calm demeanor a reflex action learned in training, he was, in fact, petrified. Scurry and Felps accompanied him to the scooter, patting him on the back and reminding him that what he was doing was not thankless.

Felps bent over, allowing Buster to use his back as a boost to climb into the seat of the scooter. Once in place, Buster pressed a button on the left side of the handle bars and steadied himself as the scooter came to life, travelling at the insane speed of five kilometers an hour. Buster struggled to keep a straight course, holding the handle bars with all his strength as the scooter bounced and rocked over the loose dirt and boulders leading into the foothills of a nearby mountain range. The dirt kicked into the air, clouded him in a perpetual sand storm. He wiped down his face plate, squinting into the distance, searching for high ground.

You're afraid, said the other part of himself.

Yes, he thought. I am afraid there is no possibility in the necessity.

You remind me of something I once read. 'Get me possibility, get me possibility that I may live again.' This planet still has a number for a name, and you're already at war with it.

I'm not at war with anything, he thought. Because

I'm starting to think you're right. There is no going back. We're all alone here. Stuck. And I don't want to die. So by simple logic I want to live here. On this planet. I want to live. I want it to want me to live here. I want it to protect me. But it's probably going to kill me.

Hours later, he pulled to a stop. With the dust being kicked into the air, there was a chance he rolled right by another site. As soon as he turned the scooter off, the dust dissipated, giving him a relatively clear view. He looked up at the gas giant orbited by the chunk of rock he stood on in the system of Pegasus 12. The Carolyn Summers had landed on the bright side, forever facing the giant. In the distance, ahead of him, he could make out the stars, and the darkness beyond the mountains. Contrary to his usual fears, Buster felt the dark side of the planet might offer some form of safety. Out of view of the swirling mass above.

Maybe that's why the sky screams, he thought. Maybe this entire planet is afraid.

Behind you, the other part of himself snapped.

Buster turned to see a large section of rock give way, collapse under itself. He froze with panic, instinctively covered his face plate with his hands.

It's one of those things, he shrieked.

It's moving toward us, said the other part of himself and he witnessed several more meters of ground give way.

We'll have to outrun it.

Buster once more pushed the button, turning on the scooter and pressed the accelerator pedal as far down as he could. The scooter jerked, rolled at top speed. Buster turned to see how far ahead he was. He wanted to cry. The ground continued to give way, swirling and dropping behind him as he tried to make his escape at five kilometers per hour. Strangely, the 'sink holes' kept a short distance behind him, until suddenly, the ground beside him cracked open and a large circular section collapsed not ten yards away. Buster continued to ride away from it, throwing his weight forward in an attempt to make the scooter move faster.

Finally, he made his way to the mountains. Looking back after the dust settled, the ground behind him looked as if marked by craters. Shaking and breathing spasmodically, Buster reached into one of the packs at the back of the scooter, pulled out a flair and shot it into the sky. The light from the flair reflected brilliantly off the dust in the air, seemed to travel forever.

'Out of nothing can come,' the other part of himself quoted. 'And nothing can become nothing.'

~6~

OTTO SHULTZ SNIFFED the air, studied the surroundings, looked up at the sky (visible now through massive holes blown in the ceiling), and felt something crunch under his shoe. Bracing against the remains of a column, he lifted his foot to investigate before being startled by a clamorous noise behind him. He turned to see several men in white coats hastily setting up a makeshift lab on a collapsible table placed amongst the rubble. One of the men had dropped a monitor and stooped to pick it up, checking it on all sides for any signs of damage.

Snapping on a pair of latex gloves and retrieving a pair of tweezers from the pocket of his sport coat, he turned to the men. "Are you gentlemen supposed to be here?" he asked.

"Yes sir," one of the men responded as he hooked up the cables, connecting all of the equipment. "We have to identify the bodies." He pointed to a large pile of charred flesh and bones that had earlier been collected by the initial forensic team.

"Shouldn't you be doing that in a lab?"

"Orders, sir," said the same man, pulling a folded

piece of pink paper from the inside pocket of his lab coat. "We have to separate the bones of the victims from those that were originally interred here. The government doesn't want historic remains removed from the scene."

"Yes, of course," said Shultz, twitching his nose. He bent down to scrape at the area he previously stepped at, picking up random grains with the tweezers and scrutinizing them against the light as more men in white coats moved about him carrying assorted bones to the table.

They held the bones under a laser light, drilling holes and extracting marrow, reading the DNA of each bone before tossing them carelessly into clear plastic buckets designated for each victim. A stern looking man sitting in front of the monitor called out the names with cold detachment once the information scrolled across the screen. "Alistair Diez, aged 34 years; Penny Morris, aged 38 years; Abigail Nunez, aged 26. Oh, look at this," he exclaimed as the result of a tested femur came through. "Ronald Higgins of Shropshire, aged 59. Best darn billiards player this side of the Atlantic. I've heard of him. What a shame." He shook his head and continued. "Timothy O'Dea, aged 9 years."

Shultz placed several suspicious items in a plastic bag and stood up as a local Friendly Neighbor walked over to stand next to him.

"So, what do you think?" asked the man.

Shultz squinted. "It's exactly like Rotenberg."

"You think they're connected?"

Before Shultz could respond, the man behind the

monitor shouted, "Got one." Pointing to another man holding a small bone, he said, "That metacarpal belongs to Victor Hugo."

The man holding the bone then handed it off to another man who softly and solemnly placed it into a bucket with felt lining.

"Of course they're connected," said Shultz, gazing at the pile of bones yet to be tested. "Too many similarities. The responsible party certainly knew what they were doing. Both buildings were open to the public. Both had no special significance and, so, had very little in the way of security. There was video, of course. But it was destroyed. I've already collected the video from the cameras covering the streets leading to this spot. I'll have it analyzed soon enough." He began to pace, sighed. "This definitely isn't home grown," he mused. "One would be inclined to think such a thing as both buildings were relatively easy targets. But the degree of professionalism belies that assumption. No timing device, no residue, and two seemingly insignificant locations. I just wish…," he paused, then, "Francois, your phone."

Francois, his Friendly Neighbor colleague took his cellular phone from his pocket. "Where is yours?" he asked.

"In my vehicle," Shultz declared. He grabbed the phone and dialed global information, waited, got a response. "Any region," he stated to the operator, waited till he heard the familiar click, then said, "Connect me with the Office of Development, an engineer, preferably one with an interest in historical architecture."

Silence, then several more clicks.

"Office of Development, Springfield Corporate," came an animated voice. "How might I help you, sir?"

"The Paris Pantheon," said Shultz. "I need information."

"Certainly, sir," said the voice, robotically. "The Paris Pantheon; construction began in the year 1755, the design being drafted by the architect Soufflot in the Classical style. The floor plan is that of a Greek cross 110 meters long by 85 meters wide, and the building is topped by a Latin dome reaching a height of 83 meters. The portico was modelled after the Pantheon in Rome. Construction was completed in the year 1789. Interred in the mausoleum are such notables as Mirabeau, Andre Malraux, Jean-Jacques Rousseau and Voltaire.

"Is that it?" asked Shultz, chewing his lip. "I need specifics."

"Those are the specifics, sir," responded the voice.

"I meant romantic. Apocryphal even."

There was a moment of silence on the other end, then, "You'll be wanting to speak with MacLennon, sir," replied the voice, sounding insulted. "I'll transfer you. Please hold."

Several more clicks.

"The Paris Pantheon was commissioned by Louis XV in honor of Saint Genevieve," came the unenthusiastic voice of Fordy MacLennon. "1789-- the year it was completed was also the year of the French Revolution. Another interesting footnote--the physicist Leon Foucault carried out the first of his famous pendulum experiments demonstrating the rotation of the earth on its axis. Can I be of any further service?"

"That will be all," said Shultz, hanging up and tossing the phone back to Francois. Once more, he surveyed the damage. 1789; French Revolution; Earth turning on its axis--stability and instability. He shuddered. "It was symbolic," he declared. "That's why we couldn't make any sense out of it. Because we just didn't get it."

"Symbolic of what?" asked Francois, wiping down his phone before returning it to his pocket.

Shultz meditated a moment, cleared his throat and said, "Whoever did this...wants to spark a revolution."

"A revolution," Francois repeated with dread. "So you think this will happen again."

Shultz groaned. As soon as the words left his lips he knew he had made a mistake. If he consented that there would be more explosions, the matter would be turned over to the Crime Deterrence Unit meant to prevent future crimes from happening. It would be out of his jurisdiction. Out of his hands. The rules were clear. He would have to hand over his files. If he refused, he would be violating the law himself. That is, of course, only if he consented.

But, he wondered, how can I continue with this investigation? Even if I manage to solve the crime and capture the culprit, I'll be preventing the future crimes the culprit plans to commit, and that is clearly the job of the Deterrence Police. The job of a

Friendly Neighbor is to solve crimes of a random and spontaneous nature. Crimes not meant to be repeated. But this is my case, he said to himself. And I can't be one hundred percent sure the explosions will be continuous. So, technically, I'm not out of my jurisdiction.

"That was off the record, Francois," he said, sternly. "Of course there won't be anymore. Just look around you and tell me this is anything more than a senseless act. It's barbarism, plain and simple."

Francois looked around. "But you said yourself that it was a professional job. If we were to consider for a moment that this was a revolutionary--,"

"You can get yourself in a lot of trouble with talk like that," Shultz interrupted, fidgeted. "I need to make another phone call," he said, holding up his hands as Francois once more held out his phone. "I'll use mine," he said, skirting past the rubble toward his vehicle.

Allowing the door to shut behind him, he grabbed his phone from the middle console and dialed Feldman Rose's office at Friendly Neighbor International. After several beeps, Feldman picked up. "I'm on to something," Shultz said immediately. "Can you talk?"

"I've got a couple minutes," said Feldman. "Give me what you've got."

"Identical crimes, possible motive. I don't want to go into details over the phone."

"Fair enough," said Feldman. "How much longer will you be?"

"Half hour at the most. I'll be back in Munich by

seven tonight."

"Drop by my apartment, we'll talk there. Make it eight, my wife is making spaghetti."

"Mmm."

"By the way," added Feldman. "Have you checked your messages?"

Shultz peered at the screen on his phone. It read three missed calls. "No, I haven't."

"We got something out of Ersterblumen. His blood alcohol index was 0.3%. The man was *inebriated*."

Shultz pondered this. "The Spaten breweries," he said. "Ersterblumen *was* in Nuremberg."

"That's cause," said Feldman. "And your ticket in. You wanted it, you got it."

"Thank you, sir," said Shultz, smiling.

"See you at eight," said Feldman, cutting the connection.

Feldman Rose leaned against his bathroom door with an enormous sense of guilt as his wife Amelia cleaned the dinner table. He could hear Shultz inside the bathroom, struggling with the night's meal. "Is there anything I can get you?" he asked, speaking just loud enough to be heard through the door, but not loud enough for his wife to hear in the other room.

"Nothing," came Shultz's strained response.

"This sometimes happens," said Feldman. "She can be a bit experimental with spice."

He heard the toilet flush, followed by the sound of an aerosol freshener and stepped away from the door as Shultz pulled it open, his face haggard. "How do I look?" he asked, drying his hands on his trousers. "Is it bad?" He turned to look at himself in the oversized mirror covering an entire wall of the bathroom, pulled the flesh down under his eyeball. "My eyes are red. Do you have a dropper?"

Feldman laughed quietly, patted Shultz on the back. "Don't worry," he said. "I told her you were upset by what you saw in Paris. She won't even think to blame it on her cooking." His hand still pressed to Shultz's back, he led him through the spacious living room toward a pair of sliding glass doors, pulled back the burgundy silk curtains and beckoned Shultz out onto the terrace. "Now," said Feldman, sliding the doors closed behind him, "let's have a talk."

Shultz leaned over the railing, looked down at the city below until a fiery streak trailed across the night sky, grabbing his attention. He pointed. "There goes another one," he said. "I wonder where this one is going."

Feldman looked up as well. "Why those people choose such a life is beyond me," he said. "Though, I do suppose it has its attractions. Adventure. Risk. Amelia watches the reports every week. Sometimes she records them. Her cousin set off on one of those ships. He's supposed to be heading for some rock orbiting Mu Arae in the Ara constellation. But he only left three years ago, I don't think he's arrived yet." He shielded his eyes as a billboard advertising winter wear situated atop a neighboring skyscraper lit up, flooding his terrace in alternating shades of neon blues and reds. "Otto, listen," he said, lowering his voice and motioning to Shultz to have a seat in one of several fashionable deck chairs that betrayed his prestigious position. "You understand there is a fine line separating the functions of various law enforcement," he said, covering his mouth with his hand to keep his words from being read by any of the thousands of observation cameras mounted here and there. "And you, my friend, are very near to crossing that line. Now, tell me why I shouldn't order you off this case."

Shultz, covering his mouth as well, answered, "Because you can't order me off a case based on my own hunch. And," he said, pointing, "Nobody is more capable to solve this than me."

"Not necessarily," Feldman replied. "The deterrence police have many methods with which to conduct such an investigation that would place them in a much better position than us to solve these crimes."

"Methods that some consider to be inhumane," countered Shultz.

"Nonetheless," said Feldman. "They get the job done." He stood up, stared at his wife through the curtains. "What happens if you slip up? What happens if you cannot catch whoever is responsible before there is yet another explosion?"

"If we hand it over to the Deterrence Police, they'll simply allow another explosion in the hopes that it would render up more clues."

"Such is the nature of law enforcement," offered Feldman.

"But we are not law enforcement. We solve crimes. And what greater crime has been committed in the last two centuries?" said Shultz.

Feldman held up his hands and smiled wryly. "Calm yourself, Otto. I am on your side. However, I am not all-powerful. I can buy you only so much time." He sat back down. "Go to Nuremberg. Follow your nose. But just you know, if there is another explosion, you will have to hand over your files." He added soberly, "And more than likely, your badge."

Shultz nodded.

Feldman continued, "I wonder, though, why these particular crimes have struck a chord with you. The distinction between the departments exists for a reason, Otto. Why push it? Is it for the glory? The honor? Otto Shultz gets his man?" He waved his finger. "The people in Nuremberg may very well desire to see our system fail, but, remember, the best way for us to defend our system is to play by its rules."

"I haven't broken any rules," Shultz declared. "I just want to stop this before it gets any worse."

"Before you go, I have some things for you," Feldman said absently.

"We have built a world where there is very little uncertainty," said Shultz.

Feldman stood up from his chair. "Hold on, I'll go get them," he said, going back inside.

"Uncertainty is a cancer," Shultz continued with his sermon. "A cancer that has to be cut out, just like they had to do when people actually developed cancers. It rots the spirit, and soon after that, the flesh. It weighs down on the soul until a person begins to doubt whether or not life is even worth living. The success of our society stems from its absolute certitude."

Feldman returned holding a small box, and sat back down. "You'll need these if you have any hopes at all in passing through their gates," he said, holding out several items. "False papers and identification. You'll be Herr Flint out of Cologne, you're a porcelain wholesaler. Also, a false moustache," he said, holding up the thin strip of hair.

Shultz pointed at the box. "What's that?"

"Lederhosen," said Feldman.

"That won't do," said Shultz. "Nuremberg is historically Franconian. Lederhosen is more of a Bavarian custom."

"But Nuremberg was part of Bavaria in the old Federal days, a lot of people confuse the issue," said Feldman. "If you wear these," he said, spreading the lederhosen, "they would not think to suspect you are one of us. No real detective would make such a mistake, right?"

"A sort of reverse psychology, I get it," said Shultz, accepting the box.

"Any ideas on what you're going to do once you're in?"

Shultz fingered the false moustache. "At the moment, let's just concentrate on my getting in at all."

~7~

THE SPEAKER ON the wall next to the bed buzzed and Marvin Dennis woke up groggily, wiped the spittle from his mouth and checked the time. Six o'clock a.m., Eastern Standard Time. He pressed a button, turning on the view screen and sat up as the screen warmed to life, showing a stilled photographic image of the building supervisor, Uhaul Malone. "What is it?" asked Marvin, his voice hoarse with sleep. "It's early."

The stilled photo of Uhaul Malone slowly faded and was replaced by another photo--this one showing a much younger image of the man, lean faced and smiling. "There is a man to see you, Mister Dennis," Malone's voice came through the speaker. The image on the screen changed once more. This one capturing Uhaul Malone on the beach, flexing his muscles comically, a toothy smile on his face.

Marvin looked behind him as Flora turned unconsciously in her sleep. "Don't admit him," he said quietly. "It's too early for visitors."

"The man is already on his way up, Mister Dennis," said Malone, the speaker popping with static.

"What? Why did you let him in without my

permission?" asked Marvin, harshly. "That's contrary to our lease agreement."

The picture changed again, the man's face took up the whole screen, giving an insight to his nasal passage. Apparently the building supervisor was a man of good humor. "I am sorry, Mister Dennis," he said. "But the man coming to see you is with the Federal Board of Psychiatry. By law I--,"

"Fine," said Marvin, tartly, cutting the connection. The view screen went blank.

Flora turned once more, moaned tiredly and repositioned her pillow. She could sleep through just about anything. Marvin placed his hand on her shoulder and gently shook. "Flora," he whispered. "Flora, there's a psychiatrist on his way up."

Flora moaned again, opened her eyes. "Hmm...what?" she asked.

"Did you call for a psychiatrist?"

Flora shook her head as her brain tried to waken enough to fully understand. "No," she answered at length. "I don't think so."

"You don't think so?--"

The bell rang at the door.

"Who's that?" mumbled Flora, yawning.

"Never mind," said Marvin, pulling himself out of bed. He threw on a pair of pants and went to answer the door.

"Good morning, Mister Dennis," said the psychiatrist, a tall, thin man with ruddy cheeks. He wore a brown suit and held his hat in his hands. "Rutherford Haskell, practicing psychiatrist. I trust your building supervisor informed you of my presence. May I come inside?"

"Well, I'm obligated by law, aren't I?" said Marvin, holding the door open and waving the man inside.

"Not necessarily," said Rutherford Haskell, stepping inside and seating himself on Marvin Dennis' couch. "But refusing is frowned upon. In your case, though, it would hardly make a difference."

"What's that supposed to mean?" asked Marvin stepping into his kitchen to prepare water for coffee.

"We'll get to that in a moment, Mister Dennis. Might I call you Marvin?"

"Why not?" said Marvin. "Can I ask why you're here? And so early?"

"We have found it is best to conduct these interviews in the early morning," said Haskell. "Before the subject is able to secure his psychological defenses. Umm…if you wouldn't mind," he said, turning, "skipping the coffee. Any stimulates will complicate matters."

Marvin sighed, put the coffee away and grabbed another can. "Decaf?" he asked.

"Certainly," Haskell replied. "If you wouldn't mind--,"

"Cream or sugar?" asked Marvin with a sigh.

"Cream, please," said Haskell, satisfied.

Marvin moved into the living room, placed Haskell's cup on the coffee table in front of the couch and sat down on a matching easy chair, taking a sip from his own cup. Haskell stared down at the cup on the coffee table and smiled, leaned over to pick it up. Marvin locked eyes with him briefly, then looked away.

"You're body language speaks volumes," said Haskell, wryly, taking a sip.

Marvin stifled a yawn. "I suppose you're referring to the fact that I did not hand you the cup," he said.

"I was referring to your gait; the way you opened the door, fixed the coffee, sat down. You're an erratic person with a pessimistic vision of the future that keeps you from acting out. You see no positive consequences for any actions that you feel compelled to commit so instead you do nothing. You're energy bounces around kinetically but it is never released. You stifle it, hide it away, much like one does with a bad memory, until it seems you have no energy at all. You feel lackluster, complacent, but in truth, you are constantly teetering on the brink of catastrophe. You believe yourself to be a good man because you do no wrong, when in reality you do no wrong because you are simply afraid to do it. This does not mean you are a good man, it means you are just the opposite, only, unfulfilled." He took another sip of his coffee. "You're not handing me the cup was merely... well, bad manners."

Marvin finished his coffee, rose nervously to get another cup. "Why is it, exactly, you are here?" he asked, trying to keep the quiver out of his voice.

Haskell sat back. "It has come to our attention that you have recently been categorized PC108," he said. "Ineligible. I am here to see that you are taking it well."

Marvin felt his heart skip a beat. "That's impossible," he said. "My only restriction consists of insufficient funds. I can't be categorized ineligible because of that. That can always change."

"Yes," Haskell agreed. "But your psychology cannot. And that is what ultimately decides categorization, more so even than skin color or physical deformity."

Marvin slumped back down in the easy chair. It looked as if every muscle in his face had atrophied. He stared blankly at the floor, ignoring Haskell now, then looked up as Flora stepped out of the bedroom, her robe wrapped firmly about her.

"For the sake of your blood pressure, Mister Dennis," said Haskell as Flora knelt down beside Marvin and took his hand. "Do not feel obligated to hide your emotions. Let them out, I will understand. It is painful news."

Marvin did nothing. He merely stared ahead, blankly.

"What news? Marvin, what is he talking about?" asked Flora waving her hand in front of his face, trying for a response.

"Mrs. Dennis," said Haskell, "It seems to me that your husband was entirely unaware that he has been categorized PC108. I regret being the barer of this news, but I was sure he had been informed. How could he not know?" he asked quietly, almost to himself. "Heh…it's an awkward situation, to be sure," he said.

"I don't understand," said Flora. "What is a PC108?"

"Well, to put it simply, Mrs. Dennis. It means your husband is legally unable to procreate."

"That's not true!" yelled Marvin, venomously, frightening even Flora. He stood up and began to pace around the living room, cupping his hands over his ears as if Haskell were still speaking, destroying him with his words, as he had done. Then, suddenly, he lurched over the coffee table, his arms outstretched toward Haskell. Missing the psychiatrist, the coffee table slid out from under him, sending him flailing halfway to the floor. Swiftly, and with absolute calm, Haskell grabbed a hypodermic needle from his pocket and jabbed it into Marvin's arm. Flora screamed as her husband went limp.

"Don't be alarmed, Mrs. Dennis," said Haskell, picking Marvin up and hauling his slack form into the easy chair. "He's quite alright." Flora watched through teary eyes, covering her mouth as Haskell placed Marvin's arms on the arm rests of the chair, bent one leg over the other and stood his head up. Then, sitting back down on the couch, Haskell said loudly, "Mister Dennis, can you hear me?"

Marvin opened his eyes, turned his head a bit to look around the room and said, "What the hell have you done to me? Flora, what's happened?"

"You see, Mrs. Dennis," said Haskell. "He's perfectly fine." He turned back to Marvin. "You have been given a muscle relaxer, Mister Dennis. I always have a few handy for such occasions. Now, I am going to ask you a series of questions. Answer as best you can, the muscle relaxer will not hamper your thought process, it only calms the body. Will this be easier for you if your wife leaves the room?"

Marvin struggled to turn his head, looked

pathetically at his wife. "No," he said. "She can stay. I want her to stay."

Flora smiled as best she could under the circumstances. A tear rolled down her cheek.

"Okay, Mister Dennis, are you ready to begin?"

"You asked me earlier if you could call me Marvin," said Marvin.

"Would that make you more comfortable?"

Marvin nodded, stared down at his hands and wiggled his fingers experimentally.

"Okay, Marvin," said Haskell, smiling. "Are you currently taking any medications?"

"No," said Marvin. "Wouldn't that be in my file?"

Haskell picked at the lint on his pant cuff. "PC108's are more likely to…how should I say it, go outside the law? Try things that haven't been approved by the Surgeon General. Have you done anything like that? Don't be afraid to tell me. It's only a minor crime."

"I told you, I'm not on anything. And anyway, I just found out I was a…PC108."

"Of course," replied Haskell, somberly, then continued, "Would you like me to proscribe something, then? Something to take the edge off. We have many anti-depressants available."

Marvin shook his head.

Haskell waited just in case he changed his mind. Hoped for it. Nothing. "Okay, Marvin, how about suicide? Have you thought of that at all?"

Marvin hesitated, looked at his wife, nodded. Flora continued to cry silently. Marvin was always amazed by her strength. Man, how does she do it, he asked himself. How does she stick with me? After all I've put her through. Am putting her through.

"In that case," Haskell continued. "If you decide to explore the issue further, I can recommend several firms that are both inexpensive and humane." He pulled several business cards from his shirt pocket and held them out. Flora took them, held them close.

Is she trying to keep them from me, Marvin wondered? Or did she merely take them knowing my body is in an extremely relaxed state and it would have been much too difficult for me to take them myself? A wave of blissful happiness overtook him as he stared at his wife, teary eyed and clutching the suicide cards. No one had ever loved him so much.

"If you do visit one of those firms, if you wouldn't mind letting them know it was I who referred you to them, it would be much appreciated," said Haskell smiling once more.

"Is this almost over?" Flora asked impotently.

"Just one more thing," said Haskell. "Marvin, as you may know, we are always in need of organ donors. Will you give any thought--,"

"I could go for that," he said, surprised at himself for the speed of his response.

"In a sense, it's almost as good as procreation," Haskell continued with his pitch. "You get to live on through another."

"I said that's fine," said Marvin, the feeling of relaxation beginning to wear off, his body tingling all over, as if it were being held closely to an electrical outlet. It was somehow soothing.

Haskell said, "Great. I'll add that to your file.

You've been very pleasant." He rose, put his hat on his head. "Marvin, Mrs. Dennis, I'll see myself out." He moved toward the door, opened it. "Thanks for the decaf coffee," he said, stepping out and closing the door behind him.

With Rutherford Haskell's departure, the apartment seemed much smaller, as if the social importance of the man had enlarged it somehow with his presence, opened it up to the world outside. But now--

Marvin and Flora sat in silence, neither one moving, as if the walls had suddenly caved in, trapping them, hindering their ability to move. Marvin found it difficult to breathe. Even that one small, involuntary response had become too much of a chore.

Finally, he managed to say, "What time is it?"

Flora gazed at a clock in the kitchen. "It's almost seven," she said.

"I have to get ready for work," he said in a monotone. "Would you mind fetching my uniform?"

Flora stood up reluctantly and walked into the bedroom. She returned with Marvin's neatly pressed uniform and helped him to dress. "Don't go," she said, tying his shoes for him. "Call in sick, anything."

With a mighty effort, Marvin managed to stand. "I can't, Flora," he said. "After all, the waste needs managing. Apparently that's my purpose in life."

Flora's eyes welled with tears as Marvin made for the door. He turned, smiled weakly. "I love you," he said, and meant it.

Flora clasped her hands over her chest and mouthed the words back.

Once outside the building, Marvin walked

sluggishly down the sidewalk. I suppose, he thought, now that I have no chance of getting a procrete license, I can use our meagre savings to purchase a vehicle. Yeah, he thought. No more walking. No more taxi cabs and their disinterested drivers. I guess it's not all that bad. I can start riding to work like everyone else. Maybe that will help my self-esteem, he thought. A whole new world of velocity and relaxation. A life no longer limited to a few city blocks. I can go to Connecticut if I want. Rhode Island. Or even New York. Flora and I could have picnics at the beach. Why not.

Aww, who am I kidding. I would never qualify for a loan. I can't even have a vehicle. He cursed. This entire society is built upon the vehicle. A person is practically a nonentity without one. I don't understand. They should just give everyone a vehicle at birth. They're a necessity, like food and water, oxygen. I don't match any of the criteria to being a productive human being. Who needs someone like me around?

Maybe I should just kill myself, he thought, then.

Why haven't I? He wondered. You would think by now--

Is it because of Flora? No. Killing myself would be the biggest favor I ever did for her. But, maybe not. Maybe she's gotten so used to my suicidal disposition, it has become her purpose in life to make sure I'm still alive. Maybe she would have left long ago, except for the worry that I would probably do myself in shortly after. She doesn't stay because she believes I'd kill myself because she left, but because I would probably do it regardless and she feels my life is her responsibility. Cripes, I'm like a child that has to be constantly watched after. I'm not even a good failure. How she must feel. She thought she was marrying a man, but look what she's gotten herself into. I know why she stays, he thought. It's because I'm the next best thing to an infant!

He came to an intersection, waited for the light to change at the crosswalk.

It's not Flora, he said to himself. I know what it is. It's exactly like that psychiatrist said. I have such a pessimistic nature, I'm afraid if I do manage to kill myself, I'll open my eyes and find myself in the same exact situation. Like they used to believe in the old days. A sort of purgatory. I wouldn't even realize I was dead. Wouldn't remember a thing. I would just go on and on, hating myself, hating life, only I would already be dead. He froze, shuddered. Maybe I have already done it.

"You may cross now," said the signal light.

Marvin did not move. He caught something out of the corner of his eye. An Extra Solar Pioneer recruiting office. Packed in between a sandwich shop and a news stand. Lethargically, he made his way for it.

It was a small office, filled with brochures and posters. A gumball machine sat in the corner, half empty. There was no secretary. A man sat behind a single desk in the middle of the office. He always imagined these recruitment centers to be bustling with life, but this place was strangely calm.

"Come on in," said the man behind the desk,

motioning to a chair. "Have a seat.

The man was tall, powerful looking. Virile. He had stubble on his face! Marvin sat, scrutinized the man, picking out everything about the man that was unlike himself. Unlike anybody he had ever met. The man had an air of utter confidence, stern, yet, excepting.

"Before you say anything, let me ask you this," said the man, staring out the window as if talking to himself, chewing a wad of gum; his jaw muscles stood out with every bite. Marvin bit down, rubbed the side of his face to feel his own. "Are you tired of the hustle and bustle?" asked the man. "The cramped compartments. Fresh water rationing?"

Marvin nodded. Incredible, he thought. I am tired of all those things.

"Then let me tell you why being an Extra Solar Pioneer is what you want to be." The man held up a finger. "Peaceful surroundings with a limited number of companions. All trained and specialized to fulfil a specific purpose that is absolutely necessary. What do you do?"

Marvin hesitated. "I'm in waste management," he said.

"Perfect," said the man. "That's exactly the kind of skill we're looking for. I know how it is. I could hear it when you said it. You feel unsatisfied with your job."

Again, Marvin nodded.

"That's because earth society looks down on waste management. They don't realize the importance of such a skill. Not a job, a skill. But on a new planet, young and underdeveloped, the colonies need, absolutely need waste managers. Number two," he held up a second finger. "Each Extra Solar Landing Craft has separate compartments for each member of the crew approximately 1,500 square feet."

"That much?" Marvin interrupted, amazed.

"That much," said the man, smiling surly. He held up a third finger. "Three--All the fresh water you want, delivered regularly by supply satellites. That's why we ration down here, you know," said the man. "Because we need it up there."

"I have heard that," said Marvin. Once again, he scrutinized the man, almost homo-erotically. He was everything Marvin wanted to be. Everything he was not. He had never seen a government official quite like this man. So unlike the people he usually saw, robotic and soft, permanent smiles on their faces. Is this the true face of our government, he wondered. Strong, confident and secure? And the way the man spoke, not cold, authoritatively, like most government men. This man spoke with brashness, as if what he were saying could be wrong, but probably wasn't.

As if reading Marvin's thoughts, the man reached into his desk, slid a photograph across to him. Marvin picked it up. It was a photograph of the man, only younger, smaller, a despondent look on his face. "This is you?" he asked.

The man nodded. "I've been out there," he said. "That was me before signing up."

"Wow," Marvin exclaimed.

"Have a look at this," said the man, standing and swaggering over to the brochure stand. He picked one up and handed it to Marvin. It read 'HD1487-

Puppis, your new home.' The brochure was filled with pictures.

"Is this the actual planet?" he asked.

"That is an artistic representation," said the man. "We haven't set down there yet. But if you sign up, that is where you could be. The first man to set foot on HD1487. How does that sound?"

Marvin continued to read. 'HD1487 is a rocky moon orbiting a gas giant fifth from a 3rd magnitude super giant star in the Argo Navis. Imagine the beautiful nights accompanying a 248 day rotational year! Bring along a scarf, though, Pioneer, you'll need it.'

He put down the brochure. "If I were to sign up, when could I go?"

"I believe HD1487 is scheduled for October."

"October," said Marvin, disappointed. "I thought the Pioneer Rockets took off once a month. It's still May."

"Those are the supply satellites," said the man. "The Pioneer crews lift off every six months. Last month we sent a colony to Aldebaran."

Marvin ruminated. "I have a wife," he said. "Can she sign up too?"

"No women," said the man. "It would be immoral to put women in such precarious situations. It can be dangerous out there. But that is one of the charms."

"But…how do you sustain a colony without women?"

"Each Extra Solar Landing Craft is equipped with a full science lab, including an incubation chamber. The crew engineers children using their own seed.

78

That is reason number four." He held up four fingers. "As many children as you want. Another perk to being an Extra Solar Pioneer. No more psyche tests. No more licenses."

"Goodness." Marvin was amazed.

The man pulled a set of paperwork from his desk. "So, what do you say? Shall I sign you up?"

Marvin paused. "Can I think about it?"

"Sure," said the man, trying to hide his disappointment, putting the paperwork away. "Feel free to take the brochure with you."

"Thanks," said Marvin absently, picking up the brochure and making for the door.

"Take care," said the man.

Marvin nodded and walked out. Once outside the recruiting office, Marvin folded up the brochure and put it in his back pocket. He thought about Flora, shrugged, and then stepped in front of a moving vehicle.

~8~

FORDY MACLENNON SAT at his desk scribbling over some inane documents that seemed to fascinate only him when his secretary appeared suddenly as if from out of nowhere. Without looking up, he sighed, asked, "What is it?"

"A visitor to see you," said the secretary.

Fordy looked up, noticed a slight reddening in her cheeks, and sighed once more. "Who is it? I'm very busy," he said, trying not to upset her self-esteem. Announcing visitors was the highlight of any secretaries' day. He didn't have the heart to begrudge her.

The secretary looked at a small pad on which she had obviously written down the name of the visitor and said with some hesitation, "A Mister Hollis Kincaid, Mister MacLennon."

Fordy tried not to choke on his saliva and slowly pushed his documents aside. He cleared his throat. "I don't believe he has an appointment," he said and checked the time. "I can't be expected to---"

He was cut off as a middle aged man with considerable girth rather impolitely pushed the secretary aside and stood at the entrance of the cubicle. He was followed by a much younger, thinner man. Fordy sat back in his chair and tried to maintain an air of control.

"Hollis Kincaid," he announced dryly.

"Can't be expected to what?" asked Kincaid, shoving his way into the office, followed again by the younger man.

The secretary opened her mouth to complain but Fordy waved her off. "Be a dear and fetch us some coffee, will you?" he asked. She left with some hesitation.

Fordy turned his attention back to Kincaid. "Have a seat," he said.

"I don't want a seat," countered Kincaid. "I want to stand. I want to pace. Written complaints don't seem to do a whole lot of good, so making you uncomfortable on my feet seems to be the only way to get anything done around here."

"It's not working," Fordy lied, crossing his arms.

Kincaid threw his arms into the air. "How could you do it?" he asked through labored breaths. "How could you refuse to sanction my Megaplex?"

Fordy closed his eyes, pretending he had to recall the information. "Oh, yes," he said. "I believe my reasons were made clear in my report."

"Report nothing," said Kincaid. "I didn't receive any report. All I got was a big fat 'no' over the phone. And by the way, thanks for not having the guts to tell me yourself and getting your stooge Strinager to do your dirty work."

"It was Strinager's case," said Fordy.

"Nevertheless, your designs were so radical, you can hardly have expected us to give you the go ahead."

Kincaid grimaced. "You development people put far too much emphasis on design," he said. "What matters most is capitol, right? The Megaplex offers the people of Cheyenne fifty-six thousand square feet of quality materials at bargain prices. It will create jobs, potentially cutting unemployment by thirty percent. What can be wrong with that?"

"Nothing is wrong with that," Fordy replied. "But the ethical lines are clear. Construction of a Megaplex that mirrors the sight of untold deaths is beyond the pale. You're lucky I didn't call the authorities."

Kincaid began to pace, then froze. He seemed on the verge of hyperventilation. "The world needs shopping malls, MacLennon. The people need them!"

"Understood," said Fordy. "But not in the shape of Flavian's Amphitheater." He tapped his fingers on the desk. "Might I make an equitable suggestion?" he asked.

Kincaid shoved his hands in his pockets, gave him his full attention.

Fordy continued. "I am not opposed to your efforts," he said. "If it is historicity you wish to maintain, I would be more than willing to sign off on a design based upon...well, let's say the Alhambra."

Kincaid's face lost all feeling as if his muscles simply fell limp. His skin turned an ashen grey and his shoulders slumped. He looked over at the younger man who had accompanied him. "Warren, do you love me like a father?" he asked.

"Absolutely," the younger man responded.

"And I you as a son," said Kincaid reaching into the inside pocket of his coat and turning back to Fordy. "You leave me no other choice," he said, his voice resounding hollowly.

Fordy rubbed his temples. "I feel I've given you many choices," he said, then, upon seeing Hollis Kincaid pull a small caliber pistol from his pocket, his voice instantly shook. "Good gracious," he said. "How did you get that past security?"

Kincaid averted his eyes away from Fordy as he screwed a silencer over the barrel. "We could have been good together," he said, then pulled the trigger, sending three bullets slamming into Fordy's chest. He slumped over onto the desk, his head making a loud thump and bouncing slightly.

Warren shrieked, "Oh, you really did it!"

Kincaid turned to the younger man and let his jaw drop open. "Crickets, Warren. Of course I did it. That was the plan all along!"

"You said as a last resort."

"Jiminy, Warren. You were standing here. He gave me no other options."

"You killed him. You killed a man." He began to sweat, shook all over.

Kincaid looked at the younger man and pushed out his lower lip. Almost pouting. "I did no such thing," he said resolutely, peeking outside the office to make sure nobody had noticed his actions. Paranoia was creeping in.

"Then what would you call it?" asked Warren.

Kincaid hesitated, wiped the sweat from his brow and looked down at the body of Fordy MacLennon. A small pool of blood began to form at the center of the desk. "Suicide," he said, struck by a sudden inspiration. "Keep an eye out," he said to the younger man as he stooped down over the body and, wiping clean the butt of the pistol, he placed it gingerly into Fordy's cold hand. "Now," he said, standing up straight, his confidence renewed. "To make our escape."

"Murder," Warren groaned.

"Toughen up," Kincaid ordered. "The rest of our lives depends on our grim determination to forget the last three minutes. Warren, give me a hug."

Absent-mindedly, Warren embraced Hollis' wide figure. Kincaid grabbed the younger man by the shoulders and held him at arm's length. "Are you with me?" he asked.

Warren nodded, speechless.

At that moment, the secretary returned with the diversionary coffee, immediately spotted Fordy's punctured body and, dropping the coffee onto the floor, prepared her throat for a scream. Kincaid, fast on his feet, pre-empted this with a quick back handed smack to her mouth.

"Grab her feet!" Kincaid hissed to Warren as she fell dazed to the floor.

Warren did so, bending over and dragging the secretary into the office and placing her behind Fordy's desk. Tears came to his eyes.

"Good boy, Warren," Kincaid lauded. "Now, give her a good kick to the sides. I don't think that smack was enough to keep her out."

Warren hesitated. Wiped snot from his nose. "I can't do that, Hollis." he moaned. "Violence!"

"Crickets, Warren. Kick her in the sides!"

Warren kicked her in the sides. The secretary, wheezed, coughed, then lost consciousness. Kincaid pushed Warren aside, bent down and studied her breathing. He stroked his chin. "One more for good measure," he said.

Warren took a step back. He felt a strong compulsion to run out of the office. "I can't," he managed to say at last.

Kincaid spread his arms beseechingly. "This woman is the only witness to our arrival," he said. "If we're going to make it out of here we need to be absolutely certain she can't give us away. We need time to at least make it out of the building!"

A chill shot up Warren's spine as he found himself almost instinctually lifting his leg to deliver another blow to the poor secretary when--

"What on earth is going on here?" Cole Strinager demanded, standing at the entrance of the office. Warren froze with his foot in the air as Hollis Kincaid began to cough uncontrollably.

Strinager stepped foot into the office and, seemingly without fear, placed his hands firmly on his hips and shook his head. The reactions of surprised, desperate people always struck him as childish and, instead of having a sense of shock at the sight now confronting him, he instead felt a sense of patriarchal obligation toward the two other men.

"This is about the Megaplex, isn't it?" he asked. He

stole a glance at Fordy and the secretary. "I had a feeling something like this might happen." Then, holding out his hand, he made his move. "What can you offer me as compensation?"

Kincaid, recovering, shakily reached into his pocket. "I have one-hundred thousand debt credits I was prepared to offer MacLennon," he said.

Warren's eyes widened. "You never made that offer," he said with some force.

"He wouldn't have taken it," said Kincaid. "I could see it in his eyes."

Stringer shook his head. "Debt credits are no good to me," he said, yawned.

Kincaid swallowed with disbelief. "No good," he exclaimed. "Debt credits are better than cash. It's insurance! Stringer, you never can tell when the next crash might be. Especially with these explosions that have been happening! The markets are finicky!"

"All right," said Stringer with some resignation. "I suppose you do have a point. Even though the job of a development man is a rather stable affair. However, debt credits are untraceable and what's better, un-taxable," he mused. "Make it two-hundred thousand and we've got a deal."

Kincaid shook his fist in the air. "Why, you bloodsucker," he squawked. Spittle flew from his mouth. But, really, he had little choice in the matter. He gave in. "Fine," he said. "But I don't have the other hundred thousand on me. Can I write you an IOU?"

Stringer stifled a laugh. "Absolutely not," he said.

"It's not entirely unreasonable," Kincaid retorted.

"If it's all the same, I would like it as an assurance that you'll keep your word. Though, I'd like to take you at face value, I really would. You've always struck me as a fair man with vision. I know if it wasn't for MacLennon, my Megaplex would have been sanctioned in a heartbeat. But you have to understand, I can't take any chances."

Stringer deliberated for a moment. "I suppose it's only fair," he said.

Kincaid smiled, handed the initial debt credits over. Stringer stuffed them into his pocket. "When can I expect the other hundred thousand?" he asked.

"I'll have it wired into your account as soon as I'm in a safe place," Kincaid replied. "I assume your bank information is on the books."

Stringer nodded. Everybody's bank information was on the books. It was part of the Public Scrutiny Act meant to deter citizens from tax evasion or other unlawful cash gains. The federal government kept track of each citizens' finances. If a large deposit was made, or if a certain citizen appeared to have too much free cash in comparison to his wages and living expenses, the government would send people to inquire and, if need be, deal with that citizen. Debt credits, though, were another matter. Not being legal tender until after a person's cash surplus dried up, they were essentially ignored by the government, and therein lye the loophole.

"Okay then," said Stringer, letting his gaze turn to Warren who remained frozen in place, chalk white and sweating. "Are you okay?" he asked.

Warren gulped, then collapsed onto Fordy's desk

and began to hyperventilate. Kincaid scooped the young man up and supported his body against his own, much as one does a wounded comrade. "He's fine," said Kincaid.

"Well, if you don't mind," Strinager continued. "You should leave now. I would like to call an ambulance for Mr. MacLennon."

"Yes, of course," Kincaid agreed.

Warren, having recovered his strength, sheepishly followed Kincaid out of the office. They made their way through the Offices of Development and down the elevator to the lobby. As they passed building security, the guard held up the packet of debt credits Kincaid had offered to him earlier for entrance into the building and, with a friendly nod, said, "Have a pleasant evening, Mister Kincaid."

~9~

OTTO SHULTZ AWOKE to the sound of several vehicle horns blaring, including his own. He had fallen asleep on the road to Nuremberg and now found himself facing down a five kilometer traffic jam on the outskirts of the city, in the middle of a snaking line of vehicles waiting to pass through the gates. He mumbles a curse and regretted having woken from his slumber.

Sighing, he pressed a button on his manifold that shut off the automatic horn signal meant to sound every three minutes if the vehicle found itself at a standstill for more than a half hour. He wished the other drivers would do the same, but most people still found the horn to hold a supernatural power to get traffic moving. The fools. He sighed once more, scratched his leg, uncomfortably left naked by the lederhosen, and checked his face in the mirror. He needed a shave.

A horn sounded from the vehicle in front of his. He rolled down his window and leaned out. "Turn it off!" he shouted.

In response, the driver switched his vehicle off

automatic and set it in reverse, lightly backing in to the front end of Shultz's vehicle.

Shultz felt a strong desire to arrest the man, but he couldn't afford to blow his cover over a minor traffic incident. Instead, he settled for flipping the bird.

The thought of falling back to sleep came through fleetingly before the impatience of solving his case overpowered his mind. Reaching into his glove box, he pulled out a long white feather and stuck it into his cap. Then, upon observing that the traffic jam was in no danger of clearing up anytime soon, he stepped out of his vehicle and began the long walk toward the city gates.

A chill wind sent goose bumps down his thighs as he walked past the line of vehicles. An hour later he found himself confronted by border security. The man looked him up and down, shook his head and smiled. The sight of tourists in lederhosen had become a bored past-time.

"What's this all about?" asked Shultz, trying to cover his annoyance with a friendly smile.

A man wearing a florescent green uniform stood at the entrance of the gates, waving traffic to the left and to the right, trying to control the flow in an evenly, efficient manner.

The border guard blew his nose into a handkerchief and responded. "This is a busy thoroughfare, sir," he said. "Unfortunately, all trade vehicles have to enter the city on the same roads as the tourists."

Shultz looked around, taking in sight of the city's stone gates, purported to be the original walls of the city dating back to medieval times. He turned back to the border guard. "Can you give me an estimate on when I can expect to pass through?" he asked.

The guard craned his neck to view the traffic. "How far back are you?" he asked.

"About five kilometers," Shultz responded.

The guard checked his watch and puffed out his cheeks. "I would have to hazard a guess, of course," he said. "But I would say another two or three hours."

Shultz stomped his foot and dropped his cap. "Fine," he said, recovering his posture and smiling to the guard. He replaced the cap and headed back to his vehicle.

Once back in his vehicle his mobile rang. He answered.

"This is a cross reference update," said a robotic, feminine voice.

Shultz cursed once more.

"On the third of this month," came the same robotic voice. "You dialed Global Information in request for a number to--." Now his own voice, "Offices of Development, any region." The robotic voice continued. "After which you were referred to Springfield Corporate. The man you spoke to, Fordy MacLennon, was admitted to the emergency room this afternoon at precisely 2 p.m. eastern standard time. The cause being three gunshot wounds to the chest. This has been a priority cross reference update to Otto Shultz, thank you." A clicking noise ended the update. Shultz hung up the phone and found himself very confused. What was the significance of this new information? Was it connected to the case?

Was Fordy MacLennon somehow involved with the recent terrorist activity? Well, whatever it was, he would have to figure it out later.

The line began to move. His vehicle began to crawl forward. The guard was mistaken, Shultz said to himself. At this pace, he would be reaching the gates within the hour.

Three hours later, he found himself once more in front of the Border Guard and showed his false papers.

"Good evening, Herr Flint," said the guard, not showing him any recognition. "What is the cause of your visit?"

Shultz hesitated. He had not anticipated the need for a cause. "Um," he said.

The border guard waited patiently for a response and Shultz began to panic when, all of a sudden, the passenger side door of his vehicle opened and a smart looking fellow with close cropped blonde hair and a dark suit climbed inside. He leaned past Shultz and flashed a badge at the guard.

"Give this fellow a pass," he said to the guard. "He's with channel 4 news, here to do a retrospective on the imperial electorate."

The guard peered closely at the badge and nodded, stamped the false papers and waved Shultz through the Am Hallertor gates. The traffic controller in the florescent uniform waved him toward a gigantic circular parking ramp.

"Can't I park inside the city?" asked Shultz, ignoring for the moment the peculiar presence of the man sitting beside him.

"No vehicles are allowed inside the city," said the man. "As you can understand, space is extremely limited in Nuremberg. That's why we've built these extensive parking ramps circling the gates. So our citizens can walk freely throughout the city."

Shultz pulled his vehicle into an empty space on the third level, put it in park and turned to his passenger. "Okay, who are you?" he asked.

The man smiled. "I'm sure you have a lot of pre-conceived notions about us, Herr Flint," said the man. "But that is to be expected." He opened his door and slid one leg out. "For my own gratification, though," he continued. "Would you mind, Herr Shultz, if I called you by your real name?"

Shultz grabbed the man by the shoulder to keep him in the vehicle. "How did you know?" he asked.

The man smiled again. "We have quite an extensive network, Herr Shultz," he replied. "Regardless of what you might think, we're not savages."

"Who are you with?" Shultz demanded.

The man showed him his badge. "Detective Schiller, Nuremberg polizei," said the man. "I anticipated the Friendly Neighbors' might be paying us a visit." He stepped out of the vehicle. "I believe we might be able to help one another."

Shultz stepped out of the vehicle, made an effort to pull down the lederhosen.

Schiller stuck his hands in his pockets and watched Shultz struggle with the costume. "I had some difficulty seeing through your disguise," he said. "Luckily I knew you were coming. Otherwise you never would have made it past the gates."

Shultz was suspicious, naturally. "And why would I not have made it past the gates if the Nuremberg polizei wishes to work with me?"

"I did not say the Polizei wishes to cooperate," said Schiller. "What I meant was that you and I might be able to work together. You see, this is all off the record. In recent weeks I have stumbled across something that my superiors would rather I had not. This is a…private investigation, Herr Shultz."

"You wouldn't have happened across any information about the recent bombings, would you?" asked Shultz.

Schiller began walking down the ramp toward the street, motioned for Shultz to follow. Shultz lingered behind, began to pull off the false moustache.

"No. Leave it on," said Schiller. "You must not be found out."

Shultz quickened his pace to catch up with the policeman. "Listen, Schiller," he said. "My presence here is serious business and I don't have time to fool around. Lives depend on my ability to find answers. So if you have any information to share on the bombings you better come out with it. Otherwise, I have no time to spare with whatever internal problems this city may have."

Schiller laughed quietly, knowingly. It was somehow unnerving. "You don't like us very much, do you?" he asked. "Most of you don't. Though, I suppose it is nothing worth complaining about. Your government's vilification of us, if anything, has made you people quite curious. Thirty percent of our national revenue is based upon tourism. The corporate world comes in droves to see how we small people live. I sometimes believe they expect us to be cavorting around in loin cloths and beating each other with sticks." He laughed again, loudly. "The fact is," he said, turning to face Shultz. He continued to lead the way, walking backwards. "We are not so very different from you. For example, did you know that one-third of the Extra Solar Pioneers are from Nuremberg? In fact, our physicists are very involved with the program."

"Yes, yes, I knew that," Shultz spat out. It was almost as if the information angered him on a deeply personal level. "I don't need a lecture from you on the value of your little city. If you and I are not so very different, why is it kick your heels into the dirt in order to stay separate from us. Your selfishness upsets the entire global community."

"We cling to our identity, Herr Shultz," Schiller replied, his face losing all humour. "After all, in the end, it is all we have."

Shultz locked eyes with the man. He opened his mouth several times to speak before deciding upon something to say. What could he say to counter such an argument? The government had been trying for several decades to do just that. And he had to wonder, did he really care to try? If he were thinking straight, he could simply have stated that nobody has an identity in the end. Death conquers all. Not just the physical being, but everything there is. And there is no counter to that argument.

"Where are we going?" he asked, frustrated.

95

"Somewhere we can talk," said Schiller. "Somewhere private."

He continued to lead the way, travelling down Weintraubing before turning left on Karl Strasse, heading toward the Weinmarkt. They walked in silence. The streets were full of pedestrians and people on bicycles. Entire families were out and about simply spending time together. Most of the families seemed to include several children. Shultz marveled at the sight and his mind wavered between indignation and disgust for their system.

"Do you realize you could cut down on that monstrous traffic out there if you would only implement our policy of controlled birth?" he asked, breaking the silence and motioning with his thumb toward the several storied parking garages. "You wouldn't need that maze of space. There would be less foot traffic. People would actually be able to drive freely throughout the city."

Schiller responded without turning. "I suppose traffic is far less of a concern for us than it is for you, Herr Shultz." He added, "I don't believe I need to point out the fact that I consider some of your laws to be inhumane and downright cruel. However, unfortunately, I am a man of the law. And I believe the law should be upheld," he said rather cryptically.

They turned onto Augustinerstrasse and followed a small alley before coming out into a large open area that served as a market place. The square was bordered on three sides by a series of colorful, local businesses and, towering above the market place, seeming to dominate the mood and beauty of the entire area, stood St. Sebaldus Cathedral, Sebalduskirche, a 13th century Romanesque structure with a later constructed high gothic choir. A more secular reconstruction of the cathedral had recently been built just outside of Newark, New Jersey. It housed a shoe factory. The government in Nuremberg had made quite a fuss about that. Shultz had seen photographs of the shoe factory and had found it charming, but the ancient structure before him gave him an inexplicably strange feeling slightly reminiscent of indigestion. This was an actual, functioning house of worship. Shultz quietly passed gas. It was witchcraft! He shuddered as he realized Schiller was heading right for it.

"We can talk in here," said Schiller placing his hand on Shultz' back and beckoning him toward the large bronze doors.

Visions of being led into an underground dungeon by robed occultists flashed through Shultz' mind. "I'd rather not," he said, trying to maintain his composure.

Schiller glanced at a small group of tourists snapping a photo of the cathedral. He was anxious. Apparently, he was afraid they were being watched; as if it were something he weren't used to. "But--," he said, almost pouting. "What I need to show you is *in here*."

Shultz took a step back. "It makes me uncomfortable," he said.

Schiller seemed to understand. "If you do not fear God, then why should you fear His house?" he asked rather metaphysically.

He was challenging Shultz' reason. The backbone of his entire society. It was a textbook psychological trick and it worked. Shultz straightened his back and took a deep breath. "All right. Let's see what *you* have to show *me*," he said condescendingly and grabbed hold of the doors of the church. Schiller followed behind.

Shultz had to strain to pull the door open. As if he hadn't already felt he was doing something wrong, inappropriate, not to mention the fact that he was straddling a treasonous line, it seemed the church itself did not want him inside. He peered back at Schiller, hoping to see in the man's eyes a change of mind. "You see?" he wanted to say, but he held his tongue. Stepped inside. Schiller closed the door behind them and Shultz shivered as a cold chill overtook him. Once again he looked back to Schiller.

"It is always cold inside," he said, sensing Shultz's doubt. "Follow me," he continued. "You don't have to look at anything if you don't want to."

Shultz didn't want to. But he couldn't help his eyes from wandering as Schiller led him further into the church, past the friezes and the stained glass.

"Who are they?" asked Shultz, pointing to the small statuettes that lined the walls.

"Saints mostly," Schiller responded.

"Idolatry," said Shultz. "And not just for a god." He looked up toward a cross upon the pew. "The seeds of violence lie in the images of man," he said. "And that," he motioned to the cross. "How can you worship murder and death?"

"This place represents far more than death, Herr

Shultz," said Schiller. "It represents eternal life and love. But I didn't bring you here to convert you. I brought you here to show you the more practical side of this building. After all, isn't that what you worship?"

Shultz remained silent, secure in the fact that he didn't need to dignify the statement with an answer as Schiller led him toward what looked to be a mausoleum. He stepped through the lattice work gate and motioned for Shultz to follow. He did so. All became dark as they descended down a narrow stair. Shultz felt Schiller grab his arm and place it firmly on his shoulder. "So you don't get lost," he said. Shultz followed along, placing his trust in the man.

After several minutes on the stairs, Shultz felt his feet on even ground. Felt loose gravel and damp earth. Schiller continued to lead him through a winding passage and his eyes began to make shapes in the dark. Flashing spots and ghostly images. At one point Shultz felt Schiller's hand press down on his head. He resisted only to bang his head as the passage grew increasingly cramped. Once again, they began to descend. This time down what felt like an unnatural stair carved out of stone. Schultz felt as if he were travelling through time. Into a darkness far more sinister than the very real dark he was being led through. He actually found himself grateful for Schiller's presence. Whatever their disagreements, at least he was another human being. They stopped. He heard Schiller bang on a hard surface.

"This is it," said Schiller. His voice echoed down the passage.

"Where are we?" Shultz asked. It was a pointless question. He knew Schiller would never be able to explain past the obvious directional physicality of the place. He knew where he was physically. But he wanted to know where he <u>was</u>.

He heard Schiller snicker and felt immediately disappointed with himself. "I know what he's thinking," Shultz said to himself. "Every moment in the darkness he feels is bringing me closer to his God."

A thin red light shone suddenly in the darkness. A sensor plate. Shultz sighed with relief. That at least was something from his world. He saw Schiller's face light up as he pressed his mouth up to the light.

"Atomic engine," Schiller said into the sensor.

The light switched to green and a clicking noise resounded throughout the passage.

"Watch yourself," said Schiller pushing Shultz back a few steps. The green light illuminated Schiller faintly as he knelt down and pulled up a small square concrete block. A light shown from below and Shultz peered down. It was a well lit room with a short ladder leading down into it. It was packed wall to wall with electronic equipment and several old fashioned type machines that he did not recognize. Schiller headed down and beckoned Shultz to follow behind.

Shultz skipped the last several rungs of the ladder and allowed himself to drop if for no other reason than to feel himself once more on solid ground. He was amazed at his own superstitious-ness. He wondered if that were the true cause of his antagonism towards the people of Nuremberg. Oh well. At least he was in a semi modern room.

Schiller slapped his hands on his knees and smiled wide. "I can't believe it," he said. "It worked. It took my partner and I months to get that password." He practically danced around the room. In the far corner were stacks of plastic crates. He walked over to them and opened them up. "Here, come have a look at this," he said, waving Shultz over.

The crates were filled with loose sheets of paper bound with cord. "What is it?" asked Shultz.

"Just look."

Shultz picked up a ream. A chill shot down his spine.

"Are these what I think they are?"

"Scandalous, isn't it?" said Schiller. He laughed.

Shultz waved the ream of papers in the air. "This isn't funny. How long have you known about this?"

"We've known for quite some time," said Schiller. "Of course we didn't have any proof. But that all changes now."

"These are procrete licenses," said Shultz in disbelief.

"No, they're not. They're forgeries."

Shultz cut the cord and pulled several sheets from the ream. Studied them. "They're perfect." He shot an accusing stare at Schiller. "Why weren't we informed about this earlier?"

"Because it's not against any of our laws," said Schiller. "Simply put, our government does not care. But as I said, I am a man of the law. This is a happy coincidence for you."

Shultz weighed the forged licenses in his hand with the thoughts in his mind. It didn't add up. "But I'm here to investigate the bombings," he said pathetically.

Schiller was indignant. "Forget the bombings. That's not even your responsibility. Don't you have a special unit to take care of intended crimes?"

"Yes, but by its nature, these documents are intended for future crimes so I don't think I can be of any real help here."

"These crimes are proof of crimes already committed," countered Schiller. "For all we know, these documents are merely left over from the bulk." He lowered his voice. "I brought you here to help. My partner and I have put ourselves into considerable danger."

Shultz sighed. "These documents could disrupt our entire society. Who knows how many people are out there procreating illegally. All we need is one mentally retarded child to shake confidence in the system." He shook his head.

A ringing interrupted his thoughts. Schiller took his mobile from his pocket and answered. He listened intently to the speaker on the other end. Shultz noticed as Schiller began to perspire. His hand was shaking as he hung up.

"We have to go," he said with some urgency. "Bring those," he said indicating the documents Shultz still held.

"What's wrong?"

"The code was a plant," said Schiller heading for the ladder. "Meant to inform the conspirators of a false entry. They may be here any minute."

Shultz stuffed the forged documents into his waist line, tucked them under his shirt as he began to follow Schiller out. "Was that your partner on the other end?"

"Quiet!" Schiller yelled and shoved Shultz back into the hole. He jumped down after and looked nervously for a place to hide. "I hear voices."

Shultz listened for the voices and heard a faint echo. Schiller pulled several of the crates containing the false documents slightly from the wall. "Hide behind these," he said. Shultz squeezed between the crates and the wall.

"Just show them your badge," said Shultz. "What are you afraid of?"

Schiller continued to search for a place to hide himself, said quietly, "Our people aren't like yours," he said. "Police can die in Nuremberg." Seeing there was no place to hide, Schiller pulled his pistol from its holster. "Whatever happens, stay out of sight. I'll have to hold them off." He ran over to Shultz and knelt down. "If I don't make it, meet my partner at the corner of Unter and Hoch. His name is Hoyt. They'll be looking for you. He will help you get out."

Voices could be plainly heard now. Whoever was coming was at the entrance. Schiller placed himself behind a printing machine and levelled his gun.

"Come on out, policeman," said a harsh, sinister voice. "You have no chance."

Schiller wiped sweat from his brow. "This is Officer Schiller of the Nuremberg polizei," he said with an authority masking his fear. "I hold in my hand a Luger type ten. It fires multiple ten ounce pellets that can take the head off of any man. I don't want to hurt anybody. Come down the ladder slowly and give yourselves up. As a final warning, I have the firepower to take on a small army. It is your choice."

Laughter echoed down from the chamber. Shultz wanted to wet himself. Never had he been in such a position. He had no control. I don't want to die in this hole, he thought. And even if Schiller were telling the truth about his firearm, which he highly doubted, he didn't want to see a man's head blown clean off either. It was a no win situation.

What am I doing here?

All the same, though, Schiller seemed confident. At least on the surface. It was enough to lend Shultz a bit of hope.

Schiller shouted, "I'm going to count to five and after that I'm coming up shooting. Or you can do yourselves a favor and climb down. I'm a crack shot, I promise you."

"Okay, we're coming down," came the same sinister voice, only this time with an air of caution. Schiller's bluff seemed to be paying off. A black booted foot appeared on the top rung of the ladder. Someone was climbing down, slowly, until--

Suddenly, the person on the ladder jumped down, skipping the rest of the rungs. Several more shadowy figures followed quickly behind. They reached Schiller in a hurry, taking him completely by surprise. He didn't have time to fire even a single shot.

"Traitor!" one of the men shouted as they knocked Schiller off his feet.

Shultz closed his eyes and would have covered his ears if he weren't so afraid to move. Schiller gave out a deathly moan and Shultz observed one of the shadowy men tucking a bloodied knife into his cloak. Schiller grabbed hold of one of the men as they began to climb the ladder back to the top. The man kicked him away and spat on him before climbing up himself.

Shultz waited in terror as the cover to the room was replaced. Fear had wholly taken over him. He was buried alive. In the same room with a dying man.

~10~

BUSTER MACREADY SCANNED the horizon for any sign of life. Nothing. He shot another flair into the sky and tried to ignore the presence at his side.

Before you were born, I knew you, it said. For the last thirty days, Buster had been trying his hardest to remind himself that the figure beside him was nothing more than his imagination. A psychotic reaction to the endless space around him. But no matter how many times he closed his eyes and counted to ten, the figure remained. No longer just a voice in his head. It reminded him of the dangers surrounding him, and the hopeless mission he found himself trying to accomplish.

There is nobody; no one to find; no one to save. You're all alone.

You just want me to give up, Buster said to the figure. Forget about everyone and fend for myself.

You are all you have, said the figure.

Maybe physically, Buster replied. Without the

others I am nothing. Just matter. It is through others I live. After all, isn't man a social creature?

Man survives through competition with others of his kind, said the figure. Violence, greed, selfishness, would not exist without a collective. Do you really want to be part of that collective? Do you really want to perpetuate violence and greed? Wouldn't it be easier to give up? Wouldn't it be more godly?

Buster clasped his hands over his ears. Deceit, he said. I'm not listening to you.

I have been with you, said the figure, from the beginning. When you were on earth; when you were journeying here. I have been with you always. And I will be here long after you are gone. If you search your heart, you will see the need for my wisdom. Just lie down here. I will show you the gates of forever.

If I lay down I'll die, said Buster. I still have three flares left. There's always a chance.

A chance for what, asked the figure. More failure? More disappointment? More hate and anger? If you stop now, humanities ills will not take hold of this planet!

Shut up.

This planet is pure! Do you really want to spread this poison?

Buster fell to his knees and burst into tears. It would be so easy to give up. The planet was completely dead. Aside from a few square centimeters of ground collapsing every hour or so, there was no movement at all.

How can you say this planet is pure, Buster asked, when the only action it makes is a symptom of self-destruction? Is this the only true nature? The basic component to life? Self-destruction? If man, a purely reactional creature, had not learned to assert himself aggressively, would we ever have evolved beyond the simple ape? Is this the way of the universe? Would we be able to found a sustainable colony on a world truly at peace?

Humanity is antonymous with peace, said the figure. A struggle is symptomatic of negativity. Life is a struggle. Give up life, give up the struggle. All else is positive.

Why is it so hard? Buster whined above the roar of the atmosphere.

It's not as hard as it might seem, said a distant voice. Buster looked around, the figure had disappeared. He brought the scooter to a halt and scanned the horizon once more. Another figure, robed and far taller than the last, stood upon a great precipice in the distance. Buster could barely make out the figure's silhouette through the dusty haze. He brought his hands up to his eyes, hoping for a clearer vision.

The figure waved to him, seeming to move in slow motion, then circled its hands about its mouth as if to shout. But its words came softly to Buster's ears.

In the end, there are no questions, It said. No reasons. No time. Only answers. Your mission is one of selfishness, not sacrifice. You struggle only to fulfil your own selfish motivations. Failing your comrades brings with it only the negative connotations of failure. This is what motivates you. Not the desire to see to your comrades' wellbeing. Do not give into selfishness. Lie down, and allow yourself to merge with the ethereal.

Buster felt the already thin air growing thinner. He moved to put on his helmet when the feeling overtook him that it might somehow be wrong. "No!" he shouted.

Or maybe you're simply making a power-play, said another figure, appearing suddenly at Buster's side. Its voice was harsh with aggravated hate. Buster jumped away from the figure, falling off the scooter and rolling several yards. His head bounced off the ground, a rock split the skin right above his eye.

Your only desire in accomplishing this 'mission' is to put yourself in a much more powerful position in the soon to be developed hierarchy of this planet, the figure continued, bending obscenely over Buster's flailing form. Buster covered his ears and tried to rebound away from the figure. At a quick glance, the figure was beautiful. But when Buster took a longer look, his body froze in horror at the monstrosity before him. The figure had three faces on a single head, with fiery tongues darting from each mouth. Its eyes were vacant, hollow, but there nonetheless. Its fingers were long, at least seven inches, and curved along with the serpentine motions of the body.

You are envious of the others and want revenge, It said. Admit it!

Buster turned away from the figure and began to race after the scooter which had sprung back to life after his fall. For a moment, he was able to forget the figure and give thanks, for once, of the scooter's slow speed. Apparently, that split second of forgetfulness was enough. The figure vanished. Buster felt a small sense of victory before the scooter's left wheel brushed up against a boulder, causing it to veer to the right. Buster's foot slipped from the high step and he fell once more to the ground. After a slight moment of hesitation, Buster felt his fall continuing. The ground had given way below him. As he tumbled to the bottom of the newly created cavern, he just barely escaped being crushed by the scooter which followed him down. As the dust settled, he coughed and rubbed his eyes. The scooter, remaining active, whirred as it rammed continuously into the walls of the cavern. The sound of its machinery echoed in the darkness; off the dust and rocks.

2

(DISOBEDIANCE)

~   BUSTER DOUBLED OVER as his dust filled lungs attempted to heave out the waste. He felt cold all over and a certain amount of fear gave him an urge to pray for his life. There was no calm in the stillness of the hole that swallowed him up. If it weren't for the hollow hum of the scooter and the immense pain racking his entire body Buster would begin to doubt whether or not he were still alive. At the moment, though, while he knew for a certainty he was alive, he did begin to wonder if he were not in hell.

Feeling a tingling sensation on his upper thigh, Buster jumped quickly to his feet and began to dance deliriously around, for fear of whatever it was that was crawling up his leg. He brushed furiously at his leg and stomped. Whatever it was had gotten into his suit. He screamed out in terror. Then--

A woman's hand reached around from behind and stroked his face tenderly. Buster opened his eyes wide and turned slowly. The woman smiled faintly and held a finger to his lips.

Shhh…

Buster forgot his fear in his adoration of the woman as she laid her hands on his shoulders and pressed him gently to the ground. He continued to stare, fixated, as the woman rubbed her fingers down the length of his body, lightly tapping them as if gently stroking the keys of a piano. She reached into the waistline of his suit and, to Buster's disbelief, pulled out a creature roughly resembling a centipede. She gave a sweet sigh and held the creature close to Buster's face, then giggled as he recoiled.

With a subtle movement, the woman dropped the creature and crushed it beneath her bare heel. Buster shut his eyes as a black liquid escaped from the crushed form.

The woman moved intimately closer to Buster and waited patiently for him to open his eyes.

There is life here already, she said in a musical voice. Life requires a creator.

Buster opened his eyes. It was almost impossible to breathe. He needed his helmet. He waved his arm upon the ground in search for it.

Your presence here interrupts the plan of the creator, said the woman. Why would you want to do something like that? Who are you to even try?

His eyes having adjusted to the dark, Buster spotted his helmet several feet away. He leaned forward in an attempt to stand, but the woman pushed him back down. Her lips receded angrily.

Who are you to even try? She asked again with utter malice. You are nothing! Less than this worm!

She bent and picked up the remains of the creature and dangled them in his face. Buster closed his eyes once more and bit down so hard his face shook. He was beginning to gasp for air. With his eyes still closed, Buster lifted his arm to push the woman away, but he felt nothing. He opened his eyes. The woman had vanished. Along with the crushed worm.

With a haggard moan, Buster dove over to his helmet and quickly pulled it over his head. Able to breathe once more, he took several deep breaths and fell down dizzy. On the ground, he searched for any sign of the woman. Seeing nothing, he covered his

114

faceplate with his hands.

It's not fair, he moaned.

Suddenly, a bright light flashed in the sky overhead, lighting the cavern in a ghostly red. Buster looked up and began to cry.

What now, he asked himself. Then-

As the light filtered away, Buster imagined a shape moving dexterously in the dark. Moving as if it were following the shadows caused by the light. Trying to stay in the dark. Buster strained his eyes to make out the shape, but the light faded away and he could see now less than he could before. He waved his arms in the dark as the warmth of his labored breaths returned to him from his faceplate. The breathing apparatus was not working correctly. It wasn't circulating the air properly. Moisture clung to his faceplate, blinding him more than he already was. He heard a noise and backed instinctively against the wall of the cavern.

Give me strength, he prayed.

At that moment, loose dirt sprinkled his helmet. Buster quickly looked up and tried to wipe his faceplate, knowing as he did so that the problem lay on the inside.

"Leave me alone!" he shouted. "What do you want?"

"What are you doing down there?" came a voice from above.

Buster tried to recoil away from the voice, tried to find a place to hide. He followed the sound of the scooter, desperate to find something recognizable to hold onto. Something to keep him grounded in reality. Safe.

"Are you alone?" asked the voice.

"Alone," Buster repeated to himself. "All alone. Here in the dark."

"I'm lowering a rope," said the voice. "Try and pull yourself up."

Buster felt something brush against him. It was the rope. He grabbed it blindly and gripped it tightly with his hands as if testing its reality. It was real. He felt joy overtaking him. But he was cautious.

"Who are you?" he asked.

Several seconds later came the response. "Name's Stevenson. I'm a crew member of the Extra Solar Craft: Heidi Irregular. Climb the rope."

"I can't see you," said Buster. "I can't see anything."

"Take off your helmet."

I can't take off my helmet, thought Buster. I can't breathe. "I can't take it off," he said aloud.

"Take it off and look up here," said the voice, sternly.

Buster closed his eyes and took several deep breaths. What did he have to lose, really? Suddenly determined, he put his hands up and pulled off the helmet. Looked up.

Stevenson knelt over the edge of the cavern, holding the other end of the rope tightly in his hands. Waiting for Buster to pull himself up. Buster stared in disbelief. Was this another illusion? Another temptation? Stevenson's mouth moved but Buster could not hear him. Then, remembering he had removed his helmet, he recovered the microphone from its inner pocket.

"--long have you been out here?" came the belated voice of Stevenson through the microphone. "Is there anybody else with you? Where is the rest of your crew?"

Buster looked up in awe. Stevenson was real. "I've found you," he said.

Stevenson removed his own helmet, revealing a wise, weather beaten face, and steadied himself as Buster began climbing the rope. "No," he said. "I have   found   you."

~11~

AN UNASSUMING MAN sat at the edge of a high-rise, looking down. His head moved side to side, slowly, as if searching for a particular light out of the billions that shone below. The lights reflected in his eyes, giving them the appearance of life; kinetic and dancing; though the eyes seemed to hold a natural glaze, so that if the lights were dimmed, the eyes would seem those of a dead man, fit only to match the expressionless features of the face.

The wind blew strongly so high up, blowing back the man's cloak, revealing a rather thin figure. It was a wonder the wind did not carry the man over. But, then again, maybe the wind found him unassuming as well.

Knob Hill could be seen not too far off in the distance. As well as the Golden Gate Bridge, the Justice Building, Alcatraz, too, with its newly renovated condos-built specifically for local politicos-only twenty stories high.

The Financial Building that he stood atop of swayed slightly with the breeze and a whale could be heard singing somewhere off in the Bay; its sad song riding the calm waters to shore. The man listened for a moment the best he could over the wind, seemed to want to cry, and closed his eyes to better imagine what humble request the ancient creature might be making.

He turned then to walk to the other side of the building. One step in the dark sent a flock of frightened pigeons fluttering violently away in the night sky. The man lost his balance for a moment, bent at the knee to correct himself, and gave a low, chilling laugh at his own expense. To be killed by pigeons, nature's most benign creature, would be an irony.

On reaching the other side of the building, looking down now at the piers and wharfs, there was little light to dance in the man's eyes. He let out a slow breath and, standing rigidly suddenly, covered his face with a gloved hand as a dozen motion sensor security cameras attached to the adjacent building clicked to life, rotating up in his direction. He had not anticipated them. Thought the buildings too far apart. Luckily, he was able to cover his face in time, before they could alter their lenses. Nevertheless, they would have to be dealt with.

There was a better view of the Golden Gate Bridge on this side of the building, as well as Alcatraz. He gazed far off into the water for a moment, hoping to catch sight of the whale, but soon gave up. It was far too dark out there over the water. Still, the thought of a whale wandering into the Bay was fantastic. Even after all this time. After the water had receded so far. Had he not heard it, he would not have believed it.

Or, maybe he would have.

He let his eyes follow the water, back toward dry land, until letting them fall on the massive wall that seemed to hold back the water from the city. The wall that announced, ever so famously, the Port of San Francisco.

The man closed his eyes, whispered quietly, "Fiery Angels fall to the shore, look up to the sky and cry once more."

Then, with a sigh, he put his hand in his pocket and pushed a button, thunderously lighting up the night sky.

~12~

MARVIN DENNIS WOKE up several minutes before opening his eyes. He had been dreaming and was trying to keep hold of the lucidity brought on by the long sleep. He felt it vanish as his body became heavy. His limbs. His heart.

He opened his eyes. Flora stood above him, looking down. Her eyes were red from lack of sleep and her lips were chapped. She seemed to have aged a decade. Marvin began to wonder how long he had been asleep.

"You're awake," Flora said, a slight quiver of relief in her voice.

Marvin smiled.

"Don't try to move. The doctor will be here any moment."

"How long was I out?" he asked.

Flora smiled tenderly and grabbed his hand as a short man with spectacles and receding hair entered the room. He said nothing to either Flora or Marvin. Checked the monitors at Marvin's bedside and stroked his chin. After reading the monitors, the man made several strange gestures with his face, clasped his hands behind his back then leaned over Marvin to prop his eye lids open. Marvin rolled his pupils to keep them from drying out as the man stared long and hard into them. After the man let go, Marvin had to close his eyes for several seconds to stop them from burning.

The man turned to Flora. "He'll be fine," he said matter of fact. Then, turning once more to Marvin. "You'll be fine, Mister Dennis. Thanks for wasting our time."

The man exited the room without another word. Apparently he was in a foul mood.

"How long was I out?" Marvin asked again. "What happened?"

"I'll tell you what happened," came the aggravated voice of Rutherford Haskell. Marvin turned his head to see the government psychiatrist enter the room. "You've proven yourself to be not only a man of short temper and depressed demeanor, but you're also a filthy liar." He stepped up to the bed, shot Flora a quick smile and laid his briefcase down on the floor. "Mister Dennis, did I not ask you just a half hour before you decided to jump into traffic if you were or were not interested in suicide? Did I not recommend several reputable firms if you were interested? You know, suicide is legal for a reason, Mister Dennis. It is legal so that people like you do not endanger the lives of others because you decide to do something rash. You could have killed the man riding in the vehicle that hit you, Mister Dennis. Is that any solution? People dive off the roof of their apartment buildings, they don't care who they hit on the way down. People overdose on medications, giving no thought to that medication going to another who needs it. Another who actually wants to live. This, my friend, is why you were deemed unfit to parent a child." Haskell took a breath, smiled once more at Flora and moved to the side of Marvin's bed, grimaced. "What is worse, Mister Dennis," he continued. "You take up the precious time of these fine hospital workers. Fortunately, you weren't all that badly hurt so you didn't waste too many resources. Now, Mister Dennis, I am obligated to ask you this while we are on the premises. Do you in fact want to die?"

Marvin narrowed his eyes. "No," he said quietly.

Strange, he thought. I actually do not want to die. He looked up at Flora. She smiled and tears were in her eyes. She's always crying.

"You're absolutely sure?"

Marvin nodded.

Haskell seemed disappointed. "Well, I can't pretend to understand. I'll tell you what I'm going to do though," he said bending down close. "Last night a patient was brought in, shot three times, very rare. A very important man, too. If you would be willing to, let's say, donate to this man one of your lungs, I might be able to pull a few strings and allow you to process the paperwork for a dog. It would give you and your wife at least the appearances of being eligible. It would be very good for your public identity. And, might I remind you, you did allow yourself to be designated a donor."

It's not that I don't want to die, Marvin thought to

himself, his brain functioning in a strangely calculated manner. It was an unusual sensation. He would have to adjust to it. It's just that I don't really care to live. I just don't care anymore. What does anything matter?

He felt a new sensation in his body. A sort of intensity. A powerful feeling brought on by coldness to the world.

"Take the lung if you want it," Marvin said, his voice clear and full. "But you can keep the dog. I don't need any scraps from you or anybody like you. I am a human being in case you haven't noticed. I'm tired of being treated like some animal. Worse than an animal. At least they get a little respect."

Haskell was taken aback. "Mister Dennis--"

"And stop calling me 'Mister Dennis'," Marvin interrupted. "I told you at the apartment you could call me Marvin. I don't like your feigned politeness. It masks your utter contempt for me. Why can't anybody in this world just be honest? Why are we always playing games with one another?"

Haskell bent down and picked up his briefcase. "I'll notify the doctors about your decision to donate," he said coldly. He made for the door but stopped to look at Flora. "Mrs. Dennis, I suggest you file for divorce immediately. With my connections I can have it filed in twenty-four hours. With luck you might remarry in as little as a month. Another man. A man with a future." With that said, he exited the room.

Flora waited for him to go before leaning over her husband. She stroked his forehead gently and wiped spittle from the sides of his mouth with the sleeve of her blouse.

"If you donate, you'll have to have surgery," she said.

"What's the matter with that?"

"It's just," she said, searching for the words. "I'm worried."

"Nonsense."

"They don't usually extricate organs from living donors. What if they forget how to do it? What if they really don't care about you because they think you're a suicide freak? They might not even try to keep you alive. They could take more than your lung."

"Flora, it doesn't matter," said Marvin with a sigh. "Do you think I don't know they don't care about me? They only care about that other guy. The one who got shot." He tried to sit up. "It's funny isn't it? Nobody cares about me. But everybody cares about the other guy. Apparently he's not that great of a fellow if somebody was willing to shoot him. When was the last time somebody got shot anyway? Nobody wants to shoot me. I'm a good person. But nobody cares about me."

Flora's eyes welled with tears again as she bent over to kiss his cheek. "I care about you," she said.

My goodness, thought Marvin. I almost forgot. I suppose I've gotten so used to Flora's love it almost seems like it is supposed to be there. Almost like it doesn't matter in the greater scheme of things.

He smiled. Looked up at her. "That's right," he said.

In a separate wing of the hospital, several doctors and nurses crowded around the prone form of Fordy MacLennon as his body struggled to survive. It seemed everyone in the hospital was curious to see him. The man who had been shot. It was mysterious. Something new. The female nurses found themselves strangely attracted to the man. Regardless of the tubes and wires sticking out of him.

"Make way," said a young, confident doctor as he entered the room holding the signed paperwork indicating Marvin's willingness to donate. The crowd separated, allowing the doctor to approach MacLennon.

"Good news," said the doctor knowing full well Fordy was unable to hear. "You're going to live."

~13~

SHLUTZ LEANED IN close to check Schiller's pulse as he lay dying. He hesitated a moment before pressing his fingers to the policeman's neck. He had never seen a man on the verge of death before. Never even been close to it, really. Even after all his years as a Friendly Neighbor. Squeamishly, he checked the pulse. Schiller wasn't moving. Barely breathing. And when he did breathe, blood sprayed from his mouth, powdering his chin and the tip of his nose. Shultz had the impression of touching raw, tenderized pork. Caring for the well-being of a dying man is sometimes extremely unappealing. It was a challenge Shultz felt he might not be up to. When humanity is broken down to its most fragile, basic physical component, it is only natural to want to keep a distance.

Schiller coughed. "What kind of law officer are you?" he asked, making Shultz want to take a step back. His words were weak, but strangely polite. "You can't take a man's pulse with your thumb."

Shultz collected himself. Sympathy welled in his heart. It was a new feeling Shultz had difficulties to explain to himself. What sense did it make?

"I didn't know," he said.

Schiller coughed again. "They haven't taught you such things?" he asked weakly.

Shultz shook his head. "No," he said. "They didn't. Didn't think we would ever have to know."

.....

"Schiller. Schiller, how do we get out of here?"

Schiller coughed again. "It doesn't lock from the inside," he said. "But I think it might be for the best if you left me here."

"Why?"

.....

"Schiller."

Schiller closed his eyes. Stopped breathing. Shultz lifted Schiller's arm and checked the pulse on his wrist, careful not to use his thumb. Nothing. Schiller was dead. For the first time, Shultz had seen a man killed. And for what? Shultz's instincts and natural bigotry wanted to give the easy answer. Schiller was killed trying to uphold the law. It was a fact. Plain and simple. Shultz knew it. Couldn't deny it.

But for the first time he began to doubt. Doubt the certainty of his own world. Doubt the laws that led to that certainty. He tried to remind himself that he lived in a peaceful world. A world made peaceful simply by legislating man's passions. Creating a counter to his emotions.

He looked down at Schiller's body. It was a testament to the safety of his world. Only one day in Nuremberg and he'd already been in fear of his life and watched another man lose his. Killed by other men. Men who were breaking the law. Breaking the law trying to give life to others. Bringing life into this world with illegal documents.

He looked up at the concrete block with its digital locking device. That is the way out, he said to himself. The way out. Back through the long dark caverns. Back to the church. Back to danger and chance. Back to light.

A part of him wanted to stay in the room. Stay with Schiller. At least it was safe down there. Safe, like in a womb. Although Schiller was dead he was recognizable, and the machines, the boxes of illegal documents served as a reminder of the laws outside. It was something he knew. As soon as he stepped out of this hole he would be thrown back into the unknown. But there was really no decision to be made. He had to go.

Then his mobile rang. It surprised him. Snapped him back to reality.

"Shultz," he declared.

It was Friedman. "There's been another explosion. In the western hemisphere this time. America. You're off the case. The deterrence police are taking over. Come on home. I won't be able to cover for your absence for much longer."

A quiver of prideful anger flowed through him but was soon replaced by the previous feeling of terror he felt over his situation. "Friedman," he choked, and for lack of anything better to say, a thought squeezed through his racing mind, "They brought me to a *church*."

"Turtles, man. I told you not to go. Where are you

now?"

Schultz wanted to cry. Speaking with Friedman gave him a minute feeling of safety. "I don't know," he said. "I'm underground. I have to get out. Schiller said they would be looking for me. I need help."

Friedman paused. "Who's Schiller? How were you found out?" There was an urgency in his voice.

"Schiller's a cop...or, was. He's dead. They killed him."

"A cop?" He sighed. "Otto, if the Nuremburg authorities know about you, then it will be impossible to send a team to get you out. We can't risk an incident. Not now. You've really stepped into it this time, Otto."

"You've got to get me out of here," Shultz screamed into the phone. "This is serious."

A pause. "I need time, Otto. You will have to hang on until I can think of something. Don't worry, old friend. I won't abandon you."

He hung up.

Shultz began to panic once more. "Friedman don't hang up. Friedman! Don't leave me alone!"

He stared at the mobile in disbelief. One small trinket to connect him with the entire planet. Civilization. Civility. And it was cut off by pushing a single button.

All he could do was bow his head.

~14~

MARVIN DENNIS AWOKE quietly. The room was dark and his head was swimming. It was the drugs. But they weren't helping. His entire body hurt. He vaguely remembered giving the hospital permission to remove one of his lungs. He wanted to rub his torso. Maybe there was a slight indention where the lung had been.

Surprisingly, aside from the stiffness and soreness he imagined to be relative to the surgery, he felt no difference in his bodily functions. He took a deep breath. No. No difference. It felt like any other breath, except for the fact that it hurt when his chest lifted. But there was something else aside from the pain.

He felt hollow.

They took something out of me, he thought. They took a piece of me away. And there was nothing wrong with me.

They took it from me and gave it to another person. Why?

Why wasn't I good enough the way I was? Whole. The way I was born.

They gave it to somebody else. As if I didn't deserve it. Didn't deserve everything that was a part of me. Rightfully.

But, I did give them permission. Why did I do that? What made me do that? How could I just give myself away? A piece of myself.

He took another breath.

Maybe it's because I knew it didn't matter. It's easy to say things don't matter. But I proved it. I can still breathe. They don't care about me, but they needed me. And I was there when they needed me. Why? Why would I help them? Why was I willing to help people that don't care about me?

Because nobody really cares. But it's not their fault. They don't know any better. They weren't brought up to care. Only to fulfil a purpose. Purpose. So what is my purpose? They told me it was to manage the waste. But maybe they were wrong. Maybe it's my purpose to give others what they need. Something they don't have, and can't get anywhere else. Something they don't even know they need. Maybe they don't know they need to care. If I didn't care, I wouldn't have donated my lung. And a man would be dead. I saved a man's life. And they probably still don't care about me. But it's not their fault.

Or, maybe it is. Who knows?

He blinked.

Who cares?

The lights came on. He shut his eyes from the glare

and clenched his teeth.

"You seem to be recovering well," said the nurse, leaning over to inspect his bandages. "Faster than we expected, actually."

Marvin winced as she lifted one of the wrappings, the gauze having stuck to the congealed blood. It pulled a stitch. "I'm in pain," he whimpered.

"It's only natural," the nurse replied coldly.

"Isn't there something you can do?"

The nurse shook her head. "I'm afraid it is too early to up the pain medication," she said. "You'll have to wait for the doctor."

"Can you bring the doctor?"

Once more, she shook her head. "He's a very busy man, Mister...? Just try and keep still. I promise, you are receiving the absolute best care."

"I don't believe you!" Marvin shouted. "You don't even know my name. It's Dennis. Marvin Dennis. And I saved a man's life today!"

"Mister Dennis," stammered the nurse. "You must not excite yourself."

"Why didn't you know my name? Why couldn't you even know that?"

"Don't get so uppity, Mister Dennis, because you feel you saved a life today," said the nurse, her voice uncharacteristically raised. "A life isn't just a pulse or a heartbeat, you know. What did you really do?" she asked, leaning in close, her face only inches away from Marvin's. "You gave a piece of flesh to a piece of flesh. We do that here on a daily basis. What do you do? Who do you think you are? What can there possibly be about you to give you such feelings of grandeur? What exactly is it that makes you feel you have the right to feel so superior?"

Marvin zipped his lip. Whoever said turnabout was fair play?

It was just a feeling, really. But maybe the nurse was right. Maybe there was nothing special about him after all. Maybe...

A doctor stepped into the room. Marvin didn't recognize him. He sighed. At least it wasn't the other one. The one who treated him so callously. Scrutinizing the man, he felt his spirits lift slightly. This man had a kind face. He didn't look like a doctor at all.

"Almost ready, nurse," the doctor announced. "How's he doing?"

The nurse handed the doctor a clipboard and squeezed past him for the door. "Other than a slight attitude problem, he's doing well." She added as an aside as she left the room. "He claims he's in pain, though."

The doctor waited for the nurse to make her way down the hall, then moved to stand next to Marvin who stared up at him with a vague look of hope. He looked at the doctor, trying to convey through his eyes exactly how much pain he was in. Hoped he would understand.

"Can you describe the pain?" asked the doctor kindly.

Marvin shook his head. "It just hurts," he said pathetically.

"Hmm," the doctor mused. Then, leaning in close, he whispered into Marvin's ear, "There is something I can give you," he said. "Though I am obligated by law to inform you about the side effects."

"What is it?"

"A shot. A special shot that will take you away from all of this."

Marvin began to sweat. A fear began to choke at him. He's going to kill me, he thought. They want to kill me. They want to kill me because they think I wanted to commit suicide. But I didn't. I just didn't look across the street. It was a mistake.

The doctor reached into the pocket of his coat and pulled out a syringe filled with a muddy, yellow liquid. "The side effects as such," he said quietly, "are not so terrible."

He had it ready, thought Marvin. He already had it on him. The side effects are death! He tried to inch his body up on the bed. Pulled his blanket up to his neck as if it offered even the slightest protection.

"While this shot may give you a few hours of peace," the doctor continued, and began tugging at the blanket. "When it wears off, you may find your pain has intensified. But, make no mistake. It is all in the mind."

Marvin struggled to keep the blanket raised, but the doctor was too strong. Tearing the blanket away, he grasped hold of Marvin's arm. Marvin began to shake. Tried to keep his arm clutched by his side.

Sighing, the doctor bent over Marvin and jabbed his forearm with the needle. Pressed the plunger.

Tears rolled down Marvin's cheeks. "I want my wife," he said. "I want my wife."

The doctor tossed the syringe into a nearby trash

receptacle, then wiped Marvin's tears. "Don't worry, Mister Dennis," he said. "It will kick in soon. In the meantime, I'll fetch your wife."

Marvin felt his body go slack. It was near instantaneous. Every muscle simultaneously relaxed. It felt as if his body was liquefying; slowly dripping down the sides of the gurney. He imagined his spirit separating from his body.

What are we, he asked himself. Who are we but pieces of a puzzle-carefully drawn and reproduced-cut to fill a space; molded. Meant to fit together harmoniously to form an idealized vision of a landscape. What happens when we don't fit the way we were meant to? What happens when the person representing the moss on the side of a rock doesn't slide in place the way he's supposed to? He struggles and struggles. Forces himself to conform...to fit in place; pounds at himself; damaging his natural shape. A lifetime of struggle to represent nothing more than moss on a rock. And who puts it together? What is it that fits us all together-forming the image-when everyone is a piece of the puzzle? And who puts them in their place?

Fordy MacLennon woke up suddenly after having a horrible dream in which he witnessed his own body being torn apart. Habitually, he lifted his hand to rub his eyes but, finding it obstructed by the feeding tube sticking out of his nose, he suddenly panicked. His last waking memory flooded into his mind. Hollis Kincaid holding the pistol; firing at him. It made a strange noise. Unlike any he had ever heard before.

It sounded almost as if a stack of books had been dropped onto a tiled floor.

He screamed.

Then traced the feeding tube with wide eyes. Jerking the tube, he knocked over the stand holding the IV bag. It clattered to the floor, bringing a nurse into the room much faster than the sound of his scream.

The nurse entered the room to find Fordy flailing on the bed as if being attacked by countless small creatures. Calmly, instinctively, she pressed him back down on the bed and made a soothing noise by pursing her lips. Fordy looked up at the nurse with a mixture of relief and horror. Relieved to know he had obviously gotten the help he needed; horrified to realize he needed it at all. Suddenly, the world wasn't at all what he had thought it to be.

"What happened?" he asked blankly. Of course he knew. He had been shot. Wow. Strangely, he felt all the more important because of it. I got shot. Beat that.

"You were shot," said the nurse. "But don't worry. You're all better, now. Just lye still, I'll bring the doctor."

Morbidly curious, as he waited patiently for the doctor, Fordy lifted his gown to inspect his wounds. There was a large, pulpy red line tracing down from the middle of his chest to his lower abdomen. He closed his eyes in disgust. He had expected only three fleshy welts where the bullets had hit. What have they done to me?

The doctor came into the room, a smug look on his

face.

"You've deformed me," Fordy said, blinking rapidly to hold back the tears.

The doctor waved him off. "There will be a minimum of scarring," he said. "I must say, though, there was a lot of pressure. It is not too often we have cases such as yours. The entire surgical staff was clamoring to work on you." The doctor extended his hand, moved closer. "Mister MacLennon, it is indeed a privilege."

Fordy shook hands, squinted curiously.

"We get so many elderly," continued the doctor. "Do you know how many young men I have worked on in the twenty years I have been in medicine?"

Fordy shook his head. "I imagine…"

The doctor interrupted. "Three. Only three. The first was a child of four who had fallen from his bicycle. Broke his collar bone. The other two were co-workers whose vehicles guidance system went haywire. Ran them straight into the river. It was a Chinese model. I believe that company was liquidated." He lowered his eyes. Gave a faraway stare. "All three cases were very important to me. But nowhere near as important as yours." He pressed his finger to his lip. "Can you imagine the depth of satisfaction that comes with healing a man whose injuries were caused by another man? No. Probably you cannot." Tears came to his eyes. Fordy began to grow uncomfortable. "It is the reason people like me get into this profession."

Fordy stuttered. Held his hands up for emphases. "You said 'a minimum of scarring'?"

The doctor wiped his eyes, shook his head to bring himself from his stupor. "Oh, yes. You see, it could be no other way."

Fordy was reassured. "Will I have to stay much longer?"

"No, of course not," said the doctor. "You were given the best possible care. Normally, after surgery we require the patient stay on with us for at least forty-eight hours. But in your case we actually encourage you to check yourself out. There are, after all, reporters to satisfy."

"Reporters?"

"Indeed," said the doctor. "This is quite a high profile case. In fact, I believe they would like to get a few pictures of you and the donor."

"Donor?"

"Yes. Oh, but you didn't know," proclaimed the doctor. "Well, it's not so difficult to explain. Due to increased life-spans, it is becoming extremely difficult to find healthy, viable organs for younger patients. But we were lucky enough to find a man willing to donate for your case. In fact, the government has been pushing new initiatives to promote donations among the youth. They even promote it in schools, I believe. Anyhow, taking a few snapshots with the donor would be good public relations. They might even be able to build a campaign around it."

I suppose it's understandable, thought Fordy. After all, what has it been, thirty years since a man was shot? A part of him swelled with pride, yet, he couldn't help but feel a little dejected. Of all the hard work I've done, this is what I will be known for. And what's worse, it will probably double my work load. I'll get that bastard, Kincaid. He was stupefied. How could a building mean that much to somebody?

"I would like to leave as soon as possible," he said, suddenly disgusted by his stay at the hospital. He felt weak at knowing everyone in the city knew what had happened to him. Exposed. It seemed like such a personal event. And now they wanted him to go on the news. Tell everyone what it felt like to be shot by another man.

What did they want to know? Did it hurt? He couldn't remember. Is it shocking to know that you can inspire such hatred in another person? Yes. Yes, actually, it is a bit shocking. But what can you do? I was just doing my job. And I'm darn good at my job. Would you like me to tell you about it? Sure, sure, but only opaquely. What we are interested in, really, is what it feels like to be shot, Mister MacLennon. You know, just in case it happens to one of us. Is there anything you can tell us to prepare us for what human beings are capable of doing to one another?

…No.

~15~

SHULTZ MANAGED TO free himself of his underground prison and crawled back up to the light of day. After exiting the church, he marveled at the short amount of time it took him to escape. With such serious consequences and his very life on the line, he felt as if it should have taken a bit more time. It hardly seemed significant enough to represent all that was at stake. In the pouring rain, he managed to find the corner of Unter and Hoch, where he discovered officer Hoigt waiting patiently at a corner bratwurst shop.

Hoigt was a tall man with a lean but powerful build. The rain beaded on his black leather coat and his short blonde hair clung to his forehead, nearly covering his eyes. He didn't seem to mind the rain at all. As Shultz approached Hoigt, he figured the man was already well aware of his partner's death and standing in the rain with a soggy bratwurst in his hand was the only available emotional response. He approached gingerly.

"Friendly Neighbor, Shultz," Hoigt announced extending his hand. "I've taken the liberty of purchasing some supper for you."

Shultz stood close, grabbed the bratwurst and threw it to the ground. "Get me out of this city," he said.

Hoigt looked up, allowing the rain to beat down on

his face, then looked squarely at Shultz. "We should get inside where it is dry. Come," he said, opening the door to the bratwurst shop and motioning for Shultz to step inside. Shultz entered the shop and allowed Hoigt to lead him to a seat. They sat opposite one another and Hoigt scrutinized Shultz with a cold demeanor. It made him uncomfortable.

In time, Hoigt began to speak. "Schiller was foolish, but he was a well-intentioned man. I warned him not to get involved. Tried to convey to him the pointlessness of the entire investigation."

"Any idea who it was killed him?" asked Shultz.

Hoigt nodded. "Of course," he said. "It was the Polizei."

Shultz sat back in his chair. "The Polizei? Your own people? But why?"

"Because we cannot bear to become part of your world," said Hoigt. "Not in that way. There are those in this city who wish a complete separation from the corporate world. Of course they accept the financial need of cooperation, but a legal partnership would be far, far too much."

"Ridiculous," Shultz scoffed. "What you are talking about is completely irrational. The very idea that a policeman could murder a fellow officer for the sake of denying a perfectly functioning legal code is impossible to believe."

"Being rational, Herr Shultz, is sometimes the most undesirable thing of all. Sometimes, to those of us with abstract minds, rationality can seem like the most insidious of all prisons."

"You speak like a crazy person."

"Without the risk of insanity, how can a man truly be sane? Isn't the cause of freedom worth a little irrationality? Wouldn't it be nice to wake in the morning and believe for just a moment that life is worth living for yourself alone?"

"Absolutely not," Shultz replied.

Hoigt smiled. "I like you, Herr Shultz. It seems our respective nature's are in agreement."

"Get to the point, Hoigt. You're confusing me. And I've had enough of confusion. I want to get out of this city. I want to get back to a world that makes sense. I don't want to stay in this backward pit."

Hoigt held up his hand. "We'll leave soon enough," he said. "Be patient. It is impossible to pass the gates this late in the night. We might as well make ourselves comfortable and have a nice chat." They were both silent for a moment. Each staring slightly to the side of the other, not wishing to make eye contact until, clearing his throat, Hoigt began, once more, to speak, his voice only slightly above a whisper. It was harsh, strained. "Schiller was a profoundly unhappy man," he said, a faraway stare in his eye. "His entire purpose for life lay within these city walls. He was so proud of his home. It was his pride that killed him. I suppose you could find some symbolism in the fact that it was his own people that killed him. You would be hard pressed to find a more appropriate analogy." He rubbed his eyes, whether out of sadness or exhaustion, Shultz couldn't guess. Both probably. "It was different before," Hoigt continued. "Before we became so isolated. Back before Edinburgh and Moscow joined the

Corporation. Before we found ourselves cut off. Back then, it was easy to understand why we refused to join the World Government. We understood the beauty of our past. All the wonderful accomplishments made throughout the ages. We understood our place in world history. But it wasn't just the historical past. It was the buildings, the art, and the very people. We didn't want to lose what it was that made us special. We didn't want to be replaced with a system that made everybody exactly the same. Because what would that make us? Pretty soon, all the men women and children would walk down these streets and all they would see would be bricks and mortar, cobblestones. There would be no connection. No spiritual bond. It would be just another city. Any other place."

Shultz sighed. It was a tired argument. "I don't want to be redundant," he said. "But, as I'm sure you have heard, the reasoning behind the co-operative government is to rid ourselves of the very thing you are speaking of. The very idea of regional identity. Don't you realize how many wars were fought in the old days, how many lives lost, for the sake of regional identity? So what if there is no spiritual bond with a city? Pardon my abruptness, but do you not see the insanity in your argument? The very idea that you can walk these city streets and feel a spiritual connection appalls me. Did you construct these buildings? The parking garages perhaps. But did you lay the cobblestones? No, they were constructed centuries before your birth? I have just as much connection with this city as you have, by the simple fact that I am a human being, and a city is a human accomplishment."

"This I concede," said Hoigt. "I feel I should make my point clearer. This regionalism, it binds us to each other. And you would be a fool to think all a man need do to get along with his fellow man is understand that they are one and the same. But I digress. Schiller was a typical man of the city, excepting, of course, his desire to uphold the law. In the beginning, when the co-operative government began to form, we had clear reasons in refusing to join. A staunch resolution based upon principle and a studied knowledge of our history. Pride in who we were. But things are different now. Now, our identity is wrapped around the co-operative government to such an extent, we might as well not be separate from it. Instead of building upon the ingenuity of our forefathers, we began to regress. Our past is all that we are now. It is the only thing we can have pride in. Our identity is one of hatred of the co-operative government. Nothing else. The only way we can see ourselves now is, not so much as citizens of Nuremberg, but as individuals not allied to the co-operative. All that we are now…is not a part of you."

"You have justified my extreme lack of respect for your city," said Shultz. "I kind of appreciate it."

"Be that as it may," said Hoigt. "But when I walk these streets, I find an immense pleasure, a joy in my heart. This is my home, my place in the world. And the people here are my family. You cannot feel such a joy. You have an emptiness in your heart that you don't even know. You can feel it, but you can't understand it. All your talk about emotional control, it only hides the precariousness of your emotions. You act as if you feel nothing, you hide behind rationality, but in your heart, you spend every second of the day in despair. You may feel that you have a home, you can speak about the entire world being your home, the entire human race as being your family, but these things are too large. You can have no more than an abstract idea of a home, a family. I pity you, Herr Shultz. Because you are truly heartbroken."

Shultz fidgeted in his seat, began to tap his fingers on the table. "Look," he said. "When are you going to lead me out of here?"

"Soon," Hoigt answered. "But on one condition. I want you to take me with you."

"Why?" asked Shultz, genuinely surprised.

"Because citizens of Nuremberg need a chaperone to leave the city gates."

"I know, I know that. What I mean is why?"

"Because Schiller was my partner. And I do not mean to let him die in vain. Like it or not, I have an obligation to solve this case. I mean to bring these forgers to justice."

"But it's not your laws being broken. It is not practical for you to put yourself to such trouble."

"Practicality and obligation are antithetical," Hoigt responded.

Shultz had to agree.

~16~

"WHAT ARE YOU looking for?" asked Stevenson coming to a halt suddenly after leading Buster through the darkness for what seemed like hours.

They had reached the top of a dune and Buster was at pains trying to keep balance as his weight shifted on the sand. He looked up at Stevenson, confused, then remembered, "I need an eighteen millimeter socket," he responded quietly.

Stevenson laughed and shook his head, clasped his hands behind his back. "No," he said, then repeated with emphasis, "What are you looking for?"

Buster didn't respond. He stared at Stevenson and tried to figure the man out. There was something about the man…something strange. His features were sharp-strained, almost as if they had been rubbed out at some point. But his eyes were vibrant; almost mysterious. Not that the man himself was mysterious. No, Buster mused. It was more like the man knew no mystery. "I don't understand," he said at last.

Stevenson smiled, his thin lips receding, showing

yellow stained teeth. "Do you know where we are?" he asked, then pointed up to the sky, not waiting for an answer. Buster looked up. The sky was filled with stars. An infinite multitude of lights, unencumbered by the low atmosphere of the moon. It stood in contrast to the darkness on the surface. So much light out there in nothingness, thought Buster.

"Do you see that?" asked Stevenson, indicating a single speck of light amidst the stars.

Buster tried to follow Stevenson's finger, but couldn't make out just exactly where he was pointing. "What am I looking for?" he asked.

"That's Earth," Stevenson responded. "But that isn't what you are looking for is it?"

"I don't know what I'm looking for," Buster replied.

Stevenson continued to look up to the stars. "It is a strange thing, isn't it?" he asked. "Tell me, Macready, what do you feel when you look up there?"

Buster shook his head. He was growing tired. He wanted to sit down on the ground, but was afraid of how Stevenson might react. "I don't know what I feel," he said.

"Yes you do," said Stevenson, lowering his head and staring straight at Buster. "You just don't know how to articulate it."

Buster sighed with relief as Stevenson knelt down and, taking the opportunity to sit, the two men faced one another.

Stevenson continued. "I'll tell you what you felt when I pointed at that speck up there. When I showed you where our planet was." He paused, then, "You felt as if you were looking back, didn't you? Back toward something. And there was a little bit of hope, wasn't there. Almost like remembering some almost forgotten detail from your childhood. It was comforting, wasn't it?"

Buster shook his head once more. "I don't know."

"Of course you do," Stevenson said, almost shouting. "But you didn't feel that way until I told you where Earth was. Before, when you looked up at the night sky, you felt an emptiness. Something dragging at you. At your very soul. Do you know why?" he asked, pointing up in the opposite direction as before. "Because there is nothing out there. When we look ahead, we see nothing but emptiness. It confounds our very nature. We on this planet, you and I, all the others...we are on the very outskirts. Our only comfort lies behind us. We see no life when we look ahead. Before we came here, when we were still on Earth, we knew the Pioneers were creating colonies, so that when we looked up, we looked ahead and we saw life. But there is nothing ahead of us now, so we must look back. I ask you...how can we survive with such feelings? How can we have a future if our only hope comes from looking behind?"

"It's only an emotion," said Buster. "It's irrelevant to our situation."

"Yes," said Stevenson, smiling again. "That is right. Emotions for the most part are always irrelevant. By their very nature they are irrelevant." Leaning slightly, he placed his hands on Buster's shoulders. "Our humanity does not lie in our emotions," he said. "Our humanity lies in how we react to them. While our emotions may be irrelevant, how we control our emotions decides our fate. But, the real question is, why do we feel the need to control our emotions? Wouldn't it be simpler to give in to them? To live like the animals? For that is the only thing that separates us."

"You make it seem like such a small thing," said Buster.

"That's precisely my point," said Stevenson. "Do you realize just how easy it would be for us to revert to barbarism? All of us here. It would be the most natural thing. The most unquestionable thing. Just think of it...we've only been here a few months, yet we've already reverted in some ways. All of us have resorted to minor regressive habits. Our language grows harsher, we fall back to the old religions. Macready...we come from a highly cultivated society. Scientific and rational. But we cannot hope to continue such a society here on this planet. We cannot even dream such a thing."

Buster remained silent. What could he say?

"We are no longer at the edge of humanities future," Stevenson went on. "The Pioneers are supposed to represent all that is great in man. The apex of our evolution. Living proof that we are indeed something special in this universe. Not just silly creatures scurrying about a solitary rock in the cosmos. But the truth is, if we view the history of humanity as a straight line, we are no longer at point B. By coming here, we have gone back to the very beginning. Back to the very shadow of our species.

Do you understand?"

"No."

"Of course, I'll explain. If we continue to look back, whether literally or figuratively, we doom ourselves before we've even begun. We must forget that speck of light up there. Erase it from our memories. Wipe it out. We carry within us something grand. We have found a purpose in this universe. A heretofore unthinkable purpose."

Buster raised his eyes. "That's what I'm looking for," he said.

"That is what we are all looking for. That's why we came out here. It was the desire for purpose that drove us away from our homes, our lives, the cradle itself. But there was no more purpose in life back there. Life had become so controlled, so mundane. Desire became a crime. To desire became first punishable and then, in time, loathed. But they gave us a choice. They allowed us the opportunity to desire. All we had to do was sign on a dotted line and allow ourselves to be hurled multiple light years away from everything we have ever known. Light years away from them."

"But it's just the same here," said Buster. "I still haven't found a purpose."

"But life is more bearable, isn't it? I know, sometimes it doesn't seem so. But have you ever truly stopped to think about your life now? How much it differs from before? How full your heart feels. On Earth, we fooled ourselves into believing that we struggled to survive, but survival to us then was nothing more than balancing our accounts, paying our bills or slaving away at the jobs we were placed into. Yet, here, every day is a true struggle. Every second is spent struggling for true survival. Here, we struggle to breathe, struggle to move, to stay warm, cool…even to eat and drink. What happens when the food runs out? The water? These things are constantly on our minds, whether we consciously realize it or not."

"So is that our purpose? Was that our purpose all along? Just to survive. What sort of purpose is that? Doesn't the purpose of life mean anything greater than simply acting as an antonym to its opposite? Why are we here at all if life is nothing but delayed death?"

"Delay is the key word," said Stevenson. "The word itself carries connotations of the future. A sort of grammatical paradox. Just as we have become a paradox. Which brings us back to the beginning of our conversation. There can be no purpose without a future. True purpose lies only in actions appropriate to the future. To make a more elementary argument, the entire idea of a purpose is a hoax. Purpose is not inherent to existence, so sometimes a purpose must be created in order to survive, because humanity, out of all creatures, carries within it a singular hatred of itself. A desire to be something other than what it is. Self-awareness always carries within it the seed of regret. A desire to be something greater. The only thing that makes life bearable for us is the false idea that we may eventually find what it takes to transform ourselves. To overcome all our so-called weaknesses. Our perceived faults."

Buster spread his hand over the sand. "I think there is something alive on this planet," he said. "An indigenous life form."

"I want to show you something," said Stevenson rising.

Once more, Buster followed Stevenson as the man led him confidently through the wasteland, the darkness. In time, they reached the top of another dune and, with a wry smile, Stevenson beckoned Buster to look below.

What he saw amazed him. It was a camp comprised of fifteen extra solar landing craft situated in a large ring. By all appearances, it was exactly what it was supposed to be, exactly what the Pioneers were meant to build-a colony. But the sight itself seemed so foreign to the landscape, Buster couldn't help a slight feeling of horror as he looked down on it. It wasn't something he could build a rational argument around, not something he could explain with words. It was intuitive. A feeling. Something about it was *wrong*.

"You see," Stevenson said, indicating the camp with a wave of his hand. "There is no life on this planet but we here. Humanity itself, transplanted to foreign soil. But soon even that will change. Within a generation we will have already begun to acclimatize ourselves to this new world. Our bodies will adapt to the new environment. The weaker gravitational pull; the differing climates; the radiation bombarding us as we speak. Soon, it will have its effect. I wager within a few hundred years we will cease to resemble human beings at all.'

"For thousands of years, man looked up at the stars

and tried to imagine what was out there. What wonders we might find. Were there alien races with knowledge beyond our wildest dreams? Fostering great civilizations; eager to spread their knowledge. Or were there races of blood-thirsty creatures bent on ruling the universe. Well, the simple fact of the matter is this…all this time, humanity has been alone. Cold and alone. Until now. It has been a very basic yet fundamental error in our thinking. Knowing as we do the age of the universe, it only made sense to think of ourselves as children. It was only natural to view time in accordance to our relatively short existence. Not realizing that the universe itself does not measure time. But now…humanity is no longer alone in the universe. As I said before, we on this planet are changing. Soon we will be a race unto our own. Separate; divorced from humanity. From now on, when a small child back on Earth looks up to the night sky, he will know for a fact that there are living beings on other planets.'

"Macready, it took us twelve thousand years, frozen in time, to reach this system. Who knows what has happened on Earth in those twelve thousand years. Perhaps they have already forgotten about the Pioneers; forgotten the colonies. Perhaps they were ruined by global catastrophes or war."

"Or maybe we finally learned to live in peace," said Buster.

Stevenson looked long and hard at Buster as if not wanting to dignify the statement with the response he must give. "No," he said. "No, I don't think so."

~17~

"IS IT THE nature of life to be transitional? Or is it that nature itself is transitional and we are only unwitting victims of change? Or is it a transitional nature in life? Or is the very fact that life is wrapped around a continuous cloud of transition enough to cancel out the idea of transition itself. If change is constant, predictable, can life be defined as transitional?" It had been a quick decision on Fordy MacLennon's part, and he ruminated over the reasoning behind it as he made his way home. A lot of things were coming to him now for the very first time; revealing themselves as if they had always been there, in hiding, waiting for the most opportune moment to strike.

He rubbed his chest and tried to analyze his feelings about the new lung. There were mixed feelings, of course. The fact that it came from a living donor made him incredibly uncomfortable. The fact that he lived in the same building with the man. He wondered if he would feel the same had he not known the man. If only he hadn't recognized him. He felt about the new organ as if it were an unwanted houseguest that he was grateful for the attention from. It was all so very strange. What if there were no way to adapt. What if his body couldn't accept the introduction of another man's presence? Was it possible at all that he could die a young man?

He stepped off the elevator and walked down the hall, stopping in front of his door. Before opening the door, he looked down the hall and allowed his gaze to fall upon the door of Marvin Dennis. Never in his life had he felt such weight upon him. How can you possibly begin to thank someone for doing something like that? A thought flittered through his mind to relocate.

Abigail gave a look of utter confusion when Fordy entered and she immediately stepped into the kitchen. She leaned against the counter, her facial expressions changing rapidly as she tried to decide which emotion seemed the most opportune for the moment. She decided on pleasant surprise blended with calm happiness.

"You got a dog," she said with a smile.

"His name is Barns," said Fordy, placing the puppy on the carpet. "He's a Yorkshire Terrier. They're supposed to be agreeable. I bought some pads so we won't have to worry about taking him for walks."

Abigail bent over to pet the dog. It was a practiced gesture, meant more for her own satisfaction than the dogs. "Oh, but I want to take him for walks," she said, keeping her hands away from the terrier's mouth as it tried to playfully chew on her fingers.

"He's teething," said Fordy. "Apparently they like to chew on things."

"Did you name him, or did the shelter give him a name?"

"I named him," he answered.

"Why Barns, then?" she asked.

"It seemed appropriate at the time."

"How did Barns strike you as appropriate?"

"I can't remember," he said.

Fordy was already beginning to feel a certain degree of regret. He would prefer Abigail not walk the dog, but already she was beginning to sense a new social standing. Walking the dog would let everyone know her husband was at least strongly considering the idea of a child. Abigail was already anticipating the feel of her body growing, her appetite increasing and, Fordy shuddered, the newfound freedom she would earn due to her hormones. She would be able to get away with just about anything. Any cutting remark would have to be tolerated. But, he supposed as he watched her robotically trying to play with the dog, in the end, any cutting remarks she may spout out would be well deserved.

He thought to himself, I can't believe what a bastard I am.

"You must have filled out the paperwork weeks ago," Abigail said, rising and wiping her hands on her pants leg. "And you didn't tell me." She moved in close and gave him a peck on the cheek. "Thank you," she said.

Fordy squinted in thought. A curiosity came over him that he hesitated to encourage. "Were you worried about me at all?" he asked. "When I was in the hospital?"

Abigail shook her head as if flipping the hair out of her face. "What a strange question," she mused. "Why would you ask such a thing? Of course I was worried about you."

"I suppose I asked that wrong," he replied. "Of course you were worried. What I meant to ask was…were you worried about me, or were you more worried for yourself? Had I died, things could have been very inconvenient for you."

"I don't know how to answer that," said Abigail. "It was confusing. I guess I never had time to think it through. I suppose…I suppose I could have been worried more for you."

Fordy looked down at the dog. "The man who donated the lung to me…his wife came by to visit him at the hospital."

"I thought about that," said Abigail. "Of visiting you. But I guess I thought maybe you would be embarrassed had I done so."

He smiled. "You're probably right," he said. "It would have bothered me a bit. Thank you."

Abigail tilted her head to the side, smiled once more. She then looked down at the dog and watched as it began circling a spot on the carpet next to several potted plants and stared curiously as it lifted its leg to urinate. Fordy sighed with resignation as Abigail concentrated on the dark spot forming on the carpet. She seemed utterly lost. Curious, as if she hadn't realized house pets had the same bodily functions as every other living creature. "I'll take him out for a walk," she said after a moment's silence.

"What for?" said Fordy, feeling truly indignant for

the first time since leaving the hospital. He was disappointed, had hoped the attack had driven it away, but, it seemed life was going to continue as usual, at least for the next couple of weeks. "The dog has already relieved himself. There's no need to take him out now."

From the look on Abigail's face, it was apparent she wasn't getting the point.

"Are you...are you even serious?" he asked.

"Where is the leash?" she asked, already grabbing a sweater from the closet next to the door. "He came with one, right?"

Fordy sighed. Most of the time, quiet resignation was the only way to deal with Abigail. Supposedly, it was the ideal way to deal with every situation. But sometimes it just didn't work. He began to doubt the plan he had worked out after learning about Marvin Dennis. Following the plan would saddle him with Abigail for at least another year. He shivered. It was going to be horrible.

Marvin felt strange when he stepped inside his apartment three weeks after Fordy was released. It felt unfamiliar to him. Every piece of furniture, every fixture, all the tiny gadgets and knick-knacks that made a home all seemed different...or the same. He couldn't tell. Maybe he was the one who was different. He had noticed it on the way home from the hospital, how he had expected everything to have taken on an entirely different meaning since the accident. But it was all the same, except for the vague feeling in his stomach that everything should be different. The fact that it wasn't different was change enough. The lack of new meaning was change in itself. There was one thing he noticed, though, as he rubbed his fingers across the back of the couch, Flora hadn't cleaned the apartment.

"What's wrong?" he asked quietly as Flora studied the curtains.

"I'm leaving," she said, not looking him in the face.

"Why?"

"Because you tried to kill yourself," she explained.

"No I didn't," he said. "I accidentally stepped out into traffic. That doesn't mean I meant to get hit by a vehicle."

"I don't believe you," she answered. "You're not happy. I can't make you happy."

"So you solve the problem by making me more unhappy?" he asked. In his mind, this was only a sudden phase Flora found herself going through. Shock. Until she shouldered a small bag and began making her way toward the door. "Flora, wait!" he shouted. "Flora, you're all I've got, Flora. You're all I've got!"

"I'm sorry, Marvin," she said, tears beginning to flow from her eyes, as always. "I just don't know what else to do."

Marvin ran to block her exit, stood in front of the door and grabbed her by the shoulders. "Look, Flora. I'm not going to stop you. If you feel this is what you need to do then do it. I just want to know why. Why?"

"Because it's too hard," she exclaimed. "I just don't understand anything anymore. I don't know what to do. I don't know how to help." She paused. "I have spent the last three months in tears. That isn't the way it's supposed to be. Nobody else spends every day crying. Nobody else feels this way. I just want to be like everybody else."

"No you don't, Flora. Don't you understand? The only reason nobody else is ever upset is because they don't have anything to be upset about. They don't have love in their lives. You and I love each other. That's why it seems so hard, because it's the one real, true emotion. It's the one thing worth living for. Everybody else spend their whole lives without that one thing worth living for just so they can live. Don't you see how wrong that is?"

"No I don't," said Flora. "If it's so wrong, how come it's the only way that works?"

"Because it's easy," he said with some desperation. "These people don't care about anything, Flora. When you don't care about anything, everything seems easy. If you don't care, there's never anything to feel nervous about, or afraid. There's never any reason for doubt. People are always confident when they don't care. But that isn't what life is all about. Don't you get it? We aren't on this earth just to live. There has to be a reason to live to make it worth it. These people have no reason to live. They have no real meaning to their lives. No reason to breath. No reason to eat or drink or sleep. All they have is an instinctual will to live. Nothing else. Flora, please…you have to understand. You and I have a reason to live. You and I alone. It's only us now. You may feel like you're hurting all the time, but you have to believe that all those other people outside, when they're lying on their death-beds, it is they who are going to feel the real pain. They are the ones who are going to have to realize that they spent their entire lives living selfishly. Living only for themselves. No matter what they believe. They'll live till a hundred, but they're already dead."

"How can you say they live selfishly when they give up every selfish desire for the betterment of our society?" Flora countered. "Why do you judge everybody so harshly? You're trying to tell me that you and I are better than everybody else, but we're not! How can you tell me we're better than everybody else when you hate yourself so much? Because that's the real problem, you know? You hate yourself, and you blame everybody else."

"Flora…"

"I'm sorry, Marvin. I do love you," she continued. "But I can't continue living like this."

"What are you going to do?"

"I'm going to see that psychiatrist," she said. "He told me he could find me another husband quick. I have to live a normal life. I can't live like you. I can't live every day hating everybody else because they have what I want. And that's what I've been doing."

"But that's what I've been saying. They don't have what we want. We have what they want. They just don't know it yet."

"I don't know what to say," said Flora. "I think that's all in your mind."

Feeling his dignity attacked, Marvin began to pant,

actually made an attempt to keep his voice at an acceptable pitch, but it didn't work. "Go ahead then, Flora. Go ahead and leave. Go try and be one of them!"

Flora, continuing to cry, answered, "I will!"

"Because that's all you can do, Flora. You can try. But you'll never be one of them. And do you want to know why? Because you had it! You had it with me! One of the few people on this planet to have actually been loved. But you're throwing it away! You're turning your back on something good. The one good thing in this world and you're rejecting it! So you'll never be like them, as hard as you may try. You can only be worse than them! That's why I sometimes want to die. Because people just don't get it. Why is it such a hard thing to understand? People just treat each other with indifference unless there is something they can get out of them. Nobody wants to do anything for somebody. Nobody wants to bring something good into somebody else's life. It's all about themselves. It's a 'me' culture! And I don't want to live in a world like this. There has to be something better coming."

As much as she wanted to, Flora couldn't respond. She couldn't deny what Marvin was saying. He was absolutely right. But it was such an ugly revelation she couldn't bring herself to except it, and so, in order to deny it, she had to get away from the source.

She slunk past him and opened the door.

Marvin froze. "You're really going," he stated.

Flora kept her eyes lowered and nodded. She hadn't stared him in the face once throughout the entire confrontation.

Marvin shook his head, his eyes wide open. "I don't believe it," he said. "I don't believe it."

He made a last ditch effort to grab her, followed her out the apartment and halfway down the hall. "Flora, wait," he said making no attempt to hide his desperation. "Flora don't do this. Don't do this to me. To me! No other man is going to love you. You're just a business to them. You're just a way for them to keep their last name in the world! You're doing this to me!"

Flora quickened her pace and practically jumped into the elevator as Marvin stopped in his tracks, still unable to believe what he was experiencing. The only way to deny it was to stop moving. As if by not following her there would be no need to follow her. Everything would be the way it was if he just stopped moving. The elevator doors closed.

"I can't believe!" he shouted, praying his words would echo down to her. The realization struck him suddenly that every single moment for the rest of his life, Flora was going to be moving farther and farther away from him. Already he couldn't see her. He couldn't even look at her. Watch her move. The way he did when she was making breakfast, or sleeping next to him. It was all over. "I can't believe!" he shouted again. "Nobody wants to feel anything anymore, Flora! People don't remember what it's like to feel anything good anymore! But I'll turn it around! I'll turn it around!"

Before he could fall to his knees crying, as he felt compelled to do, he was startled by a door opening not too far from where he stood. He turned to see Fordy MacLennon stick his head out. The two men stared at each other in silence for a long moment. Marvin didn't seem to recognize Fordy. "I'll turn it around," he said before stumbling back to his apartment.

Fordy watched him go. He rubbed his chest again. He wasn't oblivious. He felt like a thief as he tried to ponder what Marvin was feeling, trying to find excuses to blame himself.

~18~

HOIGT SMILED SARDONICALLY as Shultz tugged at his lederhosen, then stared directly ahead to where the entrance of the massive parking garage encircling the city stood. He looked to the left and to the right, allowing his eyes to take in every detail of every inch in between the garage and the dumpster he and Shultz now hid behind.

"It looks quiet," Shultz whispered, impatient to leave Nuremberg once and for all. "I say we run for it."

Hoigt held up his hand and shook his head. "You didn't hear that?" he asked, squinting into the distance.

The rising sun was dimmed by overcast skies and the air continued to hold the moisture from the rain storm the night before. Shultz perked up his ears. "I don't hear anything," he said. "And pretty soon we won't be able to see anything either."

"Perhaps we should wait for a fog," Hoigt suggested. "I think the garages are being watched."

"If we wait for a fog we won't be able to drive out of here even if we do manage to reach the garage. I say again, we should just run for it."

"Okay," Hoigt said hesitantly. "But be on guard. I've never once stepped outside this city. I would not like to be gunned down before I have a chance to do so."

Suddenly, to the surprise of both men, a deep set voice replied from behind. "And why would you like to be outside the city, officer Hoigt?"

Hoigt turned to view the inside of a gun barrel as it pressed against his right eye, recognizing instantly the short, stocky man holding the pistol. Shultz shook his head in calm defeat. He couldn't even be angry about having been caught right as he was about to make good his escape. Normally, he would instinctively raise his hands, but instead he simply shrugged his shoulders and chuckled for want of crying.

"You have caused us quite a bit of needless concern, Randolph," said the man with the gun. "If you had only kept the best interests of your homeland in mind, there would be no need for violence."

"I hate to split hairs, captain Withers," said Hoigt, keeping a relative calm under pressure as always. "But I was very much minding my affairs until you sent your men to assassinate Schiller. He and I were partners for ten years. Of course you can understand my anxiety."

"You would sell out your country for revenge?" asked Withers seeming to be genuinely confused.

"Revenge is such a strong word," Hoigt said before surprising Withers with a punch to the groin. Shultz, seizing upon the advantage, quickly grabbed the pistol from the man's hand as Hoigt pulled him to the ground, ramming his face into the side of the dumpster as he did so.

"Quick thinking," Shultz lauded, adjusting the lederhosen once more.

Hoigt said nothing, dragged Withers' body behind the dumpster and pulled the man's trousers off with a purpose.

"What are you doing?" asked Shultz.

"For God's sake, put on these pants," said Hoigt, tossing the trousers over.

Shultz caught them, allowed himself a few seconds to understand before putting them on, and then said, "For a moment I was concerned."

"We are not barbarians, Herr Shultz," Hoigt responded. He stared down at Withers' unconscious form. "My commanding officer," he said. "I've known him since I was a child. He would not have come alone."

Shultz zipped up the trousers, bent to retrieve Withers' pistol, then asked, "How many do you think?"

"Let's find out," Hoigt replied, standing up straight and stepping out from behind the shelter of the dumpster.

"Have you lost your mind?" Shultz asked.

"This is Nuremberg," said Hoigt. "We like our confrontations to be direct."

Shultz checked the pistol for ammunition. "If you believe in being so direct, then why have we been running around like rats in a cage all night?"

"Because the certainty of death was not upon us last night," Hoigt answered matter of fact. "But now things are different. I did not suspect the captain was involved."

"I am not impressed with your skills as a guide," Shultz snapped, stepping out from behind the dumpster to stand by his side nonetheless. "Your partner was a liar."

"I suspect he was greatly mistaken," said Hoigt. "He may have over exaggerated his confidence in me. After all, look what happened to him." Then, raising his voice, he called out, "Dietrich! Come on out and let's talk!"

Shultz instinctively ducked down, trying to hide himself, however precariously, in the rising fog. Just what did Hoigt think he was doing?

After a few minutes of eerie silence, Shultz began to hear echoing footsteps approaching through the fog. Then, appearing almost as if from nowhere, a tall man wearing a dark raincoat stood before them. He smiled.

"Turning yourself in?" he asked Hoigt. "Making it easy for us? I must convey a small sense of regret. We could use the practice."

"Assuming it is not simply a compunction to duty," said Hoigt, seeming extraordinarily relaxed considering the situation. "Do you really wish to see me dead? For God's sake, we've known each other a pretty long time."

Dietrich continued to smile. "You and Schiller conspire with a police officer from the collective government; continue along with an investigation that you were given specific orders to drop; fire at fellow officers, and you ask me with all seriousness to show you leniency because of a friendship? You betray your own people, Hoigt, taking in this heathen. I have no respect left for you. And I spit on Schiller's body."

Hoigt nodded. "I just wanted to be sure," he said. "How many of you are there?"

Dietrich snorted, retrieved a handkerchief from his pocket and lifted it to his nose. "Six," he answered, then, after a pause, "Ten paces?" he asked.

"The fog will make it difficult," Hoigt responded. "But I suppose it is only fair."

"Very well then," said Dietrich, lifting his pistol and turning. Hoigt turned as well, leaning back to back with him.

Shultz stared in confusion. "What is going on here?" he asked.

"Ein!" Dietrich shouted, prompting Hoigt and himself to take a single step.

"Having us so unfairly outnumbered," Hoigt said to Shultz, "it is only honorable for him to allow us to face this massacre upfront with dignity. We think of it as fair play."

"Zwei!" Dietrich shouted, taking another step forward.

"This is medieval," said Shultz stepping with Hoigt.

"We make do with what we have," Hoigt replied, chuckled. "Anyhow, who are you to argue with a strategic handicap?"

Suddenly, Hoigt turned, pointed his weapon and fired a single shot into the small of Dietrich's back.

"Run!" he shouted to Shultz as a thunderclap of bullets began to rain down in their general direction before the body of the tall man even hit the ground.

Instinctively, Shultz ran to hide behind the dumpster once more, but Hoigt, grabbing him by the arm, pulled him forward, compelling him toward the parking garage. "Are you insane?" Shultz shouted.

"We must make it to the garage!" Hoigt replied. "We have to keep moving forward. There are only six of them. If we use the fog to our advantage we can pray for only slight injury to our persons. Get moving!"

Shultz broke into a run. Firing as he ran, he soon lost sight of Hoigt. The fog was growing thick. So thick he could barely see the tracer rounds as the bullets raced by him. Though naturally afraid for his life, he laughed to himself as he realized the ridiculousness of the manner in which he ran, bobbing and weaving as if the six Nuremberg policemen could see him clearly. He tried to remember exactly how far it was to the garage. Twenty meters? Twenty-five? He stopped firing his weapon. At this point, any shots he took served to locate him to the enemy. He highly doubted he was going to hit any of them anyway.

He stopped moving. Squinted in the fog for any sight of Hoigt. Where was he? Had he made it to the garage already? Taking a deep breath, he broke into a sprint, running in a straight line. No more bobbing and weaving. With his luck, if he continued to approach the garage in that fashion, it was more likely he would run into a bullet rather than actually be hit by one. Of course, after several yards of running in a straight line, he was hit in the leg. The shot sent him spinning to the ground.

Letting out an anguished groan, Shultz raised himself back to his feet and continued, he hoped, dragging his injured leg behind him toward the garage, having lost his sense of direction after the spin. Shots continued to ring out, echoing metallically in the air, coming ever closer to him, ricocheting off the cobblestones. Shultz put pressure on his wound, slightly below the buttock and, with a final burst of energy, began to hop rather than drag himself toward the walls of the garage.

Hopping, quickly losing his breath, hyperventilating and close to passing out, Shultz struggled to keep moving until, finally, he reached the wall; smacking into it hard face first. He felt his cheekbone collapse under the stretched skin of his face. "Oh, you Bastards!" he screamed into the fog, prompting several more shots. Blindly, Shultz lifted his pistol and fired the remainder of the clip. All firing in his direction ceased and a hollow thump sounded not too far from him, followed by a wheezing and moaning.

"Almost--almost there," came a voice muffled with pain.

It was a familiar voice. "Hoigt!" Shultz whispered harshly. "Hoigt, is that you?"

A pause. "Shultz, you shot me."

"Hoigt, we're at the wall. Quick, crawl toward me. Follow my voice."

"You crawl toward me," said Hoigt. "The entrance is over here by me."

Shultz raised himself on his elbows, crab crawled over to Hoigt. "Where is the entrance?" he asked, still unable to see anything.

"Follow me," said Hoigt, crab crawling himself.

The two men moved side by side until, very soon, Shultz made out a large, dark rectangular shape open up before them. The entrance. As soon as they entered the garage, the fog seemed to disappear. Both men were in agonizing pain. Hoigt's legs shook spasmodically as the two men took shelter behind the first of thousands of neatly parked vehicles. Shultz opened his eyes wide as he took notice of the amount of blood soaking into Hoigt's clothing.

"How many times were you hit?" he asked.

Hoigt took a short breath. "Five I think," he said weakly.

Shultz hesitated before speaking again. "Which one was me, do you think?"

"Right shoulder," Hoigt responded, coughed. "I think my collar bone is shattered."

"I can't tell you how sorry--"

"It is not fatal," Hoigt interrupted. "Anyway, to be perfectly honest, I can hardly feel it at all. I believe I am suffering from massive shock. Were you hit?"

"Yes, in the leg," Shultz answered. "I am a little embarrassed."

"Don't be," Hoigt replied. "Leg wounds can be very painful."

Shultz nodded, grimaced. "It is," he affirmed. Then, "Where are they? Why haven't they followed us? We're easy targets in here."

"With luck, it is possible they believe us not to have

173

made it this far. There is a good chance they are out there searching in the fog for our bodies." He coughed once more, tried to stifle it, causing himself even more pain. He spit out blood, looked at it on his hands. "Where is your vehicle parked?" he asked. "We should get out of here. I may need a doctor."

"This way," Shultz said, leading the way. The two men crawled, both unable to walk, leaving trails of smeared blood behind them. Once they travelled several yards, their elbows scraped and bruised from the crawl, Shultz asked, "Where is the ramp? I am on one of the upper levels."

Hoigt ceased crawling, sighed. "We can't possible make it up the ramps," he said. "We will have to use an elevator."

"Where are the elevators?" Shultz asked.

Hoigt lifted his hand, indicating with his thumb the opposite direction. "Back there," he said with some disappointment.

Shultz looked back and slumped. He wanted to cry. Then, without another word, both men slowly turned themselves around and resignedly headed back the way they had come, following their own still wet blood   trail.

~19~

"BUT WHY ON earth would you come here?" the woman asked Hollis Kincaid as he stood before the counter pouring himself a cup of coffee. For the most part ignoring the woman, he did, nonetheless, allow his eyes to gather in the sight of her. Tall and lean, the oversized lab coat wrapped around her body gave her form slightly more appeal to the naturally inquisitive Kincaid.

Twirling his moustache, he held up the coffee mug and, drawing his attention the cartoonish lettering on its side, said, "My dear, what does this say? Say it out loud. It says don't sweat the small stuff. Now that is a very appealing philosophy, wouldn't you agree?"

"Don't get me started on small stuff," the woman snapped. "My entire life is lived pouring over details. Every waking hour spent ruminating over the small stuff. And if you believe for even a minute, considering your story to be true, that what you have done falls into the category of 'small stuff', then I may have to have my head examined. I hope you're satisfied. Up until this moment I lived in relative security of my own sanity. You've given me doubts."

"And that, my dear, is something the government itself has never been able to do. I will accept it as a compliment."

"You've committed murder, Hollis."

"No, he lived," said Kincaid, shaking his head slightly. "I read it in the papers." Gulping down the coffee, he sat down on the edge of the counter. "Although I have to admit a feeling of relief, I am a bit disappointed with myself. I thought for sure I'd killed him." The woman slid her hands over her face and walked into another room, prompting Kincaid to raise his voice. "It is my first and only failure if you can believe that," he said. "A whole life spent betting against the odds and always coming out the winner. But not this time. Nope. In fact, on the surface it appears I have lost just about everything. Here I am on the run, living my life in hiding, depending on others for my very sustenance; not to mention I'm out a pretty good chunk of change. All this and I didn't even commit a crime. I mean, like I said, Fordy MacLennon survived. What can they really hold against me? And to top it off, since he survived, Cole Stringer won't be taking over as head auditor."

The woman came back into the room, her hair dripping wet. "You never have explained to me the necessity of Cole Stringer becoming head auditor."

"Did you...did you just take a shower?" Kincaid asked, staring at the woman with a confused mixture of surprise and insult.

"I was listening," she answered, ringing the water out of her hair into a small plastic container sitting next to the coffee pot.

"I doubt you've heard a word I've said," he said as he watched the water drip into the container. "Have you been recycling your hair water to make coffee?" he asked. "Is that what I've been drinking all morning?"

"It gets boiled doesn't it?" she said, preparing another pot, then stated, "Cole Strinager."

"Darn good man," said Kincaid. "Lots of ambition. Lots of spunk. Freaking thief, though, as it turns out. Well, I may be getting ahead of myself. After all, how could he know any better than I did that MacLennon was going to pull through. I put three holes in the man's torso for crying out loud. How could he have survived?"

"Why do we need Strinager?" she asked again.

"The man's predictable," Kincaid responded. "And he's greedy. Greedy men will get you any and everything you might ever possibly want if they believe you can get them any and everything they might ever possibly want. A situational relationship made all the more exploitable if that man honestly believes in his heart of hearts that any and everything he may possibly ever want is greater to the amount of any and everything you, yourself, might ever possibly want. Strinager is the foolish type. He's greedy for money. While you and I, my dear, are greedy for the stars!"

"I wasn't going to tell you this," said the woman. "But we're still missing several key components to the rocket."

"Don't you think I know that?" said Kincaid. "Why

do you think I've been trying to get funding for the multiplex?"

"I'm not talking about a launch foundation. At the moment, my workmen do not have what they need to connect the fuel injectors."

"Come out with it then. What else do you need?"

"An eighteen millimeter socket," she answered dryly.

Kincaid suppressed a cough. "Those are nearly impossible to find," he snorted. "Why on earth would you design a craft requiring a thing like that?"

"Because we didn't have the capitol to build a fuselage from scratch. I had to use one pre-manufactured by the government for the Extra Solar Pioneers. And all government pre-manufactured fuselages use eighteen millimeter sockets to clamp the fuel connectors."

Kincaid scowled. "Don't ever mention the ESP's," he grunted. "You know better than that."

"I, myself, think of them as an inspirational aide," said the woman, briefly losing the self-righteous smirk she had been wearing the entirety of the conversation. It was her way of showing she did, after all, have some empathetic feeling toward Kincaid. Something she was loathe to admit. She felt compelled to follow it with a snide remark just to save face, if only for herself but, inexplicably, she held her tongue. This self-realization made her frown.

"Let's just forget about it…for now," said Kincaid. "An eighteen millimeter socket, eh? Give me a moment to think." He rubbed his forefinger across his chin and meditated.

"I think there are some firms in Europe we can order from," said the woman.

"That's no good," countered Kincaid. "Something like that going through the post would surely draw attention. It would be better to fly over and pick one up direct," he said. "Of course then it becomes a customs issue. Difficult to hide something like that in your toiletries. No...there has got to be another way."

"I might be able to re-fabricate the fuselage," said the woman. She opened a drawer and pulled out a detailed series of blueprints, looked them over and sighed. "It will take time, though. Maybe too much time if there really is a man hunt out for you."

"Not to mention a certain liability. How much of a risk would there be to the craft if you did re-fabricate?"

"It's hard to say. Any number of difficulties could occur. Everything from electrical failure to pressurization. I would not feel comfortable taking the risk."

"That tears it then," said Kincaid, slapping his thigh. "I'll see what I can do. In fact, I do believe I know somebody with European connections. Only real trouble is coming out of hiding."

"I can go," said the woman. "Just tell me where. The last thing we need is for you to be picked up by the Friendly Neighbors."

"No, my dear. I need you right where you are if we're going to keep on schedule. But don't worry about me. I still have a trick or two up my sleeve.

Besides, it's a bit too early for you to be visiting the gynecologist."

The woman crossed her eyes, perplexed.

~20~

DOCTOR LOUIS JUDD sat at his desk trying to solve an old wooden toy puzzle. It was a hobby of his passed down to him by his grandfather who collected nostalgic toys. At first only a childish pursuit, Judd soon found they relaxed him. A good way to unwind. He had gotten into the habit of taking them wherever he went. Twenty years earlier, when he opened his first practice, he kept a variety of these toys hidden in the drawers of his desk for fear of upsetting the women whose husbands had not been issued a license. It struck him as cruel giving them their check-ups in view of children's toys. But, after a few months, it became apparent most people did not recognize the puzzles as toys and, so, he took no pains to hide them; sometimes even tried to solve them in front of his patients. This he found not only relaxing, but enjoyable in a certain covertly sadistic fashion.

A buzzer sounded.

He pressed a button on his phone. "What is it, Jenny?"

There was a stutter in Jenny's tinny response. "A

man to see you, doctor."

"Give me one minute."

"…He has a gun, doctor."

"Whaaa…? A gun?"

Kincaid came into the office dragging Jenny behind him. "She wasn't supposed to tell you that, Judd," he said, then, motioning with his hand to calm the doctor, said, "Oh, the gun isn't for you. I don't even know why I brought it. Wasn't planning to use it. That is, until your secretary here recognized me from the papers. Is she trustworthy or do I have to keep her hostage?"

Doctor Judd put down the wooden puzzle and covered his mouth with his hand. "She's harmless, Kincaid," he said. "Turtles…you gave me quite a scare."

"Completely unintentional," said Kincaid, pocketing the pistol and letting go the secretary's arm. "I need a favor, Judd. I'll wait until you catch your breath."

Doctor Judd took several deep breaths before placing his hands flat on his desk. "Okay, I'm ready."

"How much will it take for you to acquire me an eighteen millimeter socket from Birmingham, England?"

"Travel expenses included?"

"Naturally."

"I'm talking about the works, Kincaid. Meals, hotels, postcards for the family."

"I need it soon as possible."

"Afraid I'm booked for the next three weeks. Can it

wait?"

"Not three weeks."

"I'll send Jenny," said Judd. "She's never been to Europe. She handles things for me all the time. I'll book her a flight leaving tomorrow morning. How does that sound?"

"I would really prefer you to handle this personally," said Kincaid. "This is a very delicate situation."

"Mister Kincaid, my duties as a gynecologist greatly outweigh your need of me as a courier. Three weeks is the best I can do. Jenny, however, is available as we speak."

"Gall darn it, Judd, you owe me! After all our dealings, I would think you would have a bit more respect for my situation."

"Sending my secretary on your errands is no small thing, Kincaid," countered the doctor. "Do you realize the chaos that can ensue in an office such as this without a secretary around to keep things in order? You're going to have to learn to be a little less picky with whom it is doing you favors."

"Sounds like charity to me, Judd. Maybe you've forgotten certain incriminating files I hold in my possession?"

"You can't blackmail me, Kincaid. You may be a very rich man, but you're in no position to threaten a man of my standing. You think I'm such a fool I wouldn't safeguard myself against attempts at extortion?"

Kincaid slapped his knee and lowered his head. "Well, I don't want this to come between our friendship," he said. "If all you can spare is your secretary, then I suppose it will have to do." He held up his hands. "I'm not happy about it. Not one bit. But I can't afford to wait three weeks."

"Jenny is quite resourceful," said Doctor Judd. "She's more than capable of fetching your tool."

"Fine...fine. But I'm not paying for this young woman to take a holiday. I'll shell out enough to pay for two days. I think it's more than fair. One day to do the job, another to see the sights," he lectured, turning to face the secretary. "Do we have an agreement, Jenny?"

"What was that, sir?" asked Jenny.

"She hasn't been paying us attention," said doctor Judd.

Kincaid shook his head. "Do you want to go to England, Jenny?"

"I'd love to," said the secretary.

Doctor Judd placed his hands gently on the girl's shoulders. "Now listen, Jenny," he said. "This is a matter of some importance. Can you handle it?"

"You bet."

"Great," said Kincaid. "Now, listen, Jenny. Eighteen millimeter sockets are considered contraband on this side of the Atlantic. You will have to find a way to get it back here to us without being caught. So don't take it lightly. Use your head now, you understand?"

"Got it," said Jenny. "Don't worry, Mister Kincaid, I've done this sort of thing before." She turned to the doctor. "May I take the rest of the day off then, to pack?" she asked.

Doctor Judd nodded, smacked her on the behind as she left the office. "Satisfied?" he asked Kincaid.

"Immensely."

"Now, then. How are you getting out of here? I can't conceive of how you got here in the first place without being detected."

"I imagine you have a fire escape handy," said Kincaid.

"You mean to shimmy down the side of the building? Right this way," said the doctor motioning Kincaid toward the window.

Kincaid leaned his head out to witness the rusted over railing of the fire escape, felt his heart skip a beat and wiped his forehead. "It's archaic," he exclaimed. "You can't seriously expect--"

"Does it sting you at all to admit your inability to shirk the hold of gravity itself?" interrupted the doctor, leaning his head out to view the railing himself. "Have no fear. It is quite safe. They do yearly inspections on all obsolete constructs left in place for the sake of aesthetics. Or so I've been told. To tell the truth, I have never seen these safety inspectors."

"No, it's true," said Kincaid. "I have an acquaintance on the board. All the same, though, I think I would rather brave the elevator."

He stepped away from the window and straightened his cuffs, smiled at the doctor and made to leave the office when, suddenly, the door swung open, slamming into his face.

"Oh, my goodness!" exclaimed the man attempting to enter the office, tripping over Kincaid's legs and dropping the several boxes he had been carting. Stacks of loose paper scattered about the floor as Kincaid struggled to untangle himself from the man.

"Turtles, man! Why don't you watch where you're going?" yelled Kincaid, picking himself up and noticing a trickle of blood escape his nose. "Now look what you've done. What on earth is all that?" he asked, annoyed, as he watched doctor Judd furiously picking up the scattered papers.

"Never mind," said the doctor, smacking the slender man on the head. "You fool! I told you always to call first."

"My nose is bleeding, doctor," said Kincaid. "I shall be expecting an apology from your little friend."

"Fine…fine," said doctor Judd. "Er--Hans, apologize to the man so he can be on his way."

"Tut mir leid," said the slender man after a sharp bow, an apprehensive look on his youthful face.

"I'm not tooting anybody's horn today Frenchie. Can't you see my nose is bleeding?"

"Take these into the other room, Hans, while I help mister Kincaid with his injury," said the doctor handing the freshly stacked papers to the man, obviously anxious for him to leave the office. "Tilt your head back and pinch the nostrils," he ordered, pulling a handkerchief from his breast pocket and placing it under Kincaid's nose. "Just hold like this for a few minutes and you'll be okay. I apologize for the incident. Now, if you please, feel free to take your leave via the elevator."

Doctor Judd gestured Kincaid toward the elevator, pressing him slightly on the back when, Kincaid, bending over suddenly, swiped one of the papers that had escaped notice. "What's all this?" he asked, scanning over the paper.

"It's nothing!" said the doctor, trying to snatch the paper away from him.

Kincaid held the paper out of the doctor's reach. "I wonder about that little run-in," he said. "Tell me, Judd, where you more concerned about the man seeing me, or I seeing the man? Or where you in fact more concerned about my seeing this?" he said, indicating the paper.

"That is none of your business," said the doctor, his eyes bulging with anger and desperation. "Anyhow, there is nothing out of the ordinary with any of this."

"That's what upsets me the most," said Kincaid, his voice slightly higher pitched due to pinching his nose. He crumpled the paper in his hand, held it in a vice like grip. "Only an idiot would believe these to be legitimate procrete licenses," he said. "I can smell a forgery a mile away. But that's not what bothers me. What bothers me is you not cutting me in on the deal. After all we've been through. How much have you made from this little scheme? A million? Million-two? Ha! Of course, I've known you to be a bit on the crooked side, but who would ever have thought you to be this brazen? This…this is downright criminal! You've been breaking more laws than I have. And I tried to kill a man. Who would have thought it?"

"Give me that paper," said doctor Judd, gnashing his teeth, beginning to sense the end of his career. "I mean it, Kincaid. So help me…"

With a single motion, Kincaid stuffed the paper into his pocket and pulled his pistol, all the while continuing to pinch his nose with his other hand. "So help you what?" he said, pointing the weapon at the doctor. "We find ourselves at an impasse, Judd."

"You won't shoot," said the doctor. "You wouldn't dare."

"I've pulled the trigger before."

"There's a world of difference between a development man and a doctor of gynecology. Shoot me and you're not dealing with the Friendly Neighbors. It's the Deterrence Police you'll be dealing with. You might as well shoot yourself as shoot me."

"I wouldn't worry about that. I'm sure they'll show a little leniency once they find your stack of forged procrete licenses. Heck...I'm willing to bet I go down as a hero. Matter of fact, it might even be enough to clear me for shooting Fordy MacLennon. Darn it, Judd, I'm trying to search for reasons why not to shoot you."

Doctor Judd held up his hands. "Alright, Kincaid. What do you want?"

"A piece of the action."

"How much?"

"I'll settle for ten percent."

"A man like you demanding such a small percentage? Maybe you don't feel as confident as you're trying to let on."

"Oh, but, ten percent isn't all I want. No, sir."

"Well, what else do you want? Just put it on the table. That way I can tell you whether to just shoot me or not."

"I want you to go to Birmingham. No more secretary talk."

"Kincaid be reasonable!"

"You get me that eighteen millimeter socket and I'll knock it down to five percent."

"Why is it so important for you to have an eighteen millimeter socket? I can't just pack up and leave in the blink of an eye. If I get sick, the government send a special physician to judge whether I can come to the office or not. We're a rare breed. We don't exactly have freedom of movement."

Kincaid lowered the pistol. "What if you were laid up with an injury?"

Doctor Judd did a little dance and waved his hands in front of the gun. "Now, hold it! I'm not making excuses. I'm trying to make you see how things work. There are only two gynecologists authorized to grant procrete licenses in the whole of old Massachusetts. Being a man, I don't expect you to know this. Our numbers are organized on the basis of the senate under the old system. Larger territories have more, but here there are only two. Me and Carl Jasper. If I just up and disappear without an adequate excuse, he'll have to take over all my appointments and he'll throw a fit. All he has to do is make one phone call and I'm under investigation!"

"That decides the issue then," said Kincaid.

Spittle formed at the sides of doctor Judd's mouth. "Fifty percent if you wait three weeks!" he yelled.

Kincaid pulled the trigger, hitting doctor Judd slightly above the knee.

189

~21~

"WHAT ARE YOU doing?" asked Hoigt, wheezing, his blood trickling down the passenger seat of Shultz's vehicle as Shultz frantically pressed his navigational buttons, searching for the quickest route away from Nuremberg.

"You need medical attention," said Shultz. "And I'm worried you may be as equally unwelcome in Munich as I was here. I am trying to find directions to a safe house in Wurzburg until I feel it is safe enough to contact my commanding officer. He'll know what to do with you."

Hoigt tried to keep himself upright, but his body kept sliding down in the seat, slipping on the smeared blood. "Not Wurzburg. Take me to Thuringia."

"What's in Thuringia?"

"The Shwarzwald. I know a man there. Axel Tizch. I need to see him."

"The Black Forest is two hours farther than Wurzburg. I don't think you can hang on that long. Not to mention my own injury. If I don't have precise directions, I can't enter it into the navigational computer. The vehicle will have to be driven manually and I cannot manage that in my condition."

Hoigt banged his fist against the window. "Then let me out!" he shouted. "I will get to the Shwarzwald myself. I promised to get you out and that's what I did. There is no reason for us to travel together."

"Don't be stupid. If I let you out now, you will just lie down and bleed to death right where I leave you. Besides, I feel an obligation toward you for saving my life."

Hoigt began coughing uncontrollably.

"Anyway, we still have a case to work, remember?" said Shultz, his eyes glazing over with concern and a newfound sense of tenderness as he looked over at Hoigt. "For the time being, at least, we need each other."

"Take me to the Shwarzwald then," Hoigt mumbled, no longer able to project his words loudly. "Axel Tizch holds the key to the case. Maybe to both cases."

"Okay…okay. Just sit back. Try not to talk too much. I'll put in the directions to Thuringia. But you will have to tell me where to go once we get there. And I hope Axel Tizch is a doctor as well."

"He is more than that…," said Hoigt with glassed over, faraway eyes. "Some say he is all things."

"What's that supposed to mean?"

Hoigt whispered, almost as if to himself, "Icarus Craig."

"Icarus Craig the cult leader? I've heard of him. Why did you say his name?"

"Axel Tizch is Icarus Craig."

"He is, is he? And you want me to take you to see him? Cripes, Hoigt. It's one thing to believe in Christianity, but please tell me you haven't been sucked in to some mountain man's circle of freaks."

Hoigt faced the window, his eyes barely open. Aside from a slight flicker of his pupils whenever the vehicle passed a random signpost, Shultz was unable to ascertain to what degree Hoigt remained conscious. "If I were a follower of the man, I would never refer to him by his earthly name," he said quietly. "Icarus Craig is the name given him by those who desire an understanding of his philosophy."

"What philosophy? The man is a nut case."

"What do you know of it?"

"I know Icarus Craig is wanted on several counts of conspiracy. What I didn't know is that he resided in the Black Forest. I assumed he lived in Nuremberg with all the other superstitious nut cases. To think he's been living under the jurisdiction of the federal government. Right under our noses."

"He's no criminal," said Hoigt, grunting between words. "He has a cabin he never leaves. He lives in the forest. Lives off the forest."

"How do you know? How do you know anything about him if you've never been outside the garages of Nuremberg?"

Hoigt hesitated. "I don't know. I've only heard things."

"Yeah, like what?"

"Icarus Craig preaches that there are only two or three things God created man to accomplish in order to fulfil life's purpose. Two or three things to be accomplished by the whole of man...not two or three for each man. A true reason for living. But these things are practically unattainable. So hidden from us. Only the wisest man...a man of unquestionable spirit can discover just what it is that needs to be accomplished in order to justify our creation. Most men are unable to do this. We don't have the patience or desire. Our spirit has been nullified. That's why there are so many people on this planet. When they say man has a biological need to reproduce, it is not just for physical survival. Subconsciously, we know just how far away from the source we have become. We need to better the odds. The more people, the more chances one of us can discover the secret of what it is God wants us to accomplish."

"So what, Hoigt? Just because a man claims to understand the need to understand doesn't mean he's some sort of prophet. If he is so wise, why hasn't he discovered these sacred truths himself? Tell me, what is really so great about a man like Icarus Craig? Do you honestly believe he has the answers?"

"I don't know what answers Icarus Craig has," said Hoigt, his voice steady once more. "I'm only interested in the answers of Axel Tizch."

The two rode in silence, both bleeding appropriately from their various wounds; neither with the strength to argue a point, no matter how valid or righteous, until the scenery slowly began to change from industrialized flatland to a land of rolling hills and thick forest. Both men struggled to stay awake, fearing sleep would be everlasting unless given the proper medical attention until, after a few hours, it became impossible to witness anything but trees and shady growth through the windows of the vehicle. Another fog was rising as the vehicle came to a measured stop at the intersection of Kreuzstrasse and Ostmark. The borders of Thuringian province. The extent of Shultz's pre-figured directions.

Rubbing his eyes with his knuckles, he leaned over sorely and nudged Hoigt on the shoulder. "Okay. Where do I go?"

Hoigt drearily gestured. "Into the forest," he said.

"There's no road into the forest. It's a wildlife preserve."

"We will have to walk."

"Walk? I don't know if I can even stand. There has to be an easier way to this man's home. Isn't there some place we can go and call him? Preferably a hospital."

"I don't think he has a phone. Aside from that, I am not sure exactly where he lives."

"Not sure where he lives? Why didn't you tell me this in the first place?"

"All I know is he lives somewhere in there," said Hoigt pointing into the forest. "If we desire to find him, we will find him."

Shultz banged on the dashboard of his vehicle. "You didn't tell me because you knew I wouldn't have come!"

"But you were meant to come," Hoigt said calmly, pressing the button to open the passenger door. With a painful grunt, he rocked his body to the side in order to push himself out of the vehicle. Thumping to the ground, he raised himself on his elbows and tried to lift his body. Wounds that had begun to clot over, opened once again. The blood began to soak through his clothing. "Ohhh...damn," he moaned.

Shultz watched the stubborn spectacle with a mixture of indignity and respect. Shaking his head, he stumbled out of the vehicle and limped over to Hoigt. Placing his hands under Hoigt's armpits, he lifted him up, wrapped one of Hoigt's arms around him. "Where do we go?" he asked between heavy breaths, resigning himself to the new mystery.

Hoigt lifted his arm weakly in response, pointed into the forest once more.

"Just walk straight ahead?" said Shultz, looking for confirmation. "Fine," he said, wondering if he were going through everything in the hopes of finding Axel Tizch or proving Hoigt wrong. "We'll just go straight."

"We'll find him," said Hoigt under labored breaths. Tears flowed from his eyes.

Shultz took a heavy step off the road, stabilizing Hoigt with his own body. Branches cracked underneath his feet as they trudged deeper into the forest. They didn't get far before Shultz's foot caught on a downed limb. Both men fell; Hoigt's fall cushioned by Shultz; Shultz's face cushioned by the fallen pine needles. He let out a short shriek as the needles stuck into his skin.

"I can walk," said Hoigt, trying once more to lift himself. It was a good effort, though futile.

Shultz rolled himself over and stamped the ground

like a spoiled child. "I don't want to do this anymore," he cried. "What are we doing out here? This isn't normal."

Bending over, head between his knees, Shultz frantically tugged at his hair while Hoigt squirmed on the ground, his blood mixing with the dirt. Shultz took a deep breath to centre himself, watched Hoigt's slow, almost balladic movements. Tearing his eyes away, he brushed at the dirt on his knees until a cracking nose caused him to turn suddenly to the side to see a large buck run into view. The buck, upon catching sight of Shultz, froze in its tracks, its large eyes showing confused fear. It focused on Shultz for a brief moment, looked back the way it had come then ran off with a graceful sense of panic.

Shultz watched the buck disappear deeper into the forest until a loud bang caused him to jerk back around. Covering his ears and lowering to the ground, Shultz witnessed a large man appear from where the buck had earlier came. The man held a rifle and wore dark green overalls. A grey beard came to a sharp point at his chin and his moustache curled up at the sides, almost meeting with the hairline receding away from his temples.

"Auf dem teufel!" the man grunted, lowering the rifle and looking into the distance as if trying to envision the last fleeting glimpse of the buck's essence.

Shultz stared up at the man, dumbstruck. Was the man an hallucination due to loss of blood. Or was he flesh and bone. Either way, one thing, though, was for certain.

Swallowing hard, Shultz said in a cracked voice, "You just tried to kill an animal in a wildlife preserve."

The man looked down at Shultz, seemingly unsurprised to see him except for a slight twitch of his moustache. "Humph," he said, then turned to walk away when, Hoigt, rolling onto his back and craning his neck to see the man, forced a smile.

"Axel Tizch," he said.

The man stopped, secured the rifle unthreateningly under his arm, and said after a pause, his back to the men, "At your service."

~22~

AN UNASSUMING MAN walked through the damp streets of Inverness, Scotland, past a large crowd of children circled around a troupe of female dancers in colorful, flowing robes and braided hair. The dancers twirled riotously and the children, their eyes following the frantic dance, moved their heads in continuous semi circles until falling dizzy. Some of them fell to the ground with innocent laughter, while others pointed and made fun, until, in a spontaneous gesture of good humor, the dancers, themselves, plopped to the ground, joining in with the children's laughter.

The unassuming man stopped to enjoy the spectacle before moving on. Climbing a steep hill, the man turned down a small alley where scaffolding snaked up the walls of a crumbling building dating back to the year eighteen twelve. The man admired the remains of the building as he made his way down the alley and was shot through with confounded sentimentality, knowing as he did the scaffolding was put in place to help workers dismantle the building rather than repair it. A slow deconstruction. The centuries old building was not even afforded the dignity of the wrecking ball. The man raised his collar as if afraid a random passer-by might witness the look of disgust on his face.

Sucking in his chest, the man pressed the bulging area of his coat close against him in order to squeeze past a recycling bin placed at the end of the alley until stepping out and, continuing on his way, passing the library, a flat, single story building, he made his way in the direction of the bus depot-a building as equally small as the library.

Being a holiday, the bus depot was all but deserted except for a skeleton crew of maintenance workers and mechanics. The building itself cradled a small tourist centre and several local shops situated in a rectangular pattern opening on one end allowing pick-up and drop-off traffic to enter. The buses left the depot on a street behind the building connecting to the town's main thoroughfare.

Halfway to the depot, the man stopped and suspiciously scanned the area before continuing toward it. He straightened his back as several pedestrians passed casually by, walking in the opposite direction. He tipped his hat to them, hiding his face behind his collar. He was only several yards away from the depot when he heard a clanking sound behind him. He turned to see one of the pedestrians had dropped something. Nothing out of the ordinary except-the pedestrian bent over to pick up the dropped item with a bit too much speed, and the look on his face showed he was far too conscious of the act---as if he felt the entire world were watching him--some unseen power looking down on him--judging him for allowing a loose item to fall from his pockets. Some unseen power. That's when the unassuming man realized the look on the face of the other pedestrian. A look of pure desperation.

Without another moment's hesitation, the unassuming man broke into a run, determined to reach the bus depot. The two pedestrians chased after him and, as he approached the depot, the man stumbled as he found himself confronted by twelve armed men on the roof of the depot. The men on the roof, as well as the would-be pedestrians began to shout in unison but, either the unassuming man could not understand the shouts, or paid them no heed as he sprinted toward the depot doors. The maintenance workers and mechanics looked out the windows in curiosity then suddenly threw themselves to the floor as the men on the roof opened fire on the unassuming man.

If the man was hit at all, he showed no signs. Not stopping upon reaching the depot, the man continued to run alongside the building, slowing only to hurl several metallic canisters through the windows.

Breaking from the cover the bus depot offered, the man braved the hail of gunfire aimed at him in order to put as much distance between himself and the building. He got several yards before being hit in the leg. He fell, rolled and launched himself back to his feet, not stopping the momentum.

The twelve men on the roof of the bus depot fired

incessantly until the building suddenly exploded. The shock wave knocked the man to the ground. He waited for the debris to fall before picking himself back up. A helicopter came into view, hovered overhead as several black vehicles with gold trim rolled into the square. The man ran for cover as marksmen opened fire on him from the helicopter. Swarms of uniformed officers jumped from the black vehicles, blocking any conceivable escape route.

The man, seeing he was surrounded, stopped running, turned from side to side as if praying for an exit when he felt himself being thrown to the ground once more. It was the officer posing as a pedestrian-- the one who had blown his cover--that tackled him. The man fought with savagery, tearing at the man, biting until the officer was forced to let go. Once free, the man once more began to run. As the deterrence police opened fire, caring little for the safety of their comrade, the man reached into his jacket and, pulling out a handful of the same metallic canisters, began tossing them at random. Some rolled under the black vehicles, some crashed through shop windows or bounced off brick walls until all exploded in unison.

The gunfire ceased for a brief moment, but the deterrence police were not phased for long by the chaos. They reopened fire even before the black vehicles blown into the air had slammed back to the ground; before the nearby buildings crumbled to pieces.

Finally, as grey smoke began filling the sky, the unassuming man was felled by the marksman in the helicopter--a single bullet to the back of the head. The man flopped to the ground and rolled several yards. His body twitched, bucking against a pile of shattered stone.

The marksman in the helicopter gave a thumbs up to the pilot. The pilot then moved the helicopter away from the smoke and, switching the intercom, gave the word for the deterrence police to stand down. He then put in a request for a ground crew to retrieve the body and begin the relatively quick process of cleaning up the destruction left in his wake. Dust settled on the unrecognizable features of the   man's   face.

~23~

STEVENSON WALKED A circle, projecting his voice loudly to the large group of ragged pioneers huddled together to hear him speak as Buster Macready devoured a sandwich consisting only of two slices of dry bread and a bean spread of some sort. Stevenson spoke rather evenly, giving emphasis to only a few words which caused Macready to look up from his first real meal in months to pay attention. For some unknown reason, Macready tried to hide the fact that he was listening. The way Stevenson would occasionally try to lock eyes with him as he spoke-- the look of complete self-satisfaction on his face made Macready hesitant to listen at all. He gazed at the almost savage looking men sitting cross legged on either side of him and wondered at the look in their eyes. A look that seemed to completely offset the appearance of utter degeneracy in their features--or was it, in fact, the look in their eyes that gave them that appearance. Hard to tell. Stevenson was preaching. And the pioneers gathered round were his choir.

"I stand before you on this, another endless night, with but one true message. One sacred truth. That you, my brothers, you and I now find ourselves in our rightful position in the universe. The one truth that all man must find, seen clearly at last. Discovered...no, revealed to us on our long journey through that vast emptiness separating us from every physical relation we have ever been able to connect with. For what are we if not beings specially evolved to flourish on a distant planet we used to call home? Who are we if everything about us springs from having developed on that planet? Yet, there is one thing in us that did not originate on that rock. One small thing that is everything. I am talking about our very atoms. The one thing about us to originate long before that rock made us everything we are. The truth I speak of is that we are all far older than what we know of the universe. We are all the beginning. And being the beginning, we are all the end. Each and every one of us the alpha and the omega. Listen to me, my brothers, and I will teach you how to manifest this celestial truth. I will show you how to be greater than everything you have ever worshipped or feared.'

"This night, my brothers, the course we set ourselves upon, will develop and shape the beliefs, the hopes and dreams, fears, culture, language, sacrifices, the very reason for living to all that come after us. The hidden knowledge; the mystery of every question; the riddle of millennia; the answer to everything will be traced back to us. You and I, transcending space and time, we, my brothers, my already ancient converts, we are the physical conception of the spirit. The reason for life itself."

The heretofore tame pioneers, whether sensing the close of the speech, or swept up in sincere frenzy, suddenly broke into a fit of wild cheers. Macready, finishing the last bit of the sandwich, made a conscious effort to feel the same excitement, but the sound of the men's cheers, muffled by the low atmosphere, gave the scene an unnatural appearance. He wondered if the men were aware of this audible anomaly, and striving to overcome it, forced their enthusiasm. Was what Stevenson said really so great? Did it merit the ability to inspire? Was the band of pioneers really so devoted, or were they just bored and desperate. Desperate for the familiarity of being led...of following? He wanted to ask these questions aloud, but was afraid to.

Strange, he thought, all the things I find myself afraid of. All the little things I never considered, the little things I find frightening. All these little fears. Amounting to what? How have they affected me without even my understanding? How can a man face so many unseen, unrecognizable fears? What is the outcome of a man living his life believing he is brave, or, at the very least, facing his fears, to overcome, to strengthen, empower, when his subconscious mind is at every moment shuddering in fear; terrorized by nightmares unable to be dealt with? How is it I can face death in an alien wilderness but be too afraid to speak out to my own kind?

His thoughts betraying him, Macready coughed,

choking on the last crumbs of the sandwich. The pioneers grew still and Stevenson levied his eyes on him, leaned down.

"Would you like another sandwich?" he asked.

"Can you spare another sandwich?"

"We can spare whatever you need."

Buster steadied his gaze on him. "No, you can't," he said.

Stevenson laughed. "That's why I like you, Macready. You are a tried and true sceptic. Even about something as trivial as the abundance of sandwich. That's why I need you here. It's why we all need you."

"You're speaking in riddles," said Buster. "But, yes, I would like another sandwich."

Stevenson nodded, tightened his thin lips and clapped his hands, signaling to one of the pioneers to fetch the sandwich, which was done. Buster tore chunks out of the sandwich, eating it in small portions as he locked eyes with Stevenson.

You look younger now, thought Buster, imagining Stevenson could read his thoughts. Not as if you have grown more vibrant…but more childish.

It was a shallow antagonism. He allowed the thoughts to come, having a vague suspicion that Stevenson might have some psychic gift, but he decided to play it safe and keep his words unsaid.

Stevenson alternated his gaze from Buster and the pioneers who had begun to disperse; some went back to their living quarters, others went about doing chores; repairs, cooking, setting up lights to counteract the non-diurnal nature of the environment.

Stevenson watched all this, apparently pleased. Buster looked at the man, trying to discover his motives. This man who seemed to be building a civilization before his eyes. Who was he?

"What did you do on earth?" Buster asked, setting the remainder of his sandwich on the ground, no longer hungry, but also, curious to see how Stevenson would react to the wasting of food.

"I was a fireman," he said, showing no response to Buster's action. "For twenty-three years."

"How old are you?"

"That depends on how you mean it," said Stevenson. "How old am I now, or how old was I when I left earth?"

"Forget it," said Buster, picking up what was left of the sandwich and tossing it.

Stevenson watched, turned once more to the busy pioneers and waved his hand in the air. "They don't ask questions," he said, indicating the pioneers. "Not anymore. They did in the beginning. And, of course, my shipmates were curious. Small things mostly; trivial questions, as you have asked. Questions designed to seek out answers that no longer matter. How old am I? What did I do on earth?"

"If it's all relative, related to the whole, how can it not matter?"

Stevenson closed his eyes. "We don't have an eighteen millimeter socket," he said.

Buster clenched his fist. "Why didn't you tell me that before?"

"Not having the item makes it irrelevant. I have sent several men to search out the Carolyn Summers.

They will bring the rest of your crew here, where there is a working supply marker. So you see, the eighteen millimeter socket no longer matters. The need for one was merely a catalyst…like God."

"You're at it again. Speaking in riddles. And what if my crew doesn't want to be a part of your ragtag colony? They have a little pride too, you know. Not everybody wants to be part of somebody else's greater scheme."

"They really have no choice," Stevenson said soberly.

"And I suppose you expect them to haul the Carolyn Summers all this way?"

"If they so choose. But it really isn't necessary. We can take only what will be of use to us. We have begun building shelters from the rocks, so there really is no need to transplant the entire craft."

"And what about the incubation chamber? You'll be needing that won't you?"

"Do you understand why all the pioneer craft are named after women? There are several reasons. The first, and simplest is that there are no female pioneers. Giving our craft a female name is symbolic to having a female present. It keeps words representing the feminine in our vernacular. We refer to our craft as 'she' or 'her'. It is a small comfort. But the craft is also our mother. We generated in her bowels on our long journey across the space ways. Conceived by Immaculate Conception. Brought to this world whole. The first generation, men already. All those who come after will grow on this planet. And the pioneer craft--Heidi Irregular, Mary Elizabeth,

Stephanie Smith, and Carolyn Summers--and all the others will be here, bringing forth new life--until we no longer need them."

Stevenson's voice faded into silence.

I should leave. I should leave now, Buster thought. But where would I go? Is this really so bad? What is it about Stevenson that bothers me so? Is it because I don't feel important around him, when my entire reason for becoming a pioneer was to have a sense of self-importance...self-reliance. Though his words are full of meaning and he preaches of the ultimate importance of us all...I feel almost smaller...more worthless. I don't like him because he's better than me. I'm not even sure if he is human.

"This planet has its own gods," Stevenson said quietly.

"I don't want to hear about it."

"Sure you do. You're curious. You're afraid."

Buster thought, maybe I am. But what's wrong with that?

3
(TRUST)

~   Stevenson leaned in close as if revealing a close secret. "All heavenly objects have a creative agent. Some power that watches over it, protects it, or, in some cases, brings it to ruin; overseeing its degeneration, its wasting. In some cases, the power may wish to bless the object; watch it flourish, endure.   Or maybe the power has a peculiar disinterest. Perhaps this planet is unfortunate in that it is merely a moon orbiting round a much larger celestial object. Perhaps it is seen by the power as nothing more than a decoration circling its real prize. Or, maybe the power holds this small object in contempt. It sees this small moon as a blemish and in its own way, wishes for its destruction.'

"What a marvelous place this is. Yet, we may be the only creatures who can truly appreciate it. Can you imagine that glorious being, its presence so strongly felt, glimpsed only in the flickering dust; how it must feel…relegated to this lonely place? Its only charge, seeing to the continuous orbit of these beautiful orbs; in its own way and, perhaps quite against its own will, doing its small part to maintain order in the universe. What I believe, Macready, is that until now, the gods watching over this planet have mistreated it, abused it, maybe even hated it, if that is at all possible…feeling it a mirror that refuses to reflect their glory. But now they are forced to see it in a new light. Now we are here, and they look upon it with a newfound covetousness. And they will try and supplant us, or bend us to their will. But, superior to us as they are, they are making a grave miscalculation. They do not take into account that we come from a planet that is watched over by powers much greater than them in the cosmological hierarchy. The gods of earth must have been great indeed to have been designated a world so full of life. A world that, until now, was the only in the universe so blessed. And men have learned of the powers through our dealings with those especially elect. Elected by the one god that controls all others. The gods of this planet have no idea what knowledge we have; how petty they seem to us.'

"Very soon, they will declare war on us. They will try to stifle our potential, because they know that in time, it is we who will supplant them; us who will bend them to our will."

Buster shuddered inside, tried not to show it. "How do you suppose to do that?" he asked. "You honestly believe man can raise himself to equal these higher powers?"

"We are spirits, Macready. We have the inherent potential." Once more, he lowered his voice. "To answer your first question…we will win this struggle with our instinctual ability to formulate myth from simple fact. We have thousands of years of civilization as a map to guide us. It was all made clear to me the moment I set foot on this planet. The emptiness before us and the greatness behind. As I said before, future generations will have no inkling of the knowledge we possess. And generations from now, all that will be left of us are whispers in the wind. They will ponder the origin of life and meditate on God. They will build temples to a being only partially imagined and study scriptures that echo the tales of men long dead and all but forgotten…except for a few names. Of course we will pass on our knowledge of God, the creator. And perhaps Carolyn Summers will be the great mother-- the first woman."

Buster was beginning to understand. "And a man named Stevenson was the great prophet."

"Perhaps," said Stevenson, musing. He seemed to like the sound of that. "Or maybe something better. Prophets rarely pass down as myth. In the beginning, things always have to be a bit elemental. No, we need something a little…more."

Buster tilted his head. Why am I listening to this?

"Have you ever read the Goethe poem 'Prometheus'?" Stevenson asked.

"I've heard of Prometheus," Buster said, shaking his head. What gall Stevenson had.

"Prometheus, the bringer of fire. A myth that has survived millennia. But nothing in the myth connects so much to the human heart as Goethe's poem." He recited- *"Who aided me against the arrogance of the Titans? Who rescued me from certain death, from slavery?"*

Buster snorted. "That's how you see yourself?"

Stevenson smiled, continued, *"Here I sit, forming mortals after my image; a race resembling me, to suffer, to weep, to enjoy, to be glad, and thee to scorn…as I."* He smiled. "Perfect, isn't it?"

"I think you're mad," Buster accused.

Stevenson tilted his head back and laughed hoarsely, the atmosphere couldn't support his joviality. "Walk with me," he said, motioning Buster away from the others.

Buster held a slight paranoia as he hobbled behind Stevenson who once more began to speak, no longer whispering. "You have the opportunity to play a big part here," he said. "I don't believe you understand the full weight of the issue."

"I think you have enough lackeys."

"That's not what I mean," Stevenson said, his features serious all of a sudden. "That is what makes you so potentially important. You are right, I do have more than enough followers. What I do not have is a serious antagonist. A man as representative of everything opposite of what I preach. A man that can serve as the symbol of humanities jealousy and greed. A Cane to my Abel."

"You are mad."

"The others have witnessed your skepticism already. They have seen the way you look at me. Your doubt, your distrustfulness. The idea is already beginning to develop in their heads that you might not be one of us."

"I'm not one of you! I have my own crew. My own cabin in my own landing craft. I already told you, I don't want to be a part of any of this."

"You already are, Macready. Whether you want to believe it or not. It has already been made clear that you do not want to stay with us. Obviously you will leave the colony at some point. All I ask is that you prolong your departure until a more appropriate time. Leaving now will accomplish us nothing. You will only be another quitter. A lunatic freeman following his own selfish path to glory that does absolutely nothing for the betterment of mankind." He paused to catch his breath, then continued, "You really have no idea the degree of respect I hold for you. The way you constantly retreat in the face of fear. How you will allow it to place you into dangers unforeseen as long as it is unseen. You react only to what is directly before you not taking the time to realize you might be turning from one fear to face an even greater one. So you will always complain, Macready. You will always be frustrated by the things that confound your cowardly nature, because you will always find something to be afraid of. You are an animal. A cowardly, weakly animal, reminding me constantly of my purpose; driving me, pushing me. And that is why I need you to stay, if only for a short while. Because I will need you in the end."

"And just how do you need me? How can I possibly be so important if I'm nothing but a weak animal?"

"Just keep being yourself. Let the men see you denigrate me. Let them see you argue with me, ignore me…be absolutely disgusted with me. I will hold you up as my most favored companion. Whenever I speak, I will have you by my side. It will confuse the men. They will wonder at it; try to figure out why I have you by my side. Soon, they will begin to believe that it is my compassion, my faith, my wisdom that they should be contemplating. In trying to understand why I favor you so, they will try to understand more deeply everything I speak of. It is this process of understanding that will ingrain the events that will soon transpire into the deepest recesses of memory, force it into the hereditary subconscious. And when that happens, we will have our myths!'

"This is how we will supplant the gods of this planet. This is how we will deter the future generations from giving in to their instinctual fear of the unknown that leads to worshipping natural phenomena. You see, that is the only way these lonely gods know how to translate themselves into our psyche. They take advantage of our ignorance. For, while we may be far from ignorant now, when our knowledge is lost to future generations, the everlasting darkness on this side of the moon, those sublime atmospheric storms circling around that giant on the other side, the screaming of the sky--that is what men will turn to in times to come. Within a generation we will be sacrificing our own kind to placate a curious power who does nothing but make the ground fall in order to make us afraid. It is our duty, Macready, to pass down our knowledge of man's great inheritance. We must never allow man to forget that he was built in the image the greatest power. And in order to do that, we must recreate the history of man's spiritual journey. And we must do it now, before it is too late."

"Stevenson, just tell me. What does this have to do with me?"

Stevenson chewed his thin lower lip. "I need you, Macready. I need a Morning Star."

Buster stepped back, fear in his eyes. He wanted to laugh in Stevenson's face. Tell him once more that he was crazy. "You want me to be the symbol of absolute evil for the future of all mankind on this planet?"

Stevenson nodded. There was a look of doubt on his face that Buster was seeing for the first time.

"Why?"

"Because in order to take a step forward, we must take two steps back. In order to pass on our highly cultivated religious philosophy, we must take into account the inevitable barbarity of the future. Yes, it would be ideal to start anew on this planet and create a system of worship that has no words for evil. But that is not realistic. In order to save ourselves from dark ages of infanticide and cannibalism, we must speak to the uncivilized heart of those to come. They will never believe in a world without struggle and violence. So we must give them the tools that give meaning to violence. And we must allow them a symbol to counteract that violence. We must let them know now that it is a crime."

Buster stuttered. "I don't see...how," he said, his voice only slightly above a breath.

Stevenson, checking first to see if any of the pioneers were watching, grabbed Buster by the shoulders, beseechingly. "Before you start to worry about your reputation, Macready, understand that you, yourself, will not go down in history as the hated figure of all. It will only be the impression left behind by you. A fingerprint of sorts. At most there might be a prosaic image passed down for posterity; an abstract representation of you perhaps chalked on the walls of a cave. But we are lucky enough to find ourselves in an enlightened state, seeing with hindsight the future. How man evolves spiritually is in some ways a great blunder, fortunately for us, this leads to us rather safely able to assume the course it will take. Sometimes beautiful notions spring from simple mistakes. A slight misunderstanding in tone, a phrase lost in translation. Future generations will never know that you were not an evil man in life. And while you may be sacrificing the truth of the man you are, though you may be cursed for generations to come as the originator of all that is foul, you should take pride in the fact that you will be, in reality, the bringer of order and peace."

"You're rambling."

"Macready, I want you to kill me," said Stevenson.

~24~

"OH, HELLO," SAID Abigail MacLennon, trying to hide her surprise after bumping into Marvin Dennis as she exited her apartment, the little Yorkshire terrier waddling behind, nearly choking on its leash.

The sight of Marvin Dennis repulsed her somewhat. He looked not to have shaven for at least a week. His clothes were filthy, as were his fingernails, and the smell coming off of him stung her eyes. However, he was a neighbor and, though she would much preferred not running into him, it did provide her with a perfect opportunity to show off the dog. "Hello," she said again, twirling the end of the leash to draw attention.

Marvin looked down at the dog and scowled. "Humph," he said stepping into the elevator across from the MacLennon's apartment. Abigail stepped in after him, holding the dog now, cradling it against her chest. She pushed the button for the ground floor and made kissing noises at the terrier.

Marvin stretched his mouth tight and shook his head. "Aw...man," he said, and hopped out of the elevator. The doors closed in on him, pinching his arm before the safety release opened them back up. Marvin swung his arm loose from the doors, gestured angrily at them as Abigail looked on. The terrier let out a high pitched bark as the doors finally closed, allowing the elevator to descend.

Marvin stood in front of the elevator doors with his head hung low and tried to force himself to cry. For some reason it wasn't working. He shook his head again. It surprised him to realize a feeling of hatred toward Abigail. Who did she think she was showing off that dog like that? Gloating; rubbing it in his face. Fucking dog...what?

Rambling incoherently, he walked down the hall toward the emergency stairs and typed in his personal code to unlock the stairwell door. As he did this, Fordy MacLennon came out of his apartment. He caught a glimpse of Marvin entering the stairwell and, without thinking, began to follow.

Marvin had already descended three flights by the time Fordy got to the stairs. He moved with an even pace, controlling his breath. Taking the stairs was good for the nerves. Helped with frustration.

Fordy looked down to see how far ahead Marvin was getting. Peering down at the seemingly endless steps, he hesitated about following him any further. "He's going all the way down," he said aloud in wonder. It was irrational. Marvin Dennis certainly had problems. Fordy sighed, sucked it up and continued down the steps, trying his best to keep Marvin in sight, just in case he exited the stairwell on another floor.

Suddenly, Marvin looked up and, seeing he was

being followed, began jumping down the stairs, three-
-four at a time, as if being chased by dogs. Fordy
hissed and began running down after him, not at all
sure why. Soon, Fordy began to lose his breath. He
grew dizzy. The stairwell seemed like a labyrinth
designed to have no end. In his heart, Fordy cursed
the very idea of stairs. They were archaic. A
throwback to lesser days. After a while, he began to
curse his own body and all the muscles that had fallen
into disuse. And soon after, he began to curse the
civilization that would allow those muscles to
atrophy. He could no longer see Marvin Dennis, but
just knowing the man was leaps and bounds ahead of
him, racing down the stairs, he instantly developed a
new respect for him. For whatever reason, Marvin
Dennis's body still worked the way it was meant to.
He was still a man. Not just part of a machine.
Fordy's mind was growing hazy as he at last reached
the second floor. He's so much better than me, Fordy
thought before losing consciousness and tumbling
down the remainder of stairs.

Marvin lay by the exit door, curled up in a ball and
gasping for air as Fordy rolled down to meet the floor
beside him. Marvin, being too exhausted to react,
merely looked over at him to see if he were still
breathing. He was. In fact, he was relatively
unharmed. A small scrape to the forehead being his
only injury. Lying flat on his back, his chest heaving
and his legs akimbo, he craned his neck to look at
Marvin. Both men stared at one another, struggling
to catch their breath; confused both by the actions of
the other and themselves.

Finally, Marvin spoke. "You don't deserve a dog," he gasped.

Fordy's mouth was dry, he gulped painfully. "Thanks for giving me your lung," he said.

Marvin did not respond.

"I wanted to do something for you," Fordy continued. "I didn't know what to do, though. I've been trying to ignore you because I don't know what to say to you...But I wanted to do something. I can't think of anything that can possibly equal what you did for me...And I know you didn't really do it for me personally, but you did it anyway." He paused a moment to catch his breath as Marvin looked on blankly. "I was going to get you a procrete license," he said. "That's the only reason I got the dog...I used it as an excuse to see the licensing agent. I had to find a way. I found out how to get forged procrete licenses and I was going to get one for you...But then your wife left you and it screwed everything up. Even a legitimate license is useless to a divorcing couple. Had I gotten the forged license you still wouldn't be able to use it. So I don't know what else to do." He began to cry. "Now Abigail thinks I'm ready to have a kid because I got her that stupid dog."

Marvin hesitated to speak. Something told him nothing he could say would be worth it. Why should he waste his time in comforting Fordy MacLennon? The man represented everything he was against. "Why don't you just tell your wife you're sterile? She seems like the kind of person who would believe something like that."

"Not a chance. You know how it is. They test for

that kind of thing before you get married. All I wanted to do was help you out...but now I've got this to worry about."

Marvin sighed. "You don't even want a kid but the government would probably license you for as many as you could handle. Flora and I would have been great parents."

Fordy shook his head. "I'm not trying to say it is fair. But couples aren't meant to be parents these days. We're meant to be something more along the line of caretakers. It's one of the beautiful things about our society. Understanding that children are the future. That they will soon replace us...knowing the potential they have...it's our duty to raise them to be beneficial to the future of the planet. Not to raise them to replace us...but to be better than us. Individuality doesn't play into it...and love is ultimately an outward projection of individuality. It is the most purely selfish emotion. In the past, people managed to fool themselves into believing it was selfless. But it is anything but selfless. Only by taking love out of the situation can we give ourselves the proper distance to allow a purely objective attitude in raising a child, so as not to raise them in accordance with our own individualized concept of society. We must allow them the knowledge to understand their place in the world."

"All that doesn't change the fact that you're terrified," Marvin accused.

"I'm terrified of the cycle. When you have a child, your life ends. It's like your place in the world has been taken by the new life. Having a child these days symbolizes the fact that you have done everything you can do with your life. But I feel like there are things I can still do."

"It sounds like you think raising a child is an act of failure. Does it ever occur to you that raising a child can strengthen you or add something to your life...making it more complete?"

"I don't need a child to make my life more complete. I'm satisfied with life. With my existence the way it is. I don't need a child to validate my existence. That's another reason we've taken the concept of love out of the equation. Having a child was never about consummating love between two individuals. It was about two people no longer satisfied with life. Two people full of doubt with the world...searching for answers. They use the child experimentally, to live vicariously through another being in order to see things more clearly. Using the simplicity in a child's eyes in order to see for themselves how simple life can really be. The only problem with that is they have to keep the child ignorant lest it lose its simplicity. The parents do not allow the child to grow and gain knowledge. It becomes a competition. For years, the parents, witnessing the simplicity of the child, feel themselves for the first time to have all the answers...they feel superior. And they strive to keep that superiority. Because they can't face up to the fact that they no longer matter. It is the grown child who matters. The world belongs to it now. And the parents never discover that they've grown to hate what they felt they brought into the world through love."

"You don't understand," said Marvin, rising to his feet. "We're all really worthless. People like you most of all. Because you don't know how to love." He opened the door to the stairwell, letting in the light from outside.

Fordy shielded his eyes. Except for the faintest outline of a silhouette, Marvin was all but lost in the glare. "It's not about love. It's about mutual respect and obligation. If we can't live with one another without love, then how can we live with one another at all? We shouldn't have to love one another to do what's best for them. I thought you of all people understood that. Isn't that why you did what you did for me?"

Marvin turned. "I did what I did because I love you. I love you all."

With that, he left the building. The door closed, leaving Fordy in the dark. He didn't understand anything anymore.

Marvin didn't even bother shielding his eyes from the sun as he strode down the same path he walked since moving into the district, retracing several years' worth of steps. He had it all figured out. It wasn't about comfort or vehicles or building a better life. He squinted into the sun, walking half blind. It wasn't even about the one bedroom apartment he would now have to vacate. Back to the cramped studio apartment.

Who cares, he thought. Flora sure doesn't seem to. And why should she? It's simple for a woman to find a new mate. She'll probably move right into another one bedroom. Or possibly a two bedroom if her next husband is eligible for a procrete license. She didn't even think about what would happen to me. Selfish bitch!

He punched at the air. Who cares? I'll make do. I'll paint the walls with exotic scenery. I'll increase the illusion of space with color and shade. Yeah…it's for the best. I shouldn't have to spend my life with someone who would up and leave me at the drop of a dime. Someone who lied to me! I'm glad they wouldn't give me a license. I don't want to share my genetics with someone so callous and shallow. How would that benefit the future? Maybe these people really do know what they're doing.

He saw a sign. Stopped. "Yeah," he said. "You've got it all figured out."

"How may I help you, sir?" asked the man at the desk, rising from his seat and smirking wryly.

"Sign me up," Marvin said with forced enthusiasm.

The man behind the desk held up his hands. "Now, hold on there, sir. I have a job to do." He sat back down, gestured Marvin to a chair next to the desk and rifled through the top drawer of the desk. He pulled several sheets of paper from the desk and slid them across to Marvin. "Before you read that, you should take a look at these," he said, tossing a brochure and photograph on top of the papers.

Marvin set the picture aside and glanced over the brochure--'HD 1487 Puppis--your new home!'

"I've already seen these," Marvin said, annoyed. "Turtles! You don't remember me either."

The man shrugged. "I see people every day, sir. I can't be expected to remember everyone."

227

"Well I see people every day too," said Marvin. "And I still remembered you, not to mention how to get to this office."

"This is a recruitment center, sir," the man countered. "And I am sure I have a great deal more on my mind than you, what with trying to advance the potential of the entire human race on my hands."

"You bastards," Marvin scowled. "You believe somebody has to be shot into space to have any importance."

The man smiled evenly. "Pity you feel that way. I was beginning to take a personal liking to you."

Marvin rubbed his temples to calm himself. "Where do I sign?"

"Bottom line. Where else?"

"Do you have a pen?"

The man held up a pen. "I'll have to ask a few brief questions," he said.

Marvin slumped in the seat and lifted his hands, allowed them to flop at his sides. A light, unbelieving chuckle escaped his lips.

The man nodded, licked the tip of the pen. "State your name, please. Last name first."

"Dennis, Marvin."

The man wrote down the information. "Place of birth?"

"Chicopee."

"As of this date, Mister Dennis, what is your age?"

Marvin sighed. "Thirty-two."

"At any time prior to this date have you suffered from or shown symptoms of heart burn, indigestion, upset stomach or diarrhea?"

"Of course."

The man checked a box on the paper and raised his eyes, shooting Marvin an accusative glance. Keeping his eyes on him, he continued, "Vertigo, rheumatism, heart palpitations, asthma?"

"Sometimes," Marvin replied. "I was diagnosed with asthma as a child, but I haven't had an attack since primary school."

The man checked several more boxes, smirked. "It really doesn't matter when the last time was you had an attack."

"Don't you leave any room for abstraction?"

"Oh, sure. We're surprisingly liberal in our expectations. But, if accepted, you will be required to take a six week survival course in which physical therapy plays a major role. The instructors will have an easier time planning the proper regimen for you once they know your background. It's all very mathematical."

"And what is the likelihood of my being accepting? I thought anybody could be a pioneer. That's how it's advertised on all the programs."

"Everybody has the potential to be a pioneer, Mister Dennis. It's really all up to the individual." He put the pen back to the paper. "Mister Dennis, what was your classification at the time of your last physical?"

Marvin gulped. "PC108," he said, tapping his fingers together. To his surprise, it didn't appear as if the man behind the desk judged him at all negatively after hearing this. Instead, the man smiled, almost affectionately. He seemed almost pleased. Marvin began to wonder, was this man like him after all?

The man put down the pen, "Nothing unifies like oppression," he said evenly.

Marvin levelled his eyes on the man. "I could report you," he said, genuinely shocked by the man's comment.

The man was unfazed. "Who would listen to a PC108? Who would care?" He pushed the pen over to Marvin. I'll be honest with you, Mister Dennis. Most people don't have what it takes to join the Extra Solar Pioneers. Most people are too comfortable to take the risk. And if they're not comfortable, their too afraid to chance the few things in their lives enjoy. You...you're different. You've got the guts. Sign the papers. The Buttercup Styles launches in five months."

Marvin took the pen and held it over the papers, but hesitated. Something caught his eye. A small television mounted on a corner wall of the office. It was tuned to a news program advertising breaking news. In recent days, a man believed to be responsible for numerous terrorist offences, it was reported, had been tracked down and neutralized by the Federal Deterrence Police. Several freeze frame pictures flashed across the screen showing the grim scene. In one of the photos, an officer was shown draping a large white sheet over the body of whom Marvin assumed was the terrorist. It captivated him. He found himself mesmerized by the sight of the covered body; how small it seemed. Almost as if it were a child's body under the sheet, or a dog. The sheet hid virtually all form except for a slight crease where it covered the legs. Marvin tried to juxtapose the sight of the covered body with the destruction revealed by the other photos.

Only one man, he thought. One man whom I have never met, never had any reason to know, halfway around the world...and now I see him lying there completely destroyed. As if he were an old friend whose fate I needed to discover.

Marvin had, of course, been aware of the terrorist acts, the explosions. And, though, like everyone else, he felt slightly afraid, vulnerable, if for no other reason than the reports always described the acts as random, he, also like everybody else, managed to keep the events out of mind. After all, he had never been witness to any of the explosions. He had only seen reports of them on the news. They were removed from his daily life, not affecting him at all. Of course, he always assumed the authorities would put a stop to them sooner or later. But now, watching the new report, he felt strange. He merely assumed the terrorism would cease when the terrorist was discovered, and nothing more would be heard of it. But seeing the covered body on the television suddenly made it all so very real to him. It was a man after all. A man, still unknown, whom the government was now introducing to the entire world after he had ceased to exist. A man whose presence in life was so recently felt by all had just been revealed, in death, to be an absolute nobody; a formless mass under a white sheet. It struck Marvin as odd that such a thing could occur. Suddenly, now that it was apparently over, it all seemed much more momentous. If a tree falls in the forest with nobody around to hear it, does it make a sound…and, if a man lies dead in view of millions, is he truly dead?

Without a word, Marvin dropped the pen and made a quick exit out of the office. Gazing up at the cirrus skies, Marvin asked himself, "How can the sky look exactly   as   it   did   yesterday?"

~25~

"MANY PEOPLE COME to see me these days. Looking for answers. Somehow, they have gotten the ridiculous notion that I can help them in some way."

Shultz lifted the worn green blanket covering him and stared down at his leg. His wound had been cleaned and dressed, yet the leg was left numb. Like a child, he brought his knuckles down on his upper thigh. He was thankful the pain had been dimmed, but he was left to wonder at the old man's methods, not to mention the sterility of the tools he must have used to remove the bullet.

"How do you feel?" Tizch asked, sitting comfortably in a wooden rocking chair next to the bed Shultz lay in, casually puffing on a pipe; his form roughly silhouetted against a low burning fire behind him.

"Will I regain feeling in my leg?"

"Naturally."

"Then I'm satisfied," said Shultz.

The old man blew a thick ring of smoke. "Your friend was in considerably worse shape. He has a remarkable spirit."

"Don' be fooled. He is merely stubborn."

"Stubborn people shape the world," the old man replied. "For better or worse."

Shultz examined his leg once more, tinkered with the bandage slightly, entertaining thoughts of removing it. He was curious to see what damage had been done. "The discoloration worries me," he said.

"Loss of blood," said Tizch. "Do not let it concern you."

Shultz tapped on his leg several more times, trying to discover the extent of the numbness. At length, he said, "The man that I came with is looking for answers."

The old man nodded. "Of course," he said. "As are you."

"I think he sincerely believes you are a prophet of some sort. Will you tell him he is mistaken?"

"You are a police officer, are you not?" asked the old man.

Shultz nodded.

"And will you arrest me if I entertain your friend's notion?"

Shultz stared directly at Tizch. "You are no prophet," he said with authority.

"I am inclined to agree with you," said the old man. "Yet, who can judge fairly? The worth of a thing is always judged perceptively. For instance, I can say to you with all honesty that I do not have any answers. But if a man feels he can interpret my words in such a way as to find the answers he seeks, then who am I to disagree? Perhaps there are powers working through me that I am completely and unalterably aware.

Perhaps there are powers working through each and every one of us. Perhaps I might discover a secret through you that you as a conscious being do not intend to reveal. Isn't that the burden of us all? Is that not the tragedy of our selfishness; our concept of individual pleasure? If there were a man who possessed all answers, he would cease to be a man. For what would such a creature holding no dependency toward others of his kind be? It is our dependency upon others that makes us men, not our individuality."

Shultz rubbed his forehead. "I do not want a sermon," he said. "When will my friend wake up? I would like to be leaving."

"Being desirous of a thing and 'liking' to do such a thing are two separate feelings," said the old man. Shultz frowned, began lifting himself off the bed. "You may want to leave this place very much," the old man continued, "but once you discover you cannot stand," he said as Shultz's body slammed to the ground, "you might find you would 'like' to lay back down."

Shultz sucked in the pain with a single breath and lye back down begrudgingly. He stared stone-faced at Tizch, determined not to show any loss of pride. Tizch stared back, his face devoid of any emotion. Shultz had expected at least a self-righteous smile.

"To calm your fears, that was not a psychical prediction. Simply cause and effect."

Shultz crossed his eyes. "I know that," he exclaimed. "Unlike your weak minded 'followers', I have an acute capacity for reason."

"Coupled with an enormous hostility," the old man replied, this time with a self-righteous smile. Shultz sighed. "That significantly blocks your reasoning capabilities."

Shultz winced. He knew the old man was going to say something like that. "I do not wish to make demands of you in your own home," he said. "But wouldn't you prefer my friends company over mine own?"

"Your friend is sleeping."

"Exactly. Or can you not appreciate the company of others without the Newtonian nature of conversation?"

Tizch continued to smile. "You toss scientific names around meaninglessly," he said. "Or, perhaps not so meaningless. Perhaps you are trying to waylay the metaphysical atmosphere you feel entrenches you at this moment. But this is no doing of mine. You came here with your own preconceived notions. You brought your own ideas with you, and this is what colors the underlying current of our conversation. I speak only words. The meanings of which are interpreted by yourself alone." He paused. "Now do you understand?" he asked.

Shultz did not reply. But he understood...and was strangely disappointed. "So you're not a prophet," he said. His eyes began to mist over. No matter to what degree of disbelief he held for such things...somewhere deep down inside, he enjoyed even the curious thought of such things being possible, regardless of his outward attitude. It made his life worth living. It gave him a long list of mysteries to solve. But, lately, ever since his decision to cross into Nuremberg, he had come to find that trying to solve a true mystery is not at all satisfying and, while it was in his nature to at least try and solve such things, he regretted every second of it.

"Words are our means of interpreting ideas, Herr Shultz," the old man said quietly. "How close can they ever come to the truth? A paradox," he said, raising a finger. "We have come to believe that spiritual matters are perceived most clearly by only the most highly cultivated civilizations. Yet, no matter the beauty of our language; our poetry and songs; the simple fact is the most truthful utterances of man are his grunts and growls...his vocalizations of anger and bemusement. When man first looked up at the sun in wonder, that simple sound emanating from his throat was the most honest form of expression we are ever likely to attain. From that point on, we have been locked in a cycle of regression. We lost our truths in pursuit of better ways to explain them. Because there is no explaining them." He paused casually to relight his pipe, blew a smoke ring into the stilted air. "When people come to see me...they come searching for a truth. Something universal. Something connecting them to the whole. Yet, their conscious minds demand words. So I talk with them. And most seem to feel better after speaking with me. By simple definition, this makes me a prophet. But 'prophet' is only a word, you see. What does it matter what a man labels me? There are true prophets and there is the word, just as there is true conscience and faith and the meagre words

237

corresponding to our ideas of both conscience and faith. Herr Shultz, does the word 'life' truly encompass this gift of existence?"

"Then, by that logic, existence is, as well, only a word. If words are merely an abstraction of thought; and questions of truth are formed by words, then there can be no answers, because there are no questions."

Tizch remained silent.

"It is a trick," came a haggard voice from a far off corner of the room. Both Tizch and Shultz turned to see Hoigt descending a narrow stair-case, painfully, and with some hesitation in his steps. He limped over, his back hunched, to sit next to the fire. His face was pale and his lips were blue. The fire gave him the appearance of an apparition which, in turn, in Shultz's mind, gave him an air of authority in the earthy atmosphere of the cabin equal to the old man Tizch.

"You should be resting," said Tizch, looking down at the floor.

"What do you mean, a trick?" Shultz asked.

Hoigt took several deep breaths, his hand on his chest, before answering. "If words mean nothing, then why waste time on conversation at all?" he asked, turning slightly to look at Tizch. "If words mean nothing, why are you probing Shultz? More importantly, if words are merely an aspect of the illusion of reality, an aspect in which we, in our daily lives, as social creatures, ever striving to best convey our deepest feelings of self to one another in the attempt to find connection with and through others of our kind; since the moment we climbed down from the trees, evolving, as we have, in order to project to one another every shared aspect, every shared experience; recognizing in one another, no matter the differences, the identical need to eat, drink, breath, sleep, laugh and cry--this 'illusion' that entangles us all--if it is meaningless, then why waste time searching his thoughts, reading his mannerisms? Why waste time on this process of conversion? Or have you not come to acknowledge your deepest self just enough to discover the fact that you are a charlatan?"

Hoigt paused as Tizch cleared his throat, anticipating the old man's response, but when one did not come, he continued. "You see, Shultz, it is not always a fool who follows a fool. It is not always foolish to believe the words of a man like this..."

"But I don't believe him..."

"Herr Tizch is very intelligent. His philosophy is very sound. He is indeed a man of wisdom and substance. Yet, we are faced with a difficult decision. Is Tizch really a prophet, a man holding answers to questions that confront us all? Or is he simply a lonely old man, trapped in a life of solitude; a lifestyle chosen by himself in rejection of the world around him; whose philosophy has developed over the years in order to justify the solitude?" Once more, he turned to Tizch. "Is it, Herr Tizch, that you simply enjoy the company of others? You sit here in the quiet of your own space, surrounded by the majesty of nature, dreaming of conversations that only come rarely Yet you, in your solitude, are given the opportunity most of us have not been gifted. You have the opportunity to have real, substantive conversation with your fellow man. Because your life is not filled with mindless chatter. You have put yourself in the position to speak in a manner where every word counts---yet you say words do not matter. You want to flabbergast your guests. Keep them thinking about you long after they have left your sight. You want what the rest of us want. You want to be remembered. You don't want to be forgotten. If you truly believed in your own philosophy, you wouldn't have bothered with the two of us. You wouldn't promote the little cult that has sprung up in your name, or the pilgrimages to you by those in need of 'answers'. You're all alone, Tizch. And you don't want to be alone." He turned to Shultz. "I will tell you how the word 'life' explains the meaning of our existence. Just say it aloud." He said the word, low, dragging out the middle syllable. "Life: it begins with a weak labial, followed by the long 'I', expressed with the fullness of breath...then it ends softly, gently, with the hint of an echo. What word could be more perfect?"

Tizch chuckled, looked at Shultz who stared back expectantly, as if he were waiting for a good come-back. "Your friend does not seem to like me very much," Tizch said. "And to think I saved his life."

"More of those meaningless words," Hoigt returned. "My wounds were not life threatening. And I hardly think a real prophet would feel the need to pat himself on the back."

"The both of you continue to hold it against me that some consider me a prophet. I do not refer to myself as a prophet. Indeed, I have already disowned this claim several times."

"With what you claim to be meaningless words," said Hoigt. "You can't have it both ways, Tizch. It's your actions that show your true feelings of self. You hold to a false modesty, which makes you seem all the more believable to those of lesser mind, but deep down inside, you know what you want others to believe. I'll tell you what you are, Tizch, you're just an old man who is very good at riddles."

Tizch rubbed his chin. "Your reason has found disagreement with my theories based upon my actions as a man," he said. "But that is what I am. A man. And if I were to pretend to be any other way, I would be a charlatan indeed. As we live, behavior and thought will always and forever be distinct. Only in the afterlife do we find perfect equilibrium." He paused, seemingly to collect his thoughts, which seemed to be coming with much more difficulty. "The mistake most people make when they search for answers, whether they attempt to find them through me or through another, is the attempt to find answers to what happens once we have passed to the other side. But the true answers are not found in the afterlife, but in life itself. We as a people have only one real question. How do we live well? And the only way for one to live well is to discover one's true nature. A man's nature, Herr Hoigt, is the tentative balance of the physical and the spiritual. The two aspects of man, totally and, seemingly irrevocably at odds. Have you ever recalled a childhood memory and then tried to put it down on paper? It is impossible. No matter how clearly you see the images in your head; every minutia of detail; it is impossible to formalize. The reason for this is that the event being remembered was experienced through the senses. And because our senses are aspects of our physical selves, we cannot jot that memory down in such a way as to capture its true force. Because memory is an aspect of our spiritual self. It defies the senses. We see the images without eyes; smell them without a nose; feel them without touching. Once an event occurs, there is no recovering it. It is gone forever, and the memory is something else entirely. This is why those trapped in thought sometimes feel a floating sensation. Thinking, itself, is a simple, rather elementary form of transcendence. The act of thinking is a connection of our physical self to the spiritual; almost a biological call for help. A sign that the two aspects of man can blur the distinction. And this gives us hope that transcendence is not something need be considered out of reach."

"If that is the case," Hoigt chimed in, "then Shultz's system is the closest we've come to reaching a unity of physical and spiritual. And it is the system you have run from."

"Herr Shultz's system does not represent a system of transcendence. It attempts only to stifle the spirit, not reconcile it. Man must realize for himself the best way to live with himself and others. If he is coerced into living in peace with his fellow man, he will never discover the beauty of living in peace with his fellow man. It is not the intentions I judge, rather the methods."

"The methods are always the problem," said Shultz. "People don't intentionally want to screw up the world."

"You're speaking from experience?" said Tizch.

"Well…sure."

"Would you like an example of the futility of your system? How much do you know about the Extra Solar Pioneers?"

Shultz stared blankly at the old man. "They are a testament to the ingenuity of mankind. Something to be proud of."

"You consider your world to be one of peace, order and plenty. A world in which everyone is provided for; everyone is educated, leaving nothing to be desired. Correct?"

"That just about sums it up."

"Then why do so many volunteer to be Pioneers? Why leave this world of comfort for one of infinite danger?"

"For the glory."

"Why is there a need for glory, Herr Shultz? Why are people not satisfied? Where has your system failed?"

"…"

"Because people need to overcome something. People need struggle. We are not happy when we are not in motion. Perpetual prosperity is not progress. But there is something more. Something you would not dare to dream of." He paused for effect. "You say you are not in search of answers. But would you like to know what I know?"

"Yes," said Hoigt.

"No," said Shultz. "I don't want to hear any more of this nonsense. I don't care about the Extra Solar Pioneers! The only thing I care about is terrorism! Don't you know there's a madman out there blowing things up? Hoigt! Come on! You have a case of your own to solve. What's going on here? Did we fall into a black hole or something?"

"The Extra Solar Pioneers are a fraud," said Tizch.

Shultz calmed himself.

"The Extra Solar Pioneers are a fraud," Tizch repeated. "The entire organization is a sham."

"Are you kidding? I see the ships launch all the time. I see it with my own eyes."

"I am not talking about the ships. Oh, yes, the ships are real. They are very real. But they are not bringing new life to the farthest reaches of the universe. They are death-traps. Rocket powered concentration camps meant to rid the world of subversives. Men who are not satisfied with their lot in life. Men who may wish to bring change to the system. Men of low tolerance for oppression; men not satisfied with a government that tells them who they are, what they should be, who they should marry and whether or not they can even procreate. The scientific community created the ESP's with good intentions, but the government co-opted them after all the scientists failed to discover a means to travel faster than light speed. All of those ships they launch…not one of them has reached its destination. There are hundreds of extra solar ships floating in the void that are filled with corpses."

"Ridiculous," said Shultz, beginning to shake. "We

have photographs. Video images of the Pioneers setting up colonies."

"All fabricated in government studios. Well, the colonies on Mars are real. Mars, however, is very close to the earth."

"Your government is responsible for the deaths of thousands, Shultz," said Hoigt. "They killed people for being unhappy."

"I don't believe you. Nobody in the government would do such a thing."

"Do we judge men by their actions or by their intentions? Your heads of state have found the best possible way to circumvent any criminal culpability. They do, after all, launch the ships toward an actual destination. The navigational computers do follow a clear line. They cryogenically freeze the Pioneers. In theory, it could all work out as planned. But even so...even if one of those ships were to reach its destination, it would not arrive for hundreds of thousands of years. They've been lying to everybody. And their only saving grace is that it is all volunteer."

"Even if you are telling the truth," said Shultz. "You cannot prove the government has murdered anybody. The only thing they are guilty of is fraud. They've told us the Pioneers have settled several far off planets. So they haven't yet...but they will when they finally reach their destination. The only thing they've done wrong is exaggerate the time."

"Shultz...who in their right mind would volunteer to suspend their life for thousands upon thousands of years? Even if their vital functions are maintained, how can we consider them anything but dead? They may not have choked the life out of them with their bare hands…but…"

"It's a holocaust," said Hoigt.

Shultz buried his head in his hands. "Shut up. Just shut up, both of you."

"The terrorist you're after has actually been saving lives," said Tizch. "By creating a sense of unpredictability, a small chaos, he is giving people back their sense of struggle here on earth. Filling the void of discomfort created by your government. By giving people something tangible to fear, they will not search for something to fear. I guarantee the Extra Solar Pioneers have noticed a marked decrease in volunteers over the past few months. Isn't that a remarkable aspect of humanity?"

Shultz jumped up from the bed suddenly. "I've got it," he said. "I forgot who I was with for a moment. Look at me, sitting comfortably in a cabin situated illegally in a nature preserve with a Nuremberg police officer and a crazed cult leader! Both of you have a desire to see my government fall. Ha! Wouldn't it be a coup for your cause to brainwash a Friendly Neighbor? I'll tell you what I'm going to do," he said, patting his trousers. "I'm going to put you both under arrest." He continued to pat his waste-line. "Where is my gun? You're probably in league with the terrorist!" He pointed at Tizch. "You probably are the terrorist! You and your cult!" he said, breaking suddenly into a fit of laughter before falling back onto the bed.

"Even if a Pioneer landing craft were to set down on another planet…even if there is another planet capable of sustaining human life, even rudimentarily--by the time that happens, it is almost certain there will no longer be a human presence on earth. Even if they were to survive that long frozen trek through space…they will not only be isolated by space and time…they will be completely alone in the universe. That, I believe, is the harshest punishment for those attempting to keep the human spirit alive. The ultimate betrayal."

"How do you know all this?"

"More important to you," said Tizch, "is how the terrorist knew it…before the deterrence police executed him."

"So they did get him," Shultz mused. "It figures."

"You seem disappointed," said Hoigt.

"Of course I am. It was my case. If I hadn't got caught up in your mess, I would've-"

"Doesn't it satisfy you that the terrorism is over?" asked Tizch.

"I--"

"So what do you do now?"

"I want to go home."

"Don't you want to solve your case?"

"It's in the hands of the deterrence police now."

Hoigt shook his head. "Haven't you been listening, Shultz? The deterrence police have not stopped the criminal, they have covered up the crime."

"What do you say, Herr Shultz? Are you prepared to face your true nature?"

"I don't understand what you're talking about?"

"It is all connected," Tizch continued. "The Extra Solar Pioneers, the government, terrorism, forged procrete licenses, etcetera."

"What does it all connect to?"

Tizch tapped his pipe against the arm of his chair. "I   have   a   name,"   he   said.

~26~

MARVIN DENNIS SLUMPED in the corridor, only partly watching as the workmen removed all the furniture out of his apartment. Now that Flora had left, he was being forced out of the one bedroom. The workmen (employees of the complex) would be delivering his belongings to his new efficiency apartment three blocks down the street, across the river. Not only would he have to get rid of half the furniture, acquired specifically for the purposes of filling up the one bedroom, but his walk to work would be longer as well. He didn't mind getting rid of the furniture so much. Most of it was only a reminder of Flora anyhow. They had shopped for it together. He remembered the day. It had been so enjoyable, it was like being on a date. He brought his knees up and hugged himself.

The door slammed beside him, catching his attention. Two of the workmen were lugging out the last piece, a large coffee table with a glass top, and locking the door behind them with the key card Marvin had to hand over to them earlier that morning.

Watching the workmen load the table into the

buildings freight elevator, Marvin noticed the building supervisor, Uhaul Malone, walking down the corridor, his feet skidding across the tiles. Marvin rubbed his hands down his face, folded down his lower lip with the tips of his fingers and shook his head. The sight of the supervisor shamed him.

"I'm not returning your deposit, Mr. Dennis," said the supervisor.

"I'm sorry, Mr. Malone. I would have liked to have given you more notice."

"Well, let this be a lesson to you. Don't get hitched if you can't afford it. That way you won't waste everybody else's time."

"The only time wasted was my own," Marvin said, rising to his feet. "But it was nice of you to see me off."

"Don't kid yourself. I'm only up here to fix the MacLennon's shower filter. I expected you to be long gone by now," said the supervisor, pulling the cylindrical replacement filter from his back pocket.

Marvin shook his head once more. "You're just like the rest of them," he said. "You only have time for people when they relate to your own life in some way."

"Psshht!"

"You know, I wasn't expecting never to get a raise," Marvin continued, as Uhaul Malone swiped the key card over the scanner. The door clicked and opened and Uhaul entered as the MacLennon's Yorkshire terrier began to bark.

Then it occurred to Marvin.

They were never going to give me a raise, he

thought. I was never going to earn enough to qualify for a license. And they knew it all along.

He slammed his fist into his palm, hurried toward the MacLennon's door before it closed and slipped in.

"Just what do you think you're doing, Dennis?" the supervisor asked before Marvin pushed him to the side and, his eyes ablaze, he snatched up the barking terrier and ran from the apartment.

"Stop right there!" Uhaul shouted, lurching forward, trying to grab at Marvin's pant leg. Missing him narrowly, he jumped up to chase after him. But by the time he was up on his feet, Marvin was out of the room and jumping into the elevator. Uhaul reached the corridor to see the terrier's startled expression, clutched tightly against Marvin's chest, as the elevator doors closed shut. Wasting no time, Uhaul raced to the elevator and punched a numerical code on the security plate. Within seconds, the buildings circuits cut all power from the elevator, freezing it between floors.

Marvin lost his footing and fell to the floor when the elevator stopped. He held onto the terrier as he fell, almost crushing it under his palm. The terrier, freeing itself from Marvin's grip, crawled out from under him and circled about the elevator in a panic. It began to bark incessantly as Marvin tried to pick it up again. It growled and gnashed its teeth, nipping at Marvin's fingers. Losing patience, Marvin lightly kicked the dog, stunning it enough for him to pick it back up.

"Turn the elevator back on!" Marvin screamed.

"Not on your life!" came Uhaul Malone's response,

echoing down the elevator shaft.

"Turn it back on or I'll hurt the dog!"

"Don't hurt the dog!"

Marvin looked down at the terrier. It peed on his arm and shook. It seemed silly to him at first, but of course the building supervisor cared about the dog. It was a status symbol. A virtual commodity by society's standards. As the supervisor, if the dog were harmed, all responsibility would fall on his shoulders. Not to mention they might lose a very influential tenant, Fordy MacLennon.

"Turn the power back on or I'll break its legs!" Marvin screamed, wrapping his hand around one of the terrier's tiny legs.

"Don't break its legs!"

"Then turn the power back on!"

"Give me a second!"

Marvin waited for the elevator to begin moving again. He was shaking from all the adrenaline pumping through his body. The terrier tried to nip at his nose.

"Stop!" he yelled. "No!"

A loud thumping was heard. Marvin knew what it was. It was Uhaul Malone racing down the stairwell, hoping to reactivate the elevator and meet him at the ground floor. A moment later, the power came back on and the elevator began to descend. Marvin quickly pushed the third floor button. Jumping out of the elevator, Marvin took the stairs down to the ground floor. He opened the door a crack to see Uhaul waiting in front of the elevator. He tried to sneak past him, but the dog whimpered, giving him away. Uhaul immediately began chasing him once more, but Marvin was quicker. He reached the buildings exit, reveling in the knowledge that the building supervisor had no authority outside the building. He laughed, then slammed into the exit door.

Uhaul Malone jumped on his back and was trying to wrestle him to the ground when Fordy MacLennon came in from the outside.

"What's going on here?" he shouted in surprise.

Marvin struggled to rid himself of the supervisor, continuing to grip the terrier with one hand and pressing the other into the supervisor's face.

"He's stealing your dog!" said Uhaul, his words only half audible as Marvin's palm twisted his lips.

Fordy spotted the terrier and his jaw dropped. "Huh?"

Marvin reached back and slammed his elbow into Uhaul's stomach. The supervisor gushed, but continued to hold on. "You…don't…deserve…this dog!" Marvin shrieked, finally breaking loose. He then rushed over to Fordy as he stood dumbfounded, lifted the dog up by its scruff and grabbed him by the arm. "Let's go!" he ordered.

"Go where?"

"You're going to take me to see that person you know giving out fake licenses. Now don't mess with me!" He lifted the dog again with a threatening gesture.

"I'm not taking you anywhere, Marvin," said Fordy, ripping himself away. "And you can't threaten me with that dog. That's my wife's dog. It's not mine. In fact, I don't even want it! It's all too much!"

"I'll call the authorities, mister MacLennon. You hold him!" said Uhaul Malone, rushing away to his office.

"Did you hear that? He's going to alert the Friendly Neighbors'. I'll tell them everything you told me, and then you'll just have to take *them* to see your friend. What do you want to do now, huh?"

"Okay! Okay! Just take it easy. You know, this isn't funny at all."

"It's not meant to be funny. It never was meant to be. But you all sure thought it was a joke, didn't you?"

Marvin pulled Fordy out of the building and began leading him down the street. The dog began to bark once more. "Here, damn it! You hold it!"

"Where are we going?" Fordy asked, taking the dog. It continued to struggle.

"You tell me!" Marvin screamed. "He's your guy, not mine. I don't know him!"

"Well, it's a pretty far walk. I have a vehicle, you know."

Marvin froze in his tracks, looked hesitantly down the street and back toward the parking garage. "A car?" he said, panting. "Right. We'll take your vehicle." He had never ridden in a vehicle before.

A few minutes later, the two men were heading downtown. Fordy's vehicle followed the most direct route towards their destination, running parallel to the Connecticut. Although the vehicle ran on automatic, following prelisted directions, Marvin insisted he sit behind the wheel. Fordy wrestled with the terrier on the passenger side. The little dog fought ferociously to free itself, even from the apparent security of Fordy's arms. The dog seemed not to know friend from foe anymore. It must have intuited the overwhelming sense of disdain both men felt for it, albeit for different reasons. Marvin, because it represented everything he wanted but couldn't have; Fordy, because it represented everything he could have, and couldn't help but having it, no matter how little he desired it. The dog was burdensome to his life style.

"I hate it," he groaned, trying to hold it still as it gnashed and clawed.

"What are you talking about? You can't hate your own dog."

"You wouldn't understand--ouch!" The dog bit his forearm.

"You just can't stand anything that interrupts your comfortable life," said Marvin. "You don't like anything that requires a decision you can't personally control."

Fordy laughed. "You're so ignorant, Marvin. I don't control any decision in my life."

"That's right," said Marvin. "We don't control anything. And it's not just me; it's not just people like you either. We're all just doing what we're supposed to do. Never doing what we want to do. It doesn't even matter if what we want to do would be much more beneficial to humanity. We are, every one of us, just lost children, orphaned at birth, and we followed the finger of the first decrepit old passer-by to see us crawling down the sidewalk, pointing us in the direction he saw fit at the time. It doesn't matter that he was wrong. They don't get it right all the time. How can they?" He stopped speaking, grabbed the squirming terrier and tossed it in the back seat. The dog flipped in the air before landing, then hurled itself against the back of the front seat. "They got it wrong with me, man! They got it all wrong, and they weren't going to tell me that! They don't want us to know they can be wrong. They left all that out. And I had to figure it out myself. But do you want to know the worst part? I don't make enough money, Fordy! I never made enough…and I was never going to. Do you get that?"

Fordy hesitated. "People in your line of work have been historically underpaid."

"That's my point! What's the average age of a person before he's set on a career path? Eleven years old…twelve? When I was twelve years old they knew they didn't want me to have children! They cut me out of the future when I was twelve!"

Fordy thought for a moment, then said quietly, "I…think…I've always wanted to play the flute."

"…What?"

Fordy turned to Marvin. "What happens when you're just not good enough to do the one thing you want to do more than anything else in the world?"

Marvin, anxious, alternated his gaze between Fordy and the road. "…What?" he repeated.

"Nothing," Fordy said.

Marvin stared at Fordy for some time, trying to figure out his last statement. He decided to ignore it. "Exactly who are we going to see? Who is this guy?"

~27~

DOCTOR LOUIS JUDD approached the charge telephones outside the Greater London airport, not wanting to risk using his mobile lest the call were being traced. He flashed a pre-paid card over the phones' sensor, then dialed. Several minutes passed before Hollis Kincaid picked up on the other end of the line. He was panting, as if he had run for the phone. "That you?"

"Yes, it's me," said Judd. "Now listen, because of all the activity in Inverness, all outgoing flights have been cancelled. So what am I supposed to do now?"

Kincaid responded after a pause. "Did you get the part?"

"Of course I got the part. But how am I supposed to get it to you if I can't catch a flight?"

"What's the problem? Just throw your weight around a little. Who in their right mind is going to refuse a man of your position?"

Judd looked around nervously, pressed his mouth close to the receiver. "I don't exactly want to make a scene," he said.

Another pause from Kincaid. "Where is it?" he

asked.

Again, Judd looked around. "I have it wrapped up in my briefs," he said. "And that's another thing. Thanks to Inverness, even if I were able to catch a flight, security is level red all over the island. They would search my bags."

"That's no good," said Kincaid. Another pause, then, "Could you hide it in your rectum?"

"That's enough, Kincaid. I can cash in a few markers and procure a flight, but I'm mailing you the socket!"

"No! Don't! Mail! It! That means a paper trail and it defeats the whole purpose of sending you to pick it up. You have to come up with something. We're so close to being finished with this thing!"

Judd rested the receiver on his shoulder. "It's all going too far," he said to himself, then, he felt a presence behind him. "I will be back this evening," he said, then hung up the receiver before turning around.

"Doctor Louis Judd, I presume," said Deputy Director Friedman Rose of the Friendly Neighbors holding up his badge.

Doctor Judd closed his eyes and took a deep breath. "How may I help you, director?" he asked, pointlessly.

"Are these your bags?" Friedman asked, indicating Judd's luggage.

Judd nodded.

Friedman pocketed his badge. "If you wouldn't mind coming with me," he said.

"Am I under arrest?"

"Just want to ask you a few questions."

"Concerning what?" asked Judd, picking up his bags and following behind Friedman as he led the way toward the parking garage.

Friedman's vehicle was parked in the first space. He unlocked the doors and motioned Judd into the back seat. Judd complied as Friedman took his own seat behind the wheel. As the vehicle began moving, Judd noticed that Friedman was steering it manually. Unless the Deputy Director was an old fashioned man, the fact that the vehicle's navigational system was not configured for that particular trip meant Friedman Rose was not acting on official orders. "Your name has come up in connection with several criminal acts perpetrated over the past several months," said Friedman, checking his mirror before changing lanes.

"Oh my…might I ask which criminal acts?"

Friedman looked at Judd through the rear view mirror. The man was too calm.

"What business do you have in England, Doctor?"

"Oh, I was just doing my job…controlling the fate of humanity," he said, reaching up and forcing Friedman's head into the steering column.

The safety features automatically switched the vehicle to neutral but, before it veered out of the lane, Judd shoved Friedman's body aside and took his place behind the wheel. Without even breaking a sweat, he turned the vehicle round and headed back to the airport.

On his way to the ticket counter, he pulled his mobile from his pocket and dialed a single digit number. The person on the other end picked up without an answer.

"This is Louis Judd."

A pause, then, "Authorizing," came a robotic voice, followed by several multi-layered clicking sounds, a loud humming, then, the robotic voice again, "Authorized, Louis Judd."

"Inform Inspector Murry that I require his protection. I will be returning to my office in exactly four hours via London. This is an urgent matter."

Hanging up, he approached the ticket counter.

"I am sorry, sir," said the tired looking woman behind the counter. "But all flights have been cancelled until further notice. You may contact the bureau of--"

Judd slapped his credentials on the counter. "I will be on a flight to Springfield, Massachusetts within the half hour. If you ever wish to spawn, I'd suggest you do what you can to make this happen."

The ticket woman looked closely at the credentials, began to shake. "I will have to check with central authority, "she said, then typed the order into the computer. A moment later, "There is one cross Atlantic flyer on the runway, sir," she said. "Security will show you the way."

Judd retrieved his credentials, stuffed them into his coat.   "Thank   you."

~28~

"I DON'T APPRECIATE you doing that in my vehicle," Shultz said as Hoigt downed a shot of blueberry schnapps. "I don't even know how it got in here."

"The garage attendants sneak a complimentary bottle into every vehicle parked in the visitor spaces. It is meant to be a sign of appreciation for your visit. But really, it is a mild form of rebellion. A wink of the eye to the citizens of the collected government. We started it not too long after the prohibition began." He tipped the bottle again. "I bet you didn't know that, did you."

Shultz kept his eyes on the road.

"It makes you wonder how you could not know," Hoigt continued. "I suppose nobody reports it." He passed the bottle to Shultz. "Have a drink. It will strengthen your nerves."

"I will not," Shultz said, ignoring the bottle.

Hoigt chuckled. "Try not to think about it," he said. "You will bring yourself to a panic." He mused for a moment. "Somebody was going to have to do it eventually. It might as well be us. What's wrong?"

Shultz read the time off the dashboard. "I haven't heard back from the deputy director."

"Something must have gone wrong."

"That, or he didn't believe the story. For all we know he has issued an all-points bulletin for our arrest."

"Don't be silly," said Hoigt. "We decided upon a meeting place. If anything he will just wait to arrest us there." He took another drink.

"Stop acting so gallant," said Shultz. "You're just as nervous as I am, otherwise you wouldn't be drinking so much."

"Of course I'm nervous. We're about to accuse one of the most powerful men in the world of mass murder."

Shultz sat in silence, watching the street signs pass by as the vehicle made its way toward the airport, where he and Hoigt were to meet deputy director Rose at one of the nearby hotels. He took the bottle and drank, swallowing hesitantly. "Nothing will be the same," he said.

"Everything is the same. In this world, there is only the appearance of change."

Shultz took another swig.

"How do you like it?"

"...It's good."

An hour later, the vehicle pulled off the highway and made a loop toward the airport.

"What's that?" asked Hoigt, pointing.

Shultz looked to the side to see several security vehicles and an ambulance crowded around the airport's terminal building. "I've got a bad feeling," he said.

"Let's check it out."

"What…no. Let's just get to the hotel."

"Come on. This may be something. Your boss was supposed to pick up Judd over there. Maybe something happened."

"No…Hoigt. We should…we've been drinking."

"Shultz!"

Shultz switched the vehicle to manual and turned in to the drop-off lane, driving slowly past the scene. Suddenly, he wanted to vomit. "It's Friedman!" he yelled.

"Where?"

"In the ambulance."

Shultz hit the brakes and jumped out of the vehicle, ran to the ambulance. Hoigt followed closely behind as Shultz flashed his badge to get past the security agents. Friedman Rose lay on a gurney, an oxygen mask placed over his face.

"What happened?" Shultz asked, leaning over the deputy director.

"Sir, you can't be in here," said a paramedic.

Shultz showed his badge to the paramedic. "What happened? Is he alright?"

The paramedic's face flushed and he began to stammer. "Oh, yes," he said. "He took a nasty blow to the head, but that's not the problem. Some maniac stuffed a rag in his mouth and duct taped him to the back seat of his vehicle. By the time security discovered him, he had choked on his own vomit."

Hoigt pushed his way into the ambulance. "Can we speak to him?" he asked.

The paramedic appeared confused. "But, he's unconscious, sir."

Suddenly, Friedman Rose opened his eyes and said, weakly, "You've been drinking."

Shultz leaned in again. "Friedman, what happened?"

Friedman coughed, twirled his tongue in his mouth, tasting the vomit. "You were right about Judd," he said. "The bastard is in deep."

Hoigt asked, "Where is Judd now?"

Friedman looked over at Hoigt. "Is this the cop from Nuremburg?" he asked.

"Where is he?" Shultz asked.

Friedman paused. Hoigt's presence was a difficult challenge to his prejudice. At length, he answered. "Who knows? Probably back in America by this time. It won't be difficult to find him. A man in his position doesn't need to hide."

Shultz took Friedman's hand and squeezed it. "I'm bringing him in," he said.

"Forget it. You can't take down a man like Judd. I was stupid to go along with it in the first place. He's untouchable. You're off the case."

"But sir…"

"Go home, Shultz," said Friedman, breaking into a coughing fit. The paramedic twisted a nozzle behind him, increasing the oxygen through the mask.

"Well, what's it going to be, Shultz?" Hoigt asked.

Shultz meditated on the question. He waited until Friedman's breathing returned to normal. "Sir…what happens now? How does this go?"

Friedman swallowed a large chunk of phlegm,

made a face. "There's nothing to do," he said. "Judd is completely out of our reach." He began to cough once more.

The paramedic pushed Hoigt and Shultz away. "We have to get him to the hospital," he said. "I'm sorry, sirs."

The two men climbed out of the ambulance, Shultz hesitantly, not wanting to leave his friends side.

"Shultz!" Friedman called after him. "Tell my wife I love her!" he shouted as the paramedic closed the doors. The ambulance drove off, its sirens wailing. Shultz began to pace. Hoigt stood still. "I'm doing this with or without you," he said. "Tell me now, what do you want to do?"

Shultz pondered the question. What did he want to do? What he really wanted to do was go home. But that wasn't really an option was it? I guess it's true, he thought. I guess they were right. This is what I am supposed to do.

"It's not going to be easy," he said, not so much to Hoigt as to himself.

Hoigt nodded. "It was never supposed to be," he said.

Shultz placed his hands in his pockets, looked up at the sky. For the first time since he could remember, it was quiet.

How does something like this happen? He asked himself. How do things go so far? Questions like these were beyond him. And there was another one. How does a Friendly Neighbor, in this day and age, take on the Gynecology and Licensing Bureau?

"We're in for nasty weather," he said.

~29~

"THIS IS IT? This is where you were taking me?" Marvin asked, looking up at the tall building that dwarfed all others surrounding it. A building he was all too familiar with.

"This is where I met the guy," Fordy responded, rubbing his arm. They had left the dog in the vehicle.

"This is my firm...my wife's...it was my wife's firm, but I had to report here."

"You were Doctor Judd's clients?"

"What? Uh...yeah. A few months after we married, my wife's original gynecologist retired and all his clients were referred here."

"Whew," Fordy exclaimed. "I had no idea."

"What's that supposed to mean?"

"It's nothing."

"No. What?"

"It's just that Doctor Judd is rather pricey. I'm surprised you could afford him."

"What do you mean?"

"You never look at your statements? Judd is one of

the most exclusive gynecologists in the bureau. I mean...jeez, Marvin...I never would have thought we were involved with the same firm."

Marvin looked at the building with disgust, then to Fordy. "Like how much?"

"Well, it's always a sliding scale, of course. But Doctor Judd isn't part of the federal credit act. He never charges under thirty grand."

"Thirty grand a year?" Marvin shouted. The sum echoed off the building and through the artificial trees making up a synthetic garden in which mechanical hummingbirds were sometimes seen buzzing around feeders filled with un-recycled honey water.

Fordy began to laugh.

"What's so funny?"

"You never once thought to look?" Fordy asked between guffaws. "You never once checked your statement? Crickets, Marvin...how little did you think you really made?"

Marvin squeezed his stomach. "I thought it was taxes!" he screamed. "I thought it was income tax!"

"Marvin, they don't take taxes out of your check! They haven't done that for years. Not since the credit act was passed. All taxes are pre-considered so that you take home only what you earn for take-home. The only withholdings listed on your statement are for those expenses based on personal nature...such as which firm you use...which apartment building you lease from."

"I know...I know all that!"

Fordy calmed his laughter. "Actually...it's not really funny," he said. "To think...all this time...all this anger and depression you've put yourself through…it's all because you so blindly excepted your negative world-view, that you didn't once think to check and see if things were nearly as bleak as you supposed them to be. Sure, you don't make all that much…but, Marvin…you could easily have afforded a procrete license if you had petitioned to join a cheaper firm. None of this--"

"--Would be necessary," Marvin concluded.

The two men broke into a long silence. Fordy rocked himself back and forth, balancing himself on his heels. At length, he asked, "So what are you going to do? Why did you make me bring you here?"

"I made a mistake," said Marvin, quietly. "But maybe it was supposed to be this way."

"What do you mean?"

"It's causality, I think. If I hadn't made this mistake, I never would have been put in the position to donate my lung to you. You would be dead if not for my mistake. If I weren't so flawed, you wouldn't have made it."

"…"

"You don't have to say anything," Marvin continued. "But now I know what I have to do."

"You're not going to do anything stupid, are you?"

"I'm going up there, Fordy. I'm going to walk right up to him and tell him how wrong he is. Because he's wrong and there isn't any other way to put it. And I don't think anybody has ever put it to him before."

"But how can you tell what's right or what's wrong?" asked Fordy. "When the initial judgment is always based on perspective. To those without, a man like Judd appears to be in the wrong; however, to those with, Judd is just another man."

"What do you know? To those who are unaffected--people like you, placed in a neutral perspective--you are not in the position to judge right from wrong."

"But, Marvin, my friend, that is the only way to judge. Who better to judge what is right in an action or what is wrong in a deed than those not affected by them? If everything is judged from a standpoint of personal bias, how do we keep our emotions in check? How do we solve anything with clear intentions for the better, instead of waiting until we are pushed beyond our limits, when our desperation motivates us to act irrationally? Crickets, Marvin...what were you going to do here before you found out the whole world wasn't out to get you?"

"It's not out only for me! It's controlling all of you. Men like Judd control everything. They control what we do, what eat, drink...they even control whether we breathe or not!"

Fordy replied simply, "I know."

Marvin punched him in the face. Fordy tottered, reeled back on his feet and fell to the ground. Marvin stood over him, squeezing his hand.

Fordy looked up at him. "That's what I've been trying to tell you this whole time. Why do you feel like you have to fight it?"

"Why do you defend them?" he asked.

Fordy massaged his jaw. "It's like you said--men like Judd don't just control our lives. They control who gets to procreate and who doesn't. Men like

Judd allowed my mother to carry me. They let me be born."

"Damn it! Sometimes you have to take a stand! You're so dependent on their system, but that doesn't mean you have to like it. Dependency is supposed to breed contempt. That's how we learn to stand on our own."

"I don't want to stand on my own!" Fordy countered. "I don't want to spend my life in competition with everyone else. I just want to live, Marvin. I want to be happy with what I've got, and not spend every second agonizing over things I don't have. I don't want to want anything. I just want to exist."

"Well just existing is pointless!" Marvin shouted, then broke into a run for the building doors.

"In a patriarchal society, establishing tyrannical institutions is one of the easiest things that can be done," said Doctor Louis Judd, leaning back in his chair, his feet resting on the edge of his desk. The blinds were open and he watched the sun set. "It's easy to shepherd a people when they hold a sense of obligatory thankfulness. I sometimes forget that is what we have."

"Your problem," said Unsel Kamp, chief officer of the deterrence police security section 7, ordered to watch over Doctor Judd, "is that you forgot the difference between familial parenting and the fostering of intellect. So while you may subconsciously fill the role of father figure in this so-called patriarchal society, you do very little by way of insuring how closely these people hold you to their hearts. A little more good publicity might have served as an indemnity to the situation you now find yourself in."

Judd smiled, wagged his finger. "You've been reading those books I leant to you."

The two men were close. In fact, Doctor Judd had, for a short time, been married to Kamp's wife before she and the chief officer had become acquainted. Judd had divorced her on the grounds that she was an undesirable, feeling she was mentally unfit to bear children. The chief officer, of course, did not know this. In fact, after she and the chief officer were married, Judd, newly appointed to the OB/GYN of New England, despite his misgivings, freely offered the two a procrete license. It had been a shrewd political move. A move seemingly about to pay off.

A high pitched, shrill sound suddenly tore through the office.

Judd jumped out of his seat in surprise. "What is that?" he screamed over the noise.

"The building's alarm has been tripped. We have a security breach," said the chief officer, calmly. He gripped his pistol and pressed a button on his communicator. "What's the situation?" he asked, speaking into a microphone.

A static altered voice responded. "Not sure yet, sir. The glass of the rear entrance door has been shattered. Not big enough for anybody to crawl through, though. It may just be a prank."

"Not today, it isn't," said the chief officer. "Keep your eyes open. Watch that area."

Judd said, "Maybe the alarm chased them off."

"No. It's an old trick. They set off the alarm in one area, security assumes they've used the alarm as a ruse, double up in other areas, then the perpetrator enters in the same area the alarm was triggered. It used to work, until we figured out the best way to commit a crime was to announce it first."

The chief officer seemed confident, but there was one flaw to his gut instinct. "But these men are Friendly Neighbors'. Don't they know a little about criminal tactics?"

Chief Officer Kamp straightened his mouth, pressed the button on the communicator again. "All stations report," he said. "Look for signs of sabotage in all sectors. And override that alarm!"

"Ha!" Judd laughed, sarcastically.

The alarm was silenced.

"If there are Friendly Neighbors' coming to arrest you, believe me, they'll be rogue agents. The Friendly Neighbors' as an organization would never authorize such a thing. Especially since the crimes you are alleged to have committed fall clearly within the jurisdiction of the deterrence police. And if they are rogue agents, they will not have the equipment or man-power to gain entrance into this building."

"Yes. But if these are indeed rogue agents, I promise they are not here to arrest me; for how can a few dogmatic agents arrest me, when they are in strict violation of their creed? No, Kamp. The men who are after me are not trying to arrest me...they want to kill me."

"And that is the only reason we are here, Louis. If

these men are attempting to do what you claim, then they are terrorists. And we will put them down just as we did that wacko before."

"Sir," the voice of another officer interrupted. "While overriding the alarm, the computer indicates that several men entered through the front entrance, using an active password only seconds before the alarm was tripped."

"How many men passed through, exactly?"

"Heat sensors indicate four, sir."

"And how many passwords were keyed in?"

"Just one, sir."

"Just one?" Kamp tensed up. "Keep an eye out for those men," he said, then turned to Judd. "I have to check something. Stay here and lock the door behind me."

Kamp was out of the room before Judd could say anything. He got up quickly and locked the door to his office.

Kamp took the elevator to the ground floor, met with a fellow officer. "Which door had the glass kicked out?" he asked.

"Right this way, sir," said the other man, leading Kamp to the door. Kamp leaned down to scrutinize the damage, then shot back up. "You idiots! This door wasn't kicked in. It was kicked out! By somebody already inside!"

*

Shultz and Hoigt squeezed into the elevator shaft, hoping to bypass any deterrence police stationed in the stairwell. Gaining entryway to the building hadn't been as difficult as Shultz had supposed it would be. It was a simple matter persuading Fordy MacLennon to allow them to slip inside after he entered his password into the system.

"You didn't have to threaten him with your weapon," said Shultz, his voice bouncing off the walls of the shaft. "I could have used my badge."

"We've come this far. Might as well go all the way. Besides, if we did t your way, it would have been difficult to explain hiding in the elevator shaft."

"Point taken."

Hoigt checked his watch. "Tell them to stop the elevator," he said.

Shultz nodded, raised the panel and poked his head into the elevator where Fordy and Marvin stood stock still, their nervousness overriding their motor skills. "Stop on the next floor, please," he said.

Both Marvin and Fordy reached to press the button at the same time. The elevator stopped three floors from Louis Judd's office and the doors opened. Fordy looked up. Shultz had lowered the panel. "Do we...do you want us to get out?"

Shultz raised the panel once more. "Get out, please," he said.

They did so, then stood bemused in the corridor.

"What do we do now?" Shultz asked.

Hoigt took off his jacket and wrapped it around the cord. "Follow me," he said, beginning the difficult climb. Shultz followed.

Mere seconds later, Marvin and Fordy found themselves confronted by several members of the deterrence police who had tracked the movement of the elevator. They were ordered down on their knees with their hands locked behind their heads.

"Sir, we've apprehended two of the suspects," one of the officers announced into his communicator.

"Hold until further notice," came the reply.

"You heard that," the officer said to his fellows. They nodded, then proceeded to pounce on the confused and frightened pair, kicking them and hitting them with batons.

Chief Officer Kamp made his way back to Louis Judd's office. His heart was racing, adrenaline pumping in anticipation of what might transpire in the coming moments. The deterrence police held a traditional dislike for the Friendly Neighbors'; beginning as mere professional rivalry, it soon evolved into near philosophical hatred. The Friendly Neighbors' held an aura of intellectuality about them near to snobbishness. Kamp relished in the thought of doing harm to one of their members. He sneered at the idea of them, snorted. "Tufts!" he grunted, banging on Judd's office door. "It's me," he announced.

Judd opened up, peered out. "Did you catch them?"

"We have two in custody. It won't be long before we have the others. To make it easier, I would like your pass-code in order to initiate a thermal scan of the entire building."

Judd frowned. "I'd rather not," he said. "As you are well aware, there are other rather important firms in this building, and only one pass-code shared by all board members. Giving out the code would allow you access to the other firms' data banks."

"You can change the code afterwards."

Judd thought on it. "I'll punch in the code myself."

"You would have to do that from the mainframe in the lobby. I don't want you to step foot out of this office until it is safe."

After making quite clear his reservations, Judd wrote down the pass-code and handed it off to Kamp. Kamp then travelled to the lobby where he initiated the scan.

It took several minutes for the program to begin running, then several more for the scan. Kamp watched the monitor, waiting for the results. It took ten minutes in all to scan the entire building. After the scan was completed, several options appeared on screen.

A. Show scan results in entirety.

B. Show scan results by area-level.

C. Designate area-level.

D. Show anomalies only.

Kamp chose D, then waited as the program configured the results.

Seconds later, the results appeared on screen; showing several bright red splotched on several levels--his men at their posts. He saw a grouping of splotches representing the men questioning Marvin and Fordy. He then saw something strange. Two dull, blurred splotches above Louis Judd's office. He peered closely at the monitor, trying to figure it out. The splotches did not represent objects on the level above the office, but directly above the office. Was it some sort of machinery giving off a heat suggestion? Then, the splotches cleared slightly, they appeared to be moving. Kamp's eyes widened.

"The suspects are at the office!" he yelled into his communicator, then sprinted for the elevator.

He reached Judd's office, pulled his automatic pistol and kicked the door in. Judd sitting at his desk, his hands in the air, let out a shrill, feminine sound.

"Louis, take cover!" he shouted, pointing his weapon at the ceiling and firing off a dozen rounds. Chunks dry wall and plaster fell to the floor and powdery insulation floated in the air. Kamp didn't notice Judd's desperate stare in time to defend against Hoigt tackling him from behind. The two men struggled on the floor as Shultz raised himself from behind Judd's desk, holding a pistol to the man's head.

"Alright, that's enough!" Shultz shouted. "Hoigt, get him on his feet."

Hoigt bent Kamp's arm back, forcing him to drop his weapon, then lifted him up. By the time the chief officer was to his feet, a dozen deterrence officers were at the door. Hoigt quickly yanked Kamp in front of him, using his as a shield, his arm wrapped around the chief officer's neck.

"Shoot these men where they stand!" Kamp ordered.

The men lifted their weapons. Red dots flittered about Shultz and Hoigt-the officer's taking careful aim. Shultz kneeled behind Doctor Judd, pressed the muzzle of his pistol close the gynecologist's head. "Drop your weapons," Shultz yelled. "I am placing this man under arrest."

"These men are terrorists and I order you to fire!" Kamp screamed, the veins popping out of his forehead.

Slowly, Shultz pulled his badge from his pocket and held it in the air. "I am detective Otto Shultz of the Friendly Neighbors'," he said. "Louis Judd is a criminal and I am taking him into custody."

Kamp struggled against Hoigt's grip. Hoigt kept a constant movement behind the chief officer, avoiding the tiny red dots. "Are you men going to back down to a couple of Friendly Neighbor's? A bunch of parking attendants!"

Hoigt squeezed Kamps' neck tighter, choking the man with his forearm, and slipped a sharp, jagged knife from his trousers. He slid the knife under Kamp's chin. "I'm no Friendly Neighbor," he said, menacingly. "I am an officer of the Nuremberg Polizei and I'll cut your fucking heart out."

Kamp's eyes widened as he tried to keep the knife in sight. "A Nuremberg cop!" he snorted, spittle flying from his mouth as the words struggled past his constricted throat. "Did you hear that, men? I am going to count to ten, and then I want you to take these men down."

Shultz had heard about and seen more violence in the past week since knowing Hoigt that he was beginning to understand. Although he was afraid, he knew before even entering the building that Judd wasn't going to be taken in easily. Kamp was going to count to ten. Shultz smirked. Hoigt knew this game.

Kamp began his count. He got to seven before Hoigt shoved him into the group of deterrence officers crowded in the doorway. They tumbled over like bowling pins under Kamp's weight and Shultz immediately began firing his weapon into the huddled mass. Hoigt quickly lifted Judd's large oaken desk on its side and shoved it in front of the doorway. Shultz tossed Hoigt the pistol and grabbed Judd's shirt collar. "You're coming with us, Doctor," he said, jerking the man out of his chair and pushing him to the far end of the office.

The deterrence police out in the hall opened fire, their bullets penetrating the desk and blowing out the office windows. Hoigt took cover, motioned for Shultz to get Judd out through a neighboring office. Shultz nodded, picked up Judd's desk chair and threw it against the wall with all his might. The chair crashed through the dry wall and Shultz forced Judd into the next office. Judd tripped and fell to the floor, covering his ears. The sound of gunfire was deafening.

Hoigt covered his eyes as wood chips from the desk sprayed into the air, cutting into his face. He then shot blindly through the wall, emptying the clip. The deterrence police continued firing. Hoigt could not tell if any had been hit. He reloaded, and repeated the action. This time there was a pause in the shooting coming from the hallway.

In the midst of this short relief, Hoigt noticed a large print hanging on Judd's wall. The Bestowal of Privileges. Its glass frame was shattered. Hoigt stared at the print, momentarily lost in his own mind.

He had seen the real thing before. In Rotenberg.
"Shultz!" he screamed.

*

Fordy cried like a baby. He and Marvin sat back to back, their hands clip-stripped behind their backs. He had trouble opening his right eye and the tears running down his face stung the open cuts on his face. The policemen that had been interrogating them had rushed off and now Fordy could hear gunfire not too far off.

Marvin wasn't in much better shape. He did, however, hold himself together with a bit more dignity. He squirmed, tried to position himself more comfortably. The strips were cutting into his wrists.

"Marvin, what's happening? What have we gotten into?"

"Maybe it's the end of the world," Marvin replied, sullenly.

"We have to get out of here, Marvin."

"Oh, now you want to do something."

"What's that supposed to mean?"

"Now that our lack of personal independence is made superlatively clear, you want to take action. Why not just sit still like you've done all your life. There's no difference in what's happening now to what was happening before."

"I'm tied to a chair in my wife's gynecologist's building!"

"There's no difference."

"Fine!" Fordy rocked himself forward, onto his

knees, picked himself up and hopped to the door. He turned around to twist the knob and peeked out into the hallway. The gunfire was more sporadic now, not the continuous stream as before. There was no sign of the deterrence police on the level they were on. "I think they're all gone," he said to Marvin. "Probably went to join in the fight."

Marvin shrugged. "That's good," he said, morosely.

Fordy scuttled backward to stand by Marvin. "Here, see if you can loosen these strips," he said.

Marvin looked up blankly. "What's the point?"

"Damn it, Marvin--what's with you?"

Marvin shrugged again. "Something is always getting in the way of my plans," he said. "Now I can't even tell Doctor Judd what's wrong with him. It would have taken only two minutes."

"Wha--," Fordy stomped his foot. "I'm tired of trying to figure you out, Marvin. If you want to stay here, fine--but I'm getting the freak out of here--so loosen my strips."

Marvin stared into space for some odd seconds, then inched forward and used his teeth to wrestle with the strips.

They were loosened soon enough and Fordy ripped them off. "Adios," he said, then rushed out of the office without another word.

Marvin continued to sit--apparently resigned to his fate.

*

"We've got you!-We've got you cornered!-You chicken!-German savage!" Chief Officer Kamp screamed above the gunfire. He watched his men scurry back and forth, dodging and weaving through the corridor, taking cover behind any and everything that could possibly obstruct Hoigt's bullets as they positioned themselves to lay down a suppressing fire of their own. It was exhilarating beyond his wildest dreams. It was rare for anybody to put up any kind of fight against the deterrence police. And they had never been caught off guard before. This cop from Nuremberg was everything he had been waiting for. A clear reason behind his purpose in life. Ah!--he was meant to be a policeman. Crickets! The German had taken out three of his men already. And he was shooting blindly! Kamp knew exactly what he was going to do when he got home that night; he was going to draw up plans for an invasion of Free City Nuremberg; the one last bastion of resistance to the Collected Government.

"Smith!" he yelled to the officer closest to him. "Rush him!"

Smith looked cross-eyed at Kamp. "Wouldn't you rather smoke him out first?"

"Smoke him out? Heck no! This man deserves more respect than that! Just look at how he's mowing us down, man!"

Smith did nothing.

Kamp stared at him. "Move it, Smith! Let's take this man down the hard way like he deserves."

Smith gulped, reloaded his weapon, and then rammed through what was left of the office door. He was immediately felled by a shot to the head.

Kamp was awed, overwhelmed with appreciation.

He heard a loud click and looked to his right. Two officers were loading a tactical mini rocket into a launcher, planning to blow the entire office to smithereens.

"Just what do you think you're doing?" Kamp asked, lifting his weapon and shooting the two men dead on the spot.

The four remaining officers froze, wondering what was going on. Hoigt's challenge unnerved them...and it was apparently driving their chief officer insane.

"You four go find the Friendly Neighbor," Kamp ordered. "I'll finish this one, myself."

As the other men ran off in pursuit of Shultz, Kamp a large, curved blade knife from his pack, tossed his pistol to the floor. "I'm coming in you savage! If you've got the guts, you'll drop your weapon and face me like a man!" he shouted, his voice cracking in an ever higher pitch with each word.

He waited several seconds in which Hoigt did not fire his weapon, then gripped the handle of the blade with both hands, took three deep, forceful breaths, then rushed into the office, running blindly, letting out a primal scream, almost sensual in its purity.

Hoigt watched him approach, then kicked Louis Judd's rolling chair, sending it skidding across the office, obstructing Kamp's approach. Kamp tripped, tried to keep his feet, and then went flying out Judd's office window. His sensual, primal scream continued the entire journey to the pavement below.

*

Shultz dragged Doctor Judd behind him, pulling him out of the stairwell. They ran almost the entirety of the building, like rats in a maze, in order to dodge the deterrence police. A half hour later, they were finally at ground level. Judd, seeing the lights of the city outside the doors, tried one last time to break himself free and run for it, but Shultz held on doggedly. As they wrestled with one another, the elevator doors opened with a ding and Fordy MacLennon ran out, bumping into them. Fordy fell to the floor, quickly picked himself up and ran for the door.

"Mister MacLennon, don't run off! You've got to help me!" Judd shouted after him, hoping a witness would better his odds of safety.

Fordy reached the door, turned quickly, "You overcharge!" he screamed, paused, "It's wrong!" He then made his exit.

"MacLennon!" Judd shouted once more, but his plea was cut off by a series of rapid gunfire. Bullets tore into the wall paneling and he and Shultz both ducked for cover behind the lobby desk.

"This is all your fault," Judd screamed at Shultz. "If you had just stayed where you belonged, none of this would be happening! You're crazy! You're a Friendly Neighbor, not a cop!"

Shultz pointed his pistol at him. "Shut up, you! You're the criminal here, not me. You reap what you sow." With that, he raised himself up from behind the desk and returned fire. He hit one deterrence officer full in the chest, watched him fall, and ducked back down to reload.

The three remaining policemen opened fire once more. Shultz was pinned down. Judd, his confidence raised by the knowledge that the deterrence police were not leaving him in the lurch, cackled. It would all be over soon. Then, suddenly, the entire lobby began to fill with smoke. This was followed by three evenly spaced shots.

"This is it," said Judd. "They're smoking you out. You're finished."

"Not quite yet," came a voice through the smoke. It was Hoigt. He dropped behind the desk, squeezing Judd in between himself and Shultz.

Shultz breathed a sigh of relief. "Is it over?" he asked.

Hoigt hesitated before answering. "No," he said.

Shultz fixed his grip on the pistol. "How many more are there?"

"No more," Hoigt replied.

"Well, then, let's get out of--"

"Tell me, Doctor Judd," Hoigt interrupted, leaning to the side and pulling a paper from his back pocket. "When was the last time you were in Paris?"

Shultz recognized the paper as one of the counterfeit procrete licenses. What was Hoigt up to?

Judd slumped at the sight of it, sighed. "How did you find out?" he asked.

"Hoigt, what is this?"

"Judd isn't responsible for the Extra Solar Pioneer fiasco," he answered. "He's behind the terrorism. He funds it with the sale of counterfeit licenses. Licenses without record, so there is no way to trace it back to his office. You were just doing your job, weren't you, Doctor."

Judd reached for and grabbed the phony document. "The licensing firms are powerful," he said. "But, contrary to popular belief, we can't contend with the collected government. Financing terrorism was the only way to stop what has been happening with the ESP's. At least, the only way I could think of. In order to counteract a popular phenomenon, one is forced to introduce an equally stimulating psychological alternative. You're right," he said, turning to Shultz. "I am a criminal. But which is the worst, giving people a way out of their lives, or making them think they are being offered a better life?"

Shultz pulled a pair of clip-strips from his inside pocket, wrapped them around Judd's wrists. "What is worse," he said; "giving people hope, or pretending to?"

Judd looked down at his wrists.

"You can't mask a cruel deed under the guise of noble purpose," said Hoigt, also turning to Shultz. "Do you see?" he asked. "It is all one and the same."

Shultz nodded.

Hoigt patted Judd down, discovered a long, cylindrical object under his shirt and held it up, scrutinizing it. Whatever it was, it wasn't a weapon-- unless he had hoped to bludgeon them with it. He tossed it to the ground. Judd watched it roll and clank against the door.

"Who was he?" Shultz asked.

"Who?" said Judd.

"The terrorist. The examiner couldn't identify his body. I assume he was somebody outside the system; somebody you let fall through. Who was he?"

Judd ruminated. "That's the question, isn't it?"

"You expect me to believe you didn't know?"

"He never let me see his face." He shrugged. "Could have been anybody."

"Louis Judd, you are under arrest," said Shultz.

Hoigt motioned toward the door with his head. They led Judd out of the building, closing, effectively,   both   cases.

~30~

MARVIN DID NOT so much get up, finally, to leave the office after the gun-fire had ceased; instead, his absence of conscious thought and emotional vibrancy led him to exit the office through a wholly natural inclination not at all connected to what was happening in his immediate presence; and this natural inclination just happened to lead him to the lobby just as Hoigt and Shultz were carrying Doctor Judd away.

Marvin walked to the door and looked through the glass, watching them absently as they departed the scene. He opened the door and, looking down, his eyes fell upon the cylindrical object taken from Judd and tossed so carelessly away by Hoigt. Continuously inattentive now, Marvin picked up the object for no particular reason. He held it in his hands, half-heartedly studying it, then walked out of the building.

The sun was rising. Early morning traffic began to form as Springfield commuters started their day.

Living their lives in ignorance of the night's events; ignorant of life. Going off to their jobs, earning their keep; leaving their family and homes so they could continue their ambiguous existence.

Marvin ignored the traffic and began walking. As he made to cross to the opposite side of the street, against the light, he was suddenly obstructed by a vehicle. The vehicle came to a screeching halt as Marvin made no move to get out of its way. The occupant rolled down his window, leaned his head out. It was Hollis Kincaid.

"What are you, stupid? That's not safe, young man."

Marvin looked up, nodded, and continued his trek down the street.

Kincaid was about to press the resume command on his panel when he noticed the cylindrical object Marvin continued to hold. He shook his head, making sure he wasn't hallucinating, looked back at Marvin through the rear view mirror, then set the vehicle to Manual and put it in reverse.

He pulled up beside Marvin. "Hey, young man, where did you get that thing there?"

"What thing?" Marvin asked, sullenly.

Kincaid indicated the object. Marvin pointed toward Judd's building.

"Louis gave you that?" Kincaid asked, then, to himself; "I wonder why?" He leaned over, opened the passenger side door. "Hop in, kid. I'll give you a lift."

Marvin could care less what he did or didn't do now. It was due to no part of his decision making process to get into the vehicle. He just did, following the same natural inclination he did in leaving the building. Kincaid pulled away from the curb, drove away from Judd's building, eyeing the cylindrical object the entire time.

"So, you're a friend of Louis', I presume," Kincaid questioned, trying to discern why Marvin would have the eighteen millimeter socket he so prized.

"No," Marvin replied.

Kincaid was confused. "Do I, uh--do I just hand you the credits, then?" he asked, indicating a briefcase lying in the back seat.

"Credits?"

"For the socket. I'm assuming Judd designated you to hand it over. Probably wanted it out of his hands as quickly as possible. Always afraid of a little trouble, that one."

Marvin looked down at the socket, then out the window. He watched the neighborhood pass by. He could see his and Flora's old apartment building. But he couldn't feel his own heart beating in is chest.

He dropped the socket casually into Kincaid's lap. "You were supposed to give that briefcase to Doctor Judd?" he asked.

"I--that was the plan. But I guess…say, who are you? Did Louis send you or not?"

Marvin was silent. Kincaid's confusion was deepening.

"How did you get this?" Kincaid asked, holding the socket up.

"I don't want to go home right now," Marvin said somberly. "Do you mind if I ride with you for a while?"

Kincaid didn't know how to respond. Aw, heck. The guy seemed harmless. What could it hurt?

"Sure--sure," he said, feeling almost as if he were doing some kind service. After all, there was something about the man that made it seem as if he needed some sort of help. Whatever it was, who could say. Kincaid conjectured, maybe the guy was heartbroken.

He reconfigured the vehicle to return to where he came from, with Marvin riding along beside him. In the distance, a wavy black mass began to form on the horizon. "Looks like the crickets are coming back," he said. "I wonder how they'll try and get rid of them this time, now they've figured out the turtles won't work?"

Fordy MacLennon pulled to a stop at the entrance gate to the parking garage of his apartment building. He craned his neck out the window, looked up, and tried to figure out which window was his apartment. Strange, he thought, I don't know it. He sat in his vehicle, suddenly realizing how much of his own existence he had let drift by unobserved. How can I be so unaware of myself?

A rustling sound in the back seat made him turn round. The Yorkshire terrier stretched in its sleep. Fordy giggled slightly. He had forgotten all about it.

He watched the dog sleep and thought of his wife. The terrier was so important to her. He wondered if he should tell her about what happened. For some odd reason, he had no desire to tell her anything.

There was an appreciation for the previous night's events which the knowledge of its being secret gave him a special feeling. A secret all his own. Still, there would have to be an explanation. An explanation for his absence--pulled an all-nighter at work; the abrasions covering his body--fell down some stairs; the dog's being gone--heck with it, I want a divorce. I'm sorry, it's not you. I just don't want to have a family. It's wouldn't be fair to you.

Fordy smiled and rubbed the side of his face. A large welt was beginning to form above his right eye, but, strangely, he didn't mind.

In the back seat, the terrier began to whimper in its sleep. Fordy looked back and noticed the dog's tiny legs moving back and forth, as if it were running--in a dream. Fordy watched this for some time before bursting into laughter.

The dog woke with a start, jumped to its feet and stared curiously at Fordy, tilting its head to the side and lifting its ears.

Fordy continued to laugh. For some odd reason he was filled with joy. He stayed in the vehicle with the dog, parked out front of the garage, laughing, reveling in the unexpected feeling of joy and the release that came with it, until the time came for him to decide what to do next. If it were to come at all.

*

Marvin was still, calm; for the first time in his life, his mind seemed totally at ease; his body was relaxed, and his spirit loose. There was absolutely no thought occupying his brain. He had ridden northward with Kincaid, out of Massachusetts, and was now staring at the passing scenery of southern Maine. He watched, without observing, the sun glistening through the limbs of the trees; the light reflecting, spreading across the surface of the ocean seen in the distance. It was beautiful, and he had no desire at all to understand it, or have it explained to him. It was at this moment a single thought entered his head. One thought, encompassing all feeling and idea and world- -he was finally capable of truly loving himself.

"It's beautiful, isn't it?" said Kincaid.

The words echoed in Marvin's ears, flowed through him in ever widening pitch, until being translated through the brain. "Oh, yes," he responded, before realizing what it was he was in agreement with.

Marvin's pupils dilated and he took a breath. They weren't in the vehicle any longer. Marvin hadn't realized this until Kincaid spoke. He hadn't even realized he had gotten out of the vehicle.

He was walking, rather spirit-like, alongside Kincaid, down a winding dirt path, leading to a cleared open field. In the middle of the field was the object Kincaid had commented on prior to his sudden awakening. "What is it?" Marvin asked.

"It is the future," Kincaid answered. "The Extra Solar Craft: Kitty Kampai."

"That's an Extra Solar Craft?" Marvin asked, staring ahead at the titanic structure raised on its platform. He stopped walking. Two people approached them on the path. A young woman with an older man. "I've never seen one before," said

Marvin, speaking about the ESC.

"Until today, nobody has," said the woman.

Kincaid smiled, stepped up to the woman and smiled. "Jenny," he said, then, turning to the older man, "How are you, Edward?"

Edward Lincoln extended his hand. "Did you get it?" he asked.

Kincaid handed him the eighteen millimeter socket. The old man received the object and held it tightly to his chest. He breathed a sigh of relief and walked off and walked away. The young woman smiled. "Who is your friend?" she asked of Kincaid.

"Don't know. He was the drop-off man and he decided to ride along," he replied, motioning toward Edward Lincoln. "If you two will excuse me, I must speak with Mister Lincoln," he said, then trotted down the path like an excited child.

Marvin stood on the path next to Jenny.

"What does Kitty Kampai mean?" Marvin asked in time.

"She is me," said Jenny with a smile. "My alter ego. I built her."

"What did you mean nobody has ever seen one before?"

"A few years ago, astronomers discovered an earth like planet orbiting a star in the Hyades of Taurus. It is the only earth type planet ever found. For some reason, the government does not want people to know about it…so we're launching our own Extra Solar Craft, to spread the light of humanity among the lights of the universe. It has been my dream…my purpose in life. What I was meant to do."

Marvin meditated upon the object, looked over at the woman. "Jenny," he whispered. She looked at him. "You're beautiful," he said.

Jenny smiled, and the lowering sun offered one last reflection of light, glistening down the length of Kitty Kampai. And, quite inexplicably, the two embraced one another in the shadow of the womb of mankind's existence.

---epilogue

IF BUSTER MACREADY stared hard enough into the distance, he could make out a faint ring of light layering the horizon. He tried to imagine a bright yellow sun rising up to light the sky above, but he knew there wouldn't be. There would never be a sunrise on this side of the planet. No natural course by which to segment time and classify it. No particular time to sleep, or to wake; to eat or pray. And no new day to look forward to; no way to finalize rough times, and no way to tell yourself it will all be okay in the morning.

There was a nice ridge overlooking the colony. Buster had gotten into the habit of climbing the ridge every time he awoke from sleep, but he never looked at the colony below; he, instead, stared into the distance; looking for familiarity--something to cling to, remind him of his origins. But there was nothing. Nothing but the sound of his own breathing, the workings of his eyes and ears, his heart beating, the saliva forming under his tongue.

He stood up, brushed the dust from his leggings. And began the long, slow walk back to the camp.

Stevenson had been busy. He turned out to be a natural leader. The colony now had power throughout, and there began to develop a sort of unique camp culture amongst the pioneers. They all seemed to be adjusting quite nicely. There were even plants being grown in a greenhouse, the seeds having been planted in small bags of soil brought from earth. Surprisingly, there had yet to be a single case of disease amongst the colonists. Society was indeed developing on this mysterious, lost planet so far from home.

The sink holes, too, had been decreasing. Stevenson explained this simply. The god of man, having been carried to the planet within the souls of the pioneers, was slowly and surely beginning to weaken the gods of the planet, and they were thus unable to affect the lives of man. It appeared as if man might indeed be able to conquer the planet after all. It was all going according to plan.

Halfway to the camp, Buster sat on the ground, crossing his legs. He took off his helmet. Not far from him lay a pile of refuse. Any item the colonists were unable to use was thrown out. At this moment, there was a lot. Occasionally, one or another pioneer would discover a use for something discarded and come to retrieve it, but that was rare. It was officially a recycle mound, but it was refuse all the same. What else can you call something that will outlast you.

Then, his eyes fell upon something he had not expected to see. It was the scooter he had taken from the Carolyn Summers. It seemed like ages ago, now. Somebody had parked it beside the refuse mound.

"How are you, Macready?" a voice asked from behind. It was Stevenson. Of course it was Stevenson. Who else would it be?

Buster turned round. "I'm alive," he replied.

"Yes, you are."

"And so are you."

Stevenson did not reply.

"What are you doing out here, Macready?"

"I was thinking."

Stevenson looked toward the colony. "Now is the time," he said. "They're ready."

"Hmm. Prepared yourself, you mean."

"Don't be obtuse, Macready. You know this is the way it should be."

"Maybe," Buster replied. "Maybe if humanity is going to continue there does need to be a sacrifice."

Stevenson smiled.

"But maybe the sacrifice is not the one you imagine. Maybe, if humanity is going to continue, we have to cut out everything that is wrong about it."

"Macready…"

"But it is impossible to figure out exactly what is right and what is wrong about humanity, isn't it? So, maybe we have to get rid of everything we know about humanity. Maybe in order to reach our fullest potential, we have to stop trying to reach it. Maybe we can be now, what we wish to be in the future."

"You're spouting utopian ideals that have failed time and time again, Macready. Now is not the time to wax philosophical."

"Utopian philosophy is always preached alongside a determinate level of time. A philosophy in search of a better future."

"And?"

"Here there is no future. There is only the now. And that is all there will ever be."

"Exactly," said Stevenson. "It is as I've been

saying. We must act today for those tomorrow."

"But what if the action is the same taken since the dawn of man?"

Once again, Stevenson did not respond. Buster stood up and walked to the scooter. He reached up and stroked the seat. "Why is this here?"

"The colony is here. We are here. Why do we need a vehicle to carry us somewhere else?"

"Hmm," said Buster. "I'm not going to kill you, Stevenson," he said, then lifted himself onto the scooter.

"What?"

Buster pushed the button and started the scooter. Slowly, he began to drive it away from the camp. Stevenson walked behind. "Macready, you don't know what you're doing. You are making a fatal decision."

Buster continued to drive away, refusing to turn back to Stevenson. "If humanity is going to have a future, we have to discard what makes us human."

"What are you talking about, Macready?"

"Humanity should start anew here, Stevenson. Perhaps, for once, we can build a civilization that does not lie on a foundation of blood."

Buster pushed the pedal all the way down, increasing the scooter's speed to its maximum. Stevenson had to quicken his pace to a slow jog in order to follow.

"Macready, I need you!" he shouted. "We all need you! I can't do this myself. We must work together if we are to survive!"

The scooter tires crushed the soft rock beneath its

wheels, and the wind blew gently against his skin. It was no longer cold and harsh, but welcoming; welcoming like the stars in the sky and the winking shapes they made for the eyes of humanity. Buster steered toward the distant horizon and that faint strip of light. He could still hear Stevenson's voice calling out to him. He did not follow for long. And Buster Macready did not look back. He never did.

---end